Praise for the n

THEY D

"Mofina is one of the best

–*Library Jour*

"You'll love this. The story...

that just might turn you into a speed reader. So settle in, you won't be able to put this book down till the last page."

–*RT Book Reviews*

THE BURNING EDGE

"Rick Mofina's tense, taut writing makes every thriller he writes an adrenaline-packed ride."

–Tess Gerritsen, *New York Times* bestselling author

"Mofina keeps you on the edge of your seat... kept me up into the early morning hours–the plot is so well written that I could not put the book down!"

–*www.readertoreader.com*

IN DESPERATION

"A blisteringly paced story that cuts to the bone. It left me ripping through pages deep into the night."

–James Rollins, *New York Times* bestselling author

"A superbly written thriller.... Timely, tense and terrifying, this book is sure to be a big hit!"

–Brad Thor, #1 *New York Times* bestselling author

THE PANIC ZONE

"Taut pacing, rough action and jagged dialogue feed a relentless pace. *The Panic Zone* is written with sizzling intent."

–*Hamilton Spectator*

VENGEANCE ROAD

"*Vengeance Road* is a thriller with no speed limit! It's a great read!"

–Michael Connelly, *New York Times* bestselling author

SIX SECONDS

"*Six Seconds* should be Rick Mofina's breakout thriller. It moves like a tornado."

–James Patterson, *New York Times* bestselling author

Also by Rick Mofina

THEY DISAPPEARED
THE BURNING EDGE
IN DESPERATION
THE PANIC ZONE
VENGEANCE ROAD
SIX SECONDS

And watch for Rick Mofina's next thriller

WHIRLWIND

coming soon from Harlequin MIRA

Other books by Rick Mofina

A PERFECT GRAVE
EVERY FEAR
THE DYING HOUR
BE MINE
NO WAY BACK
BLOOD OF OTHERS
COLD FEAR
IF ANGELS FALL

RICK
MOFINA

INTO THE DARK

HARLEQUIN® MIRA®

ISBN-13: 978-0-7783-1500-1

INTO THE DARK

For questions and comments about the quality of this book, please contact us at CustomerService@Harlequin.com.

Printed in U.S.A.

This book is for Carsten Stroud,
a wise master who showed me the way.

This is an evil among all things that are done
under the sun, that there is one event unto all:
yea, also the heart of the sons of men is full of evil,
and madness is in their heart while they live,
and after that they go to the dead.

—*Ecclesiastes* 9:3

1

Temple City, California,
2007

It started with the neighbors' dog.

Tucker, the Bradfords' cocker spaniel, was barking, but Ruth Peterson, who lived next door, paid no attention to him as she got ready to run errands. Her thoughts were on the new shoes she needed for her son's graduation from Berkeley in two weeks. Then, moving through her home, she glimpsed Tucker in the Bradfords' yard.

That's odd. Why doesn't Bonnie see to him?

Ruth dismissed it, but as she collected her purse and keys, the barking made her wonder for a few seconds. Tucker was a good dog, friendly, and Bonnie Bradford's kids, Jimmy and Jessie, adored him. Ruth never heard a peep out of him, certainly not at night.

In her driveway, Ruth reached for her car door but hesitated.

Tucker's barking was stronger now as it rose from the backyard.

Ruth took stock of the Bradfords' neat ranch-style house and bit her bottom lip. She hated to disturb Bonnie, not when she was trying to meet a deadline for her latest screenplay. Bonnie's ex, the building contractor, had the kids with him in Thousand Oaks for a week and she was using the time to finish her script. At least that's what she'd told Ruth when they'd chatted over the fence the other night.

Still, Ruth grew concerned at Tucker's continual barking.

After giving it a moment, she walked over to Bonnie's front door and rang the bell. Nothing happened. Not a hint of movement inside. Bonnie's car was in the driveway.

She had to be home.

Ruth went around to the back, where Tucker greeted her on the patio with more barking before entering the house through his little dog door. It squeaked a few times, swinging in his wake.

Ruth knocked.

Nothing happened, other than Tucker resuming his barking, now with an eerie echo as if the house were vacant. Ruth knocked again harder, but this time when she struck the door, it opened, startling her.

Strange.

Catching her breath, she gripped the handle firmly and poked her head inside the entrance to the kitchen.

"Bonnie! It's Ruth Peterson, is everything okay?"

Tucker emerged, barking in the silence.

Unease swirled in Ruth's mind.

Maybe Bonnie's slept in, or left her house with a friend, or forgot to lock the door, or she's listening to music with headphones...

"Bonnie!"

Ruth stepped into the kitchen and took quick inventory. She saw nothing on the table or counter, no dishes in the sink. The stove was switched off. Nothing was on. Nothing seemed awry, except for the dog.

She lowered herself, and Tucker rushed into her arms.

"Goodness, you're trembling."

His barking evolved into a mournful yelping, then he squirmed until she set him down and watched him trot down the hallway still barking.

Ruth followed him.

She was familiar with the house. Bonnie had invited her over for tea several times and they got along well. Scanning the family room and living room, she saw nothing that looked out of place.

The air was still.

Ruth called out for Bonnie again as she walked along the hall.

The children's rooms with their movie and pop-star posters were empty, their beds were made and all toys were in place. A wide-eyed teddy bear, its mouth a permanent *O,* stared at her from Jessie's bed.

Ruth moved down the hall and stood at the entrance to Bonnie's small office. Sunlight flooded the room. Pages of script were spread over her desk and credenza. Next to her computer keyboard: a ceramic mug, half-filled with tea, with World's Greatest Mom emblazoned on it.

The desk lamp was still on.

Looks like Bonnie stepped away briefly from her work.

As Ruth moved toward Bonnie's bedroom, she detected an unusual smell. The light, pleasant citrus fragrance of Bonnie's house now contended with a coppery metallic odor.

Tucker stood at the entrance to Bonnie's bedroom,

barking as if alarmed by—*or terrified of*—what was inside.

When Ruth looked, her immediate thought was a question: Who made this awful mess in Bonnie's bed? She could not believe her eyes.

Ruth didn't remember screaming or racing from the house to the front yard. She never recalled Len Blake, the retired firefighter two doors down, dropping his garden hose and leaving it running as he rushed to her aid. Ruth had no memory of telling him over and over that she needed to get to the mall to buy shoes.

All Ruth remembered was that if he'd stopped holding her, she would surely have fallen off the face of the earth.

In the whirlwind that followed there were police, TV crews, the yellow tape sealing the house as stunned neighbors watched the moon-suited investigators come and go.

Then the detectives came with their questions.

For nearly two weeks the gruesome murder of a single mother in her middle-class suburban home remained one of L.A.'s top news stories. Pictures of the pretty screenwriter accompanied every report.

Ross Corbett, Bonnie's ex-husband, seemed devastated at her funeral.

Detectives traced her final movements in an intense effort to find a lead in the case. But they had no solid physical evidence and no suspects. Bonnie Bradford had no enemies, no debts and no unusual lifestyle networks. She lived an ordinary life and was loved by everyone who knew her.

Detectives compared her murder with other cases, looking for links, a pattern, anything. Nothing emerged. They set up a tip line, appealed to the public for help, but as weeks became months, Bonnie's death remained enveloped in mystery.

Her children never returned to their home in Temple City. Eventually the Bradford property was sold and Jessie and Jimmy moved in with their father. Ruth Peterson and her husband sold their home and moved to the Bay Area to be closer to their son.

After the first year passed, the *Los Angeles Times* published an anniversary feature on the unsolved murder. Investigators, hopeful that it might jar someone's memory and yield a tip, were disappointed.

In the years that followed, the primary detective on the case retired. Eight months later, his partner died of a heart attack.

The case grew colder.

It looked like Bonnie Bradford's killer had gone free.

2

Commerce, California

The image on the computer screen resembled a child's crude painting of an outstretched hand.

Ghostly and somewhat grotesque: five misshapen fingerprints stood out from five reddish-brownish rivers that meandered amid smudges down the white page.

It was feathered amid the kid art, the take-out menus, a calendar, notes, business cards, a snapshot of mother, daughter and son beaming at the Santa Monica Pier, all pinned to the family bulletin board in the kitchen.

Typical of a young, happy family, Detective Joe Tanner thought.

It was getting late. He was expecting a call at any moment. While he waited he went back to his work.

The board stood in innocent juxtaposition to the outrage down the hall. Down the hall is where a neighbor had discovered the body of Bonnie Catherine Bradford in the bedroom of her home in Temple City, nearly six years ago.

Bradford, a thirty-four-year-old divorced mother of two children, had been tied spread-eagled to her bed and—well, the crime scene photos illustrated what the killer had done. Tanner clicked his mouse, opening more photos on his computer monitor.

The walls, the bed, "frenzied overkill," one of the reports said.

It didn't matter how many times he'd looked at the pictures in the past few weeks, Tanner still seethed at the fact that whoever did this in 2007 had gotten away with it.

The Bradford killing had now fallen to Tanner and the detectives with the Los Angeles County Sheriff's Cold Case Unit. It was among the hundreds of other cases they oversaw. And in that time a few tips had surfaced: people heard talk on the street, in a bar or a jail cell, but ultimately all of them dead-ended.

Even as leads turned cold, the Bradford case, like the others, was always there, calling out to be solved. But no matter how frustrating it was for cold case investigators, it was brutal for the survivors who called or wrote, struggling to make sure the death of their loved one would never be forgotten, that one day, justice would be done.

Bonnie Bradford's ex-husband, Ross Corbett, who'd long been cleared as a suspect, called Tanner on anniversary days, the day they were married, the day Bonnie was murdered or Bonnie's birthday.

"We had our troubles, but I always loved her," he'd say as Tanner listened with sincere compassion. "Are you any closer? Is there anything I can do to help?" Corbett always asked the same thing.

But it was Corbett's last call, some three weeks ago, that hit a nerve. He'd told Tanner how the kids at his son's school had said that the cops were never going to find the guy who killed Jimmy's mom.

Tanner knew better than anyone that there were certain types of killers you couldn't stop—*like the one who took my wife*—but the one who murdered Bonnie Bradford was not one of them.

This case was solvable and it was his duty to clear it.

The question was: How?

After Corbett's call, Tanner and his partner, Harvey Zurn, set out once more to take another, "fresh" look at the case by first pulling out the thick accordion files. They also delved into the unit's database for the computerized files of the Bradford case and reviewed all the witness statements given by those who knew or had any dealings with Bonnie in the weeks before her death. They went through files and reports going back in the last year of her life. They consulted file notes about her habits, hobbies, the patterns of her life, who she had contact with. They called up people and re-interviewed them, even challenged the validity of statements that seemed questionable.

Tanner followed the creed of a long-retired detective who'd told him that in most cases, the key you need is right in front of you.

And something surfaced.

Tanner had been examining the crime scene photos, doing his neo-Sherlockian best enlarging them on his computer screen. The victim's hands and fingers were bloodstained owing to defensive wounds, the reports had noted.

Studying a file of photos the scene people had taken of the rest of the home, he'd come across a family bulletin board in the kitchen, plastered with a calendar, business cards, notes and works of kid art. In the Bradford collection he saw a colored pencil drawing of a cat, another one of sunflowers, a single page with a handprint in paint and then a small paint-by-numbers of dolphins.

The handprint.

Something about it struck Tanner as odd. Call it instinct, or a gut feeling but it just seemed out of place, even though it was neatly overlapped by the children's work.

Where did that handprint come from? The inventory sheets indicated that while appointment notes from the calendar were followed up on, nothing from the bulletin board had been processed. Where was that handprint now?

Tanner called Ross Corbett.

"We need to see the artwork from the bulletin board that was in the kitchen. I hope you didn't throw it out?" Tanner asked him.

"No, we had a moving company collect most things and move them into storage," Corbett said. "We wouldn't have even looked at what was on that board, we were too traumatized."

No one at the time had noticed anything different about the bulletin board.

Corbett volunteered to let Tanner and Zurn accompany him as he retrieved the artwork from the bulletin board. The drawings were stored in a file folder and were in good condition.

Jimmy Bradford, who was now thirteen, shook his head when Tanner and Zurn had asked him if he had made the handprint.

"Nope, I didn't make it. I would've remembered."

Jimmy's eleven-year-old sister, Jessie, hadn't made it.

"I drew the cat and the flowers. Jimmy made the

dolphin picture," she said. "I never saw that hand thing before."

Tanner and Zurn had sent the handprint to the crime lab for analysis days ago. Charlene Podden, a forensic technician, alerted Tanner that morning that she'd have a preliminary report to him by five today.

The waiting started gnawing at him because it underscored that this potential evidence should've been analyzed at the time of the murder but wasn't. At 5:41 his landline rang at his desk.

"It's Charlene at the lab. I'm sorry for the delay, Joe."

"You find anything on that handprint?"

"This is just a preliminary, okay? We need to do more work."

"More work? Charlene this case has been cold for six years. Tell me how come this stuff was not processed six years ago."

"Maybe it was overlooked. Maybe somebody made an assumption, or lost a report. Look, I honestly don't know. It was before my time."

"Okay, forget it. Let's get to work. What can you tell me?"

"The drawing was produced with blood, human blood."

"The victim's blood?"

"Some of it."

"Some?"

"And there are latents," Podden added, "but they have to be processed, Joe, so give us time to get to that."

"Are they good?"

"Yes, and there's more."

Tanner pressed his phone harder to his ear.

"There's something under the largest, darkest smudge,

something the artist intentionally covered or concealed on purpose—a message in tiny letters, likely scratched using the tip of a pencil."

"What does it say?"

"'I'm just getting started.'"

3

Alhambra, California

He'd been patient.

Hiding so long in the house where he'd been watching her, studying her.

His heart thundered against the bones of his rib cage. He inched toward her without making a sound until he stood over her bed as she slept

Skin tingling with excitement he fought the urge to look at himself in her mirror.

He'd taken such loving care preparing for tonight.

His face was coated in thick white makeup so bright it glowed, like some evil Kabuki force. A swath of red smeared in a downward curve across his mouth. His cheeks were a maelstrom of theatrical cuts and scars, while large smudge pools of black accentuated his hollow eyes, his left one wept a trail of painted teardrops.

He was naked.

Now, here he was, standing over her.

Watching her.

He owned her.

Amber Pratt: She was a lonely secretary, an abused, heartbroken woman.

She was prey.

He knelt beside her, drawing his face near enough to drink in her breath, his aching to touch her as silent as the flicking of a snake's tongue.

Do it now.

As he stood to take action, an inexplicable spear of doubt pierced him.

It felt so painful he wavered.

Suddenly Amber stirred, moaning and rolling over.

No, it was not right. Not yet.

He sank back into the darkness and disappeared into the night.

4

Los Angeles, California

As Claire Bowen sat at the wheel of her car on Wilshire Boulevard waiting for the light to change, she met the sweetest pair of eyes.

They belonged to the pigtailed little girl crossing the street with a woman who was pushing a stroller holding a sleeping baby. The woman must be the girl's mother, Claire judged by the resemblance.

As the trio moved across the intersection in front of Claire, she guessed the girl to be about three. One of her tiny hands gripped the stroller. The other was clamped on the stuffed bunny tucked under her arm. Her pretty eyes were locked on Claire's.

Claire gave her a small wave and a smile. The girl's little fingers holding the bunny wiggle-waved back. The mother, who'd noticed, gazed down at her daughter with wearied joy.

Will I ever know that kind of love? Claire asked herself.

It was a bittersweet moment that hammered home the fact that time was running out for her.

All Dr. LaRoy's office said was that he needed to see me this morning.

Claire knew that her chances of having a child decreased with each passing day. She was thirty-five and happily married to Robert Bowen, a pilot. She was a psychologist with a successful practice and a lot to be thankful for. But ever since she was confronted years ago with the probability that she would never have children, she felt something was slipping away. She had to hang on to the hope that things would work out.

She'd never give up.

Claire was a survivor.

A horn sounded behind her.

The light had turned green. As she continued driving, towering condo buildings rose before her. She had accepted that some things in this world were absolutes. We're born, we die, and there is only so much in between that we can control. But she was unwilling to accept that she would never be a mother.

She had gotten pregnant three times, but in each instance she'd suffered a miscarriage. She had seen many doctors and had faced countless tests, examinations, procedures and treatments.

Nothing worked.

The specialists found complications linked to her failed pregnancies. But throughout her anguish she would not give up, even when the odds mounted against her.

Even when they'd nearly destroyed her.

Claire's memory flashed to the frightening incident that had ended her first marriage a few years ago. She did not want to think about it now. One thing was certain: there was no telling what could've happened had

Robert not been there that day, which had marked the beginning of her life with him. Unlike Cliff, her first husband, Robert never made her feel as if she was less of a woman or that her infertility was her fault.

"I'll do whatever it takes," Robert said when she told him about it. "We're in this together, Claire."

Robert went through everything with her in their three years together—tests for him, new workups for her. Robert's count and motility were fine. And while they sought new doctors, new experts for Claire, the reality was sobering. Aside from Claire's problems, she knew the chances of miscarrying increased for women thirty-five and older; along with the risk of late-pregnancy complications.

As a psychologist Claire counseled herself to prepare to accept that nothing was working, that her feelings of emptiness, anger, guilt and depression were normal reactions. She'd struggled not to let her infertility dominate the good life they had built together.

But it was so hard.

The problem manifested itself every day, every time she saw a pregnant woman, or a mother pushing a stroller, every time someone in her circle announced a pregnancy, a baby shower, a birth, it was there, underscoring her isolation.

She had devoted herself to helping troubled women, women who'd been abused. She guided them through the tragedies in their lives, helped them recognize lifelines, repair the damage and take control. Because she was contending with her own secret sorrow, it made her better at her job.

Above everything, she counseled her patients to

never, ever, lose sight of the possibility that things could get better.

For Claire, her latest grasp at hope now stood before her at the edge of the Wilshire Corridor in the shape of a gleaming ten-story complex and the offices of Dr. Marlen LaRoy.

He was one of California's leading fertility experts—a pioneer specializing in controversial treatments. Claire had been seeing him for the past few months. In that time she'd undergone a series of procedures and examinations to determine if she was a candidate for a radical experimental treatment.

Claire had been surprised, and mildly annoyed, when his office called her this morning to make a sudden, unscheduled appointment without giving her a hint as to what it was about.

She steered her Toyota into a parking space, then reached for her phone. Making this appointment meant she had had to juggle sessions with her patients, which was a concern.

She called her assistant.

"Doctor Bowen's office."

"Hi, Alice, it's Claire. How is everybody doing?"

"So far so good. Except for Amber Pratt."

"Amber? I don't see her until next week."

"She said she's anxious, feels like she's being watched. She wants to push up her next session."

"Okay, see what we can do. Thanks. Gotta go."

Claire took a deep breath, then headed into the lobby and stepped into the elevator, hoping she could get back to her practice by eleven.

"Ms. Bowen." The receptionist stood to greet her. "Thank you for coming. Our apologies for such short notice, but Dr. LaRoy has to fly to a conference in Dallas today and insisted on seeing you beforehand."

The receptionist directed Claire to the doctor's office.

LaRoy was standing at the window, talking on his cell phone, and indicated for her to take the chair across from his desk. LaRoy was a thickset fifty-nine-year-old New Yorker, who'd graduated from Harvard. He had white hair and an air of sweet, gentle grumpiness. He finished his call, took his seat.

"Hello, Claire. We've got some results. I need to show you something before we talk."

LaRoy began pecking at his keyboard that faced two monitors. He swiveled one toward Claire and showed her a series of images and graphs. For the next several minutes he reviewed the goal of the previous tests and procedures Claire had undergone. As LaRoy went over every detail, pointing to the monitor and explaining other images, Claire felt her pulse quicken.

"This is all good, right?" she said.

"It's very good. Claire, this means you are receptive to the new drug and new cycle therapy. I'll need you to sign some paperwork and take some literature home and read it."

"Then what?"

"We'll start you in a few weeks."

"And then?"

"Within a few months you'll be pregnant."

"I've been pregnant before."

"Yes, but I'm quite confident that this time you'll give birth to a healthy baby."

Tears filled her eyes.

"Really?"

"We've checked your results carefully. All the indications are strong, Claire." LaRoy passed her a tissue. "Really strong."

5

Van Nuys, California

Pilot Robert Bowen eased the Gulfstream jet into the corporate hangar for ExecuGlide and cut its twin engines.

He liked the G200. It had a smart design and flew evenly no matter what the conditions were. Taxiing and landings were fluid.

God, how he loved to fly—loved the rush of power and control, *to rise above everything on earth.*

"That was a nice touchdown, Tim. Good to be home," he said to his copilot, switching everything off and unbuckling his belts.

After bidding farewell to the eight TV producers they'd flown on a multi-city charter to Seattle, Vancouver and San Francisco, Bowen collected his bag and signed off on the flight. Heading for his SUV in the parking lot, he turned on his phone to text Claire, to let her know he'd returned.

A text from her was waiting for him.

Wishing you a safe landing. Dr. LaRoy's office called me in this am. No appt—wouldn't say why. Have to scramble. Good news maybe??? Talk later.
Love C.

Bowen responded.

Good landing. Good trip. Good luck with doc—any word?

He waited several minutes.

When no response came he figured Claire was driving, or with the doctor.

After placing his bag in the rear he got into his SUV. Nothing was out of place. No disturbed maps, take-out wrappers or filthy commuter cups. It was spotless, showroom clean and still smelled new. Bowen insisted on order. The leather seats squeaked as he buckled up. He flipped on the radio and listened to traffic conditions, then decided to take Ventura to the 101, rather than swinging over to the 5.

Joining the freeway traffic, he considered Claire's text to him. He was hopeful her sudden call to see Dr. LaRoy would result in good news. How many times had they had their hopes raised only to be disappointed? It was not fair to Claire. It hurt him to see her anguish. She ached to have a baby, he wanted one, too, for her. It had cost them thousands, but he didn't care. He loved her and would do anything for her. He didn't want to lose what he had with her, the way he'd lost what he'd had with his first wife.

Cynthia.

Like Claire, Cynthia was beautiful and so giving. In his quieter moments he still thought of her. They had been so in love. At that time he was flying commercial, his schedule was brutal and he was rarely home. Cynthia began to change. She complained, grew jealous and started imagining terrible things.

It shouldn't have ended the way it did, but they couldn't continue and that was that. Why dwell on it? Sometimes, even after all these years, he'd felt something was unresolved and wished he could talk to Cynthia, to tell her he was sorry about the way it had turned out for them. But he had a new life now, a good life, and you can't go back in time.

Bowen left Ventura and got on the 101 southbound. There was more traffic, but it was moving at a good speed. He'd gone less than half a mile when something blue rocketed by in the left lane, startling him.

He cursed.

The thing must've been doing one-thirty. Looked like a pickup truck. He couldn't tell the model as it knifed through the lanes ahead, leaving a wake of brake lights and angry horns.

That idiot's going to kill somebody.

The distraction passed, and with it, Cynthia faded from his mind.

He repositioned his grip on the wheel, maintained a safe speed as his thoughts had drifted back to the first time he'd met Claire. *The scene with her and her husband.* Bowen shook his head slowly until the images of that day dissipated. Since that time all he'd wanted to do was protect Claire, let nothing hurt her again. *But how do I protect her from heartbreak—from forces that are beyond my control?*

He dragged the back of his hand across his mouth. He was forty-five, and some days he couldn't see what Claire told him she'd seen and liked: The small crinkles around his eyes, his chiseled jaw, his thick salt-and-pepper hair. He was six-one, about one-eighty. His workouts gave him an athletic build. But he didn't see the strong, decisive, capable, kind man that Claire saw. He saw a man who'd failed too many times, a man constantly at war with himself, a man unworthy of her.

At times he would steal glimpses of her when they were at home, or while he waited for her at her office. He liked how her hair curtained over her eyes when she studied her notes, or the way she slid her small silver cross back and forth on her necklace chain when she was on the phone with a patient. She was devoted to them—compassionate and caring, never allowing her own heartache to interfere.

He didn't deserve her.

As he drove, Bowen massaged his temple. A million things rushed through his head. He was tired from the flight and stressed over those rumors of looming cutbacks at the company.

He couldn't go back to commercial. He couldn't face those hours again and that kind of strain at home. He just couldn't. Look at the toll it had taken with Cynthia. He couldn't go through that with Claire.

But that was the least of his worries.

There was more, much more.

The darkness is back, stirring again.

It had been triggered by Claire when she started taking serious steps to have a baby, because in a corner of his heart he knew that would change everything.

The darkness is taking over. Sometimes at night, I feel I—

The chaos of horns and screeching tires jerked his concentration to the freeway where traffic ahead had come to a standstill.

6

Los Angeles, California

Robert stopped and got out of his SUV, joining other drivers craning their necks at the heaps of mangled metal several car lengths away.

A boy, about twelve, staggered between the stopped cars toward him. The kid's face glistened with crimson scrapes. His T-shirt with a T-Rex on it was torn, smeared with blood. Somewhere a woman was screaming.

"Por favor ayuda!" The boy's eyes, wide with shock, found Bowen's and he switched to English. "My mother, my sister, please, mister, they will die. Please save them!" Robert's mind raced.

"Por favor ayuda!" the boy pleaded again before he collapsed into the arms of a well-dressed woman who'd stepped from a Mercedes. She wrapped her Realtor's jacket around him as he sobbed, "Please! My mother… my sister…they'll die. Please, mister!"

Bowen tore off his tie and ran to the carnage.

Some motorists were calling 9-1-1 while others, uncertain what to do, stood helpless. Black smoke now curled from the wreckage.

Bowen counted three vehicles: a pickup that appeared

to be a landscaper's truck was turned around, its front smashed and air bags depleted. Mowers, tillers, tools and supplies were scattered. He saw a small green car that had flipped onto its roof. Then he saw a van; it was on its side with its hood folded open and its engine on fire. A man was climbing out of the van's driver's side. Blood oozed from his mouth as he gritted in pain. Bowen got hold of his arm and got him to the ground.

"I've got a first aid kit," said a motorist wearing a Lynyrd Skynyrd T-shirt who'd stepped forward to help.

When Bowen turned to the inverted car, something splashed at his feet. He looked down to a widening puddle with the telltale rainbow film and smelled the fumes. Fuel cans from the landscaper's truck had ruptured, spilling gasoline everywhere around the overturned car, pooling in spots. Bowen glanced at the flames licking from the van's engine a few feet from the car.

The fire was growing.

His stomach lurched. He saw a hand reaching from the car and heard a woman crying softly as someone shouted at him, "Get out of there, man! There's too much gas, it's going to blow! Back off! Get out!"

He ignored the warning and hurried to the driver's side of the car. He dropped to his hands and knees. Everything had been unfolding with dizzying speed, but it slowed the instant he saw the woman.

She was upside down. Her hands and arms hung to the ground. The air bags had deployed. She was still belted to her seat and pleading weakly.

"Please, save my baby."

Bowen's attention moved beyond the woman to the back. He saw the child, about a-year-and-a-half-old, upside down, strapped in its car seat, little arms hanging down.

"Please," the woman cried.

In a surreal moment Bowen saw how the gasoline now seeped into areas of the car. Then he noticed among bags of clothes, boxes of cereal and cans of soup, a leather-bound bible. It had splayed open, a light wind lifting the pages.

The blood rush in his ears pounded him into a trance-like state.

He found himself looking into the woman's terrified eyes.

He swelled with pleasure, his ears rang and an ancient, familiar, evil erupted inside him.

Let her die.

I hold this woman's life, and that of her child, in my hands, the power over life and death, the power to rise above everything on earth.

Go ahead and plead.

I love it.

I am the beginning and I am the end.

I'm going to let you die. Your baby, too. I'll watch you die.

"I'm sorry," Bowen said. "I can't reach you. I'm sorry."

Her eyes bulged. Her fear excited him, pushing his sensual gratification to a new level.

"Please!" she gasped.

Keep begging. Beg me for your life.

She coughed. Her voice was fading.

"Please, I beg you, please! God, someone, please save us!"

The break in her voice connected with Bowen, telling him he could not let this happen. He closed his eyes, battling himself for control as the woman's cries slowly pulled him out of his trance and back into the chaos.

"Okay," Bowen said. "Okay, ma'am, I'm going to get you out."

He maneuvered his upper body deeper into the car and, while on his knees, reached up, feeling for and finding the woman's seat belt buckle.

"Can you get your arms around my neck?" he said.

He felt her lock her arms around him, felt her trembling, she smelled of soap and sweat and was nearly choking him as he tried to depress the button to release the belt. The woman's full downward weight had created pressure and the button refused to depress.

Bowen tried but it wouldn't move.

Panicked motorists were shouting.

"Get out now!"

"It's going to go up—get out!"

He glimpsed the flames horribly large and nearing the gas pools that patched their way to the car. He reached deep into himself and with every bit of strength he had in him he lifted the woman's weight upward, taking pressure off of the belt while depressing the button with every fiber of strength he had until he heard: *click.*

The belt released.

The woman slid down onto him and he immediately dragged her out of the car where helping hands seized both of them.

"My baby!"

Bowen shook off the people pulling him to safety and crawled back into the car for the child.

"No, don't do it!" Someone shouted. "It's too late!"

The fire had now grown large enough for Bowen to

hear its roar as he scrambled inside to the baby's seat. He shifted his body, relieved to hear the child crying. He reached up, fumbled for the buckle and button, and lifted the child to ease weight from the buckle.

Click.

He got it.

Taking a deep breath, he disentangled the baby from the car seat. He started snaking backward with the child at his chest. He'd just gotten his legs out the window when someone screamed—

"Oh, my God!"

He turned to see the flames lapping the gasoline pools, felt the air spasm as the pools ignited in a chain reaction creating a blinding, churning wall of fire that swallowed them.

7

Los Angeles, California

Claire Bowen was unsure her feet even touched the ground as she left the building and got into her car. She cupped her hands to her face.

I have to tell Robert.

Glancing at the time, she reached for her cell phone and read his response to her earlier text to him.

Good landing. Good trip. Good luck with doc—any word?

Great, he's back, she thought, her fingers blurring as she texted him.

Can you call me now!!!

As the minutes passed, she scanned the literature about ovulation. Not much there she didn't already know. She glanced at her phone. Unless Robert was stuck in traffic or couldn't pull over, he was usually pretty quick at getting back to her. Two minutes passed, then three.

While waiting, Claire revisited a small concern. Over

the past few weeks he seemed to have become a little withdrawn, as if wrestling with something. Whenever she'd asked him about it, he'd tell her that he was merely lost in his thoughts, leaving her to wonder if everything really was okay with him.

Claire checked the time. Too excited to wait, she pressed her cell's keypad for his number. The phone rang twice before a woman answered.

"I'm sorry," Claire said. "I've misdialed."

"This is Robert Bowen's phone," a woman said. "Who's calling?"

What the heck?

"I'm Claire Bowen, his wife. And who are you?"

"Mrs. Bowen, I'm a nurse at Pacific Breeze Memorial Hospital. I just called your office. Your husband's just been brought in—"

"Brought in? What for? What happened?"

"He's been involved in a car accident—he's—"

"A car accident? Is he hurt? Can you put him on the phone now, please?"

Claire could hear the hospital's loudspeaker system echoing in the background.

"I can't. He's with the E.R. doctor, Mrs. Bowen—" Claire fished out her keys and turned the ignition as the nurse continued. "All I can tell you at this point is that he does not appear to have any serious injuries."

"You've seen him? You're certain?"

"Yes, I'm in the E.R. He's been brought in for observation. It's just happened now. We've got a number of trauma patients."

Claire keyed the hospital's name into her GPS. She could be there in twenty-five minutes, less if the traffic was good.

"Please tell him I'm on my way."

"Certainly, Mrs. Bowen."

"Wait, what's your name?"

"Lilly Springer."

"I'll ask for you at the desk."

When Claire ended the call, her phone rang.

"Claire, it's Alice." Alarm sounded in her voice. "The Pacific Breeze hospital just called about Robert and a car accident."

"I know. I just spoke with the E.R. nurse. She said he's okay."

"Oh, thank heaven."

"I'm on my way to the hospital."

"Okay, want me to clear your schedule for the rest of the day? You have a couple of hours until your next patient."

"Don't move anything yet. I'll have a better idea after I get to the hospital. I'll call."

Driving through the city, Claire took a few deep breaths to keep calm, never letting go of the nurse's assurance that Robert was not hurt. But it ran counter to human nature not to worry and Claire would not be assured until she saw him, until she held him.

She thought of their last moment together a few days ago and remembered his cologne, the rustle of his crisp shirt and the brush of his lips on hers. She was still in bed and he'd bent down, lifted her hair and kissed her goodbye in the early morning before he'd left for this trip.

"I love you," he'd whispered.

And now this.

This reminder of how life can change in an instant.

The web of our existence is a fragile thing.

Claire knew that too well from her own life and the lives of her patients—how dreams could be taken away or shattered. *We're on the threshold of becoming parents*—a dream they had long been denied.

Arriving at the hospital, Claire saw four ambulances at the emergency entrance. Nearby she saw a number of police vehicles and TV news trucks. She hurried through the automatic doors. Half a dozen media people had gathered around a hospital official at one side of the lobby and were pressing her for information. Claire continued to the woman seated at the reception window. Behind her, two staff members stood as they worked at computer terminals.

"May I help you?"

"I'm here to see my husband, Robert Bowen. I'm Claire Bowen, his wife. I spoke on the phone to an E.R. nurse, Lilly Springer."

The receptionist's face registered recognition and she turned to the women behind her.

"Lil?"

One of the women stepped from the counter. She was fresh-scrubbed, with a ponytail and an upturned nose.

"Hello, Mrs. Bowen, I'm Lilly." She nodded at the door to the right of the window and it buzzed. "Come through here, please."

Antiseptic smells hung heavy in the air as they moved down the polished hallway. The nurse's soft-soled shoes squeaked when they stopped at a small waiting room.

"Please have a seat, Mrs. Bowen. The doctor will be with you shortly."

"How long before I see my husband? You said he was okay?"

"Yes, it should only be a few more minutes."

"Can you tell me what happened?"

"The doctor should have more information." The nurse smiled before leaving.

Claire took stock of the room—of its brown faux leather sofas and outdated copies of *Time* and *People* on wicker tables. Still tense from the drive and worry, she sat down and inhaled slowly. On the sofa facing her, a woman with a wrinkled face bowed her head to the rosary in her gnarled fingers. The beads clicked softly and her lips moved as she prayed. Sitting beside the woman was a younger man. His T-shirt, blue jeans and work boots were stained with blotches of paint. He looked as if he'd rushed here from a work site. He stared into the worn ball cap in his lap as if it held his past and his future.

They were the only people still in the room with Claire when a man arrived, wearing a white lab coat over blue scrubs and carrying a chart.

"Mrs. Bowen, here for Robert Bowen?"

"Yes." Claire stood.

"Dr. Shaw." He shook Claire's hand. "We'll talk in the room across the hall." The room was smaller; the doctor left the door open indicating their conversation would be brief. Claire stood while he tapped a pen on the chart as he reviewed it.

"Your husband's fine." He kept reading.

"Can you tell me about his car accident?"

"As I understand it, he was not involved, but came upon it and helped rescue people. He was pulled away just as the wreckage exploded."

"Dear God."

"He's lucky. He and the people he saved are fine. He's got some abrasions and very mild shock, but he can go home. We'll give you sedatives so he can rest at home. I'll take you to him, then you can sign some papers for discharge." He smiled.

"Thank you, Dr. Shaw."

"And we understand there are some press folks who are interested in talking to him out front. That's entirely up to him of course."

They turned to leave but the doorway was blocked by the man who had been in the waiting room with Claire. He was holding his ball cap with both hands, slipping its rim through his paint-flecked fingers.

"Can I help you?" Dr. Shaw said.

"Please forgive me, but I overheard—" he nodded to Claire "—about your husband." Claire shot a questioning glance to Dr. Shaw, but the man continued. His accented English was strong. "I am Ruben Montero. My son, Alex, he is eleven and he was in the accident with my wife and daughter. They were delivering donations to our church."

"Yes," Dr. Shaw said, recognizing the name. "Alex. He's with Anne, Dr. Feldstein. Would you like me to see about him?"

"No, I've spoken to him. We're going to see my wife and daughter soon. But Alex told me what this lady's husband did for my wife, Maria, and our baby, Bonita."

"Oh, yes. He must have helped get them to safety," Claire said, surprised when Ruben Montero suddenly took her hand.

"He saved the lives of my family," Claire felt Montero's callused hand tighten on hers and looked into his face, close enough to notice his stubble. "For that, I thank him with every beat of my heart. Tell him for me."

"I will, Mr. Montero."

“You are blessed for having such a man for your husband. You are blessed because a man like this…a man like this, is rare.”

8

Los Angeles, California

Robert Bowen was alone.

He was sitting on the table of the examination room. The faint ringing in his ears had stopped. He stared at the large clock on the wall above the eye chart and scales. Outside the closed door he heard the loudspeaker's muffled dispatches over the bustle in the hall while here, in the quiet, he listened to the whir of the clock's movement.

It was only a moment ago that he'd held the baby…

...then hands grasp his legs, drag them from the car... clear, the explosion, lift the wreckage, rattle the debris, the flames, heat, hands drag them...the ensuing mayhem, the baby's cries, the sirens, the paramedics: "Can you hear me, sir? We're taking you to the hospital... The baby's going to be okay!"

Everyone had survived, they'd told him, with no life-threatening injuries.

A miracle.

The clock's minute hand swept time.

He was still shaky. His few scrapes had been cleaned and dressed. A nurse had said Claire was on her way.

The room smelled of rubbing alcohol and held a trace of gas. His white shirt, torn, streaked with road grime, along with his pants, was stuffed into a clear plastic bag in the corner. They'd given him a surgeon's T-shirt and pants to get home in.

He stared at nothing, contemplating the last few moments. Adrenaline was still rippling through him. He massaged his temples, shut his eyes and again he was cast back to the accident.

An ominous wave rolled over him then suddenly…*the hands that had grasped his legs became talons pulling him into the inferno, dragging him down, down, down, through the burning recesses, through the lava slime of every shame, to the breathing, heaving bubbling pit of every foul, cursed thought, every bestial urge. Every vile desire, until he came to... It calls to him now, demanding he answer: Why did you let the woman and her baby live?*

Bowen said nothing.

No one knew the battle raging within him.

The soft buzzing of the clock's movement filled the silence that passed.

He continued massaging his temples. For how long, he didn't know. But he kept rubbing until his heart rate slowed, his breathing slowed, until he heard the clock, the subdued sounds of the loudspeaker and activity in the hallway as the door to his room swung open and Claire entered.

"Hey," she said.

"Hey."

She hugged and kissed him.

"How are you doing?" She brushed his hair lightly, taking quick inventory of his scrapes.

"I'm fine, how about you?"

Tears filled her eyes as she nodded and smiled.

"Good. Let's get you home."

An administration staff member and a nurse helped Claire expedite Robert's discharge. As they stepped out of the hospital, Claire saw Ruben Montero turn from talking with a half a dozen reporters.

"That's him, with that lady, the man who saved my family."

Microphones and bright TV lights collected around them.

"Sir, are you Robert Bowen?"

"Yes."

"Carmen Chow, *First Witness News,*" said a woman in her twenties wearing heavy makeup. "Sir, this man says you saved his family. Do you consider yourself a hero?"

Bowen looked at Claire then at Carmen Chow.

"No, I just did what anyone would've done in the same situation."

"We're told a lot of people at the scene were afraid," one reporter said.

"Not this man." Ruben Montero beamed, taking Robert's hand and shaking it. "This man is a good man, a great hero!"

A razor-thin line of unease cut behind Bowen's smile. He knew the truth.

9

Downey, California

Standing in the kitchen of his bungalow, Joe Tanner watched the old video playing on his cell phone of his wife, Rebecca.

"Hi, Joe. I'm feeling pretty good today, I almost think I can beat this, I—" She tried to smile from under the bandana covering the fine tufts that used to be her hair. "If I don't beat this, just hug Sam today for me, okay."

As she touched a tissue to the corners of her eyes, he traced her face on the screen with his finger.

"That's it for this one, sorry," she said.

The video ended.

It was among several hundred Becky had left him, and even though it had been two years, just seeing her and hearing her gave him comfort. It helped him through the hard days, like today. He was anxious about his meeting and what he was going to do about the big break in the Bradford case.

It's what I have to do.

He checked the time on his phone. He was running late. He went to the fridge for milk and eggs, smiling at the watercolor flower framing a photograph of Becky, when she still had beautiful hair. This latest piece of art was created by Samantha Tanner, Age 6, according to the artist's signature. It was titled "My Mommy," and was fastened to the door with a banana magnet, next to Samantha's paintings of a polar bear, a house—"Our House"—and a smiling stick man and smiling stick girl holding hands, titled "Daddy and Me."

Tanner tucked his tie into his dress shirt, draped a dish towel over his shoulder and started scrambling eggs. While they cooked he went down the hall calling to his daughter.

"Come on, Sam! You're going to be late for school!"

"I can't find my socks, Dad!"

"Laundry room! Let's go!"

Back in the kitchen he poured two glasses of orange juice and checked on the eggs. Then he flipped through yesterday's mail: junk, a few bills and a letter from a local charity he'd supported after they'd lost Becky.

Dear Mr. Tanner:

As someone personally affected by the disease, we're hoping we can once again count on your participation to make this year's fundraising event…

Sure, he thought, he'd be there. He set the mail aside and checked the eggs when the phone rang. It was Kim, his sister.

"Joe, do I pick up Sam today, or tomorrow?" she asked while munching. Sounded like an apple.

"You know I hate it when you do that."

"Do what? Help my little bro?"

"Chew in my ear, wiseass."

"Somebody's tense. So—" she kept chewing "—is it today?"

"Hang on." He consulted the calendar on the fridge. The notation "Sam—dentist checkup" occupied the next day's square.

"It's tomorrow. Sign her out of school at one, and thanks."

"Got it. Then I'll take her shopping for new clothes, just us girls."

Tanner wedged the phone to his ear and served eggs from the frying pan onto two plates, then made toast.

"Oh," his sister added, "my friend Remmie is wondering if you're ever going to call her?"

"Stop trying to fix me up."

Everybody in his circle had a desire to see him paired, including his relic of a partner, Harvey Zurn. *"I keep telling you Joe, you should meet my cousin Linda, recently divorced with a little boy. She's ex-military, a good cook with a good figure."*

On the other end of the line, Tanner's sister sighed.

"You need to meet some women, Joey."

"I'm fine— *Sam, breakfast!* Listen, Kim, I love you for helping me and looking out for me but my new unit's keeping me pretty busy. Don't forget, tomorrow at one. Thanks, sis. Please finish eating before calling people. I love you. Bye."

As he set the plates down, Samantha entered the kitchen and before getting into her chair, pulled up her pant legs to reveal one blue sock and one pink sock.

"See? Everybody's doing it, Dad."

She had Becky's eyes and her curls. At times, he could hear her voice.

"You're a weird little kid." He laughed, shaking his head. "Eat up."

Afterward, while Samantha brushed her teeth and her hair, Tanner went to his small study for his badge. He then opened his gun safe for his weapon, clipped on his hip holster and collected his files.

During the drive through North Downey to Samantha's school, he stole glimpses of her in the rearview mirror, sitting in the backseat in her booster seat.

"So how are you doing today, Sam?"

"A-OK, Dad."

"Anything on your mind? You said something was bugging you?"

"How much longer do I have to sit in this seat for babies?"

"Two more years."

"Two years? That's like *forever!*"

"Don't be in too big a hurry to grow up." He grinned.

When they arrived at the school drop-off zone, Samantha climbed out of her seat and the car. Then she appeared at his window, her backpack strapped on. She drew her face to his and he leaned out to hug and kiss her.

"Love you, Daddy."

"Love you, kiddo."

He watched her enter the school, thinking how much she was like Becky. Then he looked at the files on his passenger seat and the summaries of several unsolved homicides. The first had happened ten years ago.

A wave of sadness rolled over him.

He could measure his life against these cold cases.

He couldn't stop his wife's killer, no one could. His challenge now: Would he be able to find the monster behind these slayings? He didn't know if this meeting and what he needed to do were smart moves. Given the issue of timing, dates and some long-shot theories, it looked like his only option.

He picked up the stack of folders and the note affixed to it.

Mark Harding
Reporter
AllNews Press Agency,
Los Angeles Bureau.

10

Commerce, California

"I'm Mark Harding, here to see Detective Joe Tanner."

The receptionist at the Homicide Bureau of the Los Angeles County Sheriff's Department greeted him with a weak smile and a cool assessment.

Harding stood just over five and half feet tall and was sensitive to his height and slight overbite.

"Good morning, Mark. And you're with…"

"I'm a reporter with the AllNews Press Agency."

Charmed, her smile broadened. "Are you British?"

"Yes."

"I love your accent."

The receptionist typed on her keyboard, spoke softly into her headset then looked to Harding. "You're a bit early. Please have a seat. Detective Tanner will be here shortly."

The lobby's cushioned chair gave a vinyl squeak as Harding pondered how he'd come to be here to see Tanner. He didn't know the guy and had never heard of him until a few days ago when Tanner called him.

"We understand you've been inquiring about doing a feature on homicides for your newswire service. Would you be interested in talking about some older, unsolved murders?" the detective had asked.

Tanner had been cryptic during the brief call, declining to get into details over the phone. Still, Harding had said yes because any reporter worth a damn knows that when a homicide cop invites you to a meeting, you don't say no. At the very least, he might leave with a new source.

God knows I need new sources and a kick-ass story.

He'd been working at the L.A. bureau for a few months, but in that time the pressure to break a major exclusive was mounting. Since he'd relocated back to California, he hadn't hit anything out of the park.

You blink and nearly all of your life goes by.

Harding was thirty-seven and grew up in Birmingham. He'd worked for several tabloids in London before getting a green card and landing a job with the Los Angeles bureau of *Rumored Today,* a despised but top-selling U.S. supermarket tabloid.

If reporters failed to break huge, shocking stories, they were fired. Harding hated every bit of it and got the chance to leave the sleaze behind when he broke a huge story about corruption in Hollywood. It resulted in a job with the AllNews Press Agency, the global wire service, first at its head office in New York.

Then Harding was forced to go to the dreaded Los Angeles Bureau, where he was expected to deliver huge stories.

So here I am in L.A., months without scoring a big story.

Harding rubbed his chin.

He had the idea of trying to pull off an exclusive, looking into homicides for any new breaks. In the past couple of weeks he'd put in calls, even sent letters with his card, to the LAPD, L.A. County, the FBI fishing for leads.

Nothing happened until now, when he got a call from Tanner.

Harding had to land a good story.

Sure, other people had it harder and he'd faced worse. He was reflecting on a few of the tense moments he'd had on assignments over the years when something vibrated near his heart.

He reached into his jacket for his phone and checked his messages. He had an urgent one from his boss, Magdalena Pierce, the L.A. Bureau Chief. She'd told him earlier that she disdained gritty crime stories and was reluctant to give him the morning for this meeting with an L.A. County detective. Her new text said:

We've just learned that a studio is under investigation for tax evasion. We need you here, pronto.

Harding rolled his eyes. *Same old, same old. Magda just didn't get it.*

"Excuse me, Mark Harding?"

"Yes."

He put his phone away, shook hands with a man he'd pegged at his age but about six feet. He was wearing a crisp shirt, tie, sidearm.

"Joe Tanner. Thanks for coming. Sorry to keep you waiting."

"Sure. Look," Harding said, "forgive me, I don't mean to sound rude, but my bureau chief's yanking my chain. Could we do this another time?"

"You have to go? You just got here."

"Yes, I apologize."

"I see." Tanner was taken aback. "I'm sorry to hear that. Well, I suppose I could always call the Associated Press or Reuters."

No, Harding could not let that happen.

"Hold on, wait. Can you give me a bit more so I can get my editor off my back, something to convince her this is more than a local Crime Stoppers type of cold case, something that holds national interest?"

"This concerns a number of homicides," Tanner said.

"*Homicides?* Plural?"

"That's correct and only one other person outside this building knows what I'm going to tell you."

"Who's that?"

"The person who committed them."

"Jesus," Harding said. "Let me call my desk."

11

Commerce, California

Tanner escorted Harding beyond the homicide squad bay to the Cold Case Unit and a staff kitchen that was heavy with the aroma of freshly brewed coffee.

"How do you take yours?"

"A little of both," Harding said. "I'm curious. Why did you decide to call me?"

"You showed some initiative with your letter, looking to do something on homicides. And I needed to be sure I went to the right guy for this."

"How am I the right guy?"

"We needed to go to a wire service, because their stories go everywhere. I needed someone I could trust."

"How did you decide that?"

"I remembered you from way back with the Hollywood Washington corruption story when you were with that awful rag, *Rumored Today*."

Harding had uncovered corruption and bribery between production companies, some owned by Hollywood's biggest stars and lawmakers in Washington, D.C.

His solid reporting had forced the national mainstream media to follow and credit *Rumored Today*. As the pressure for an investigation mounted, one angry superstar implicated in the scandal used a film premiere to humiliate Harding during a press conference where he was surrounded by reporters who were ignoring publicists' demands they only talk about the new movie.

The enraged star singled out Harding.

"There's the little sewer-dweller. Look at the tiny troll." The star, who was over half a foot taller, stepped closer to tower over him. "Your stories are crap, Harding. Garbage. And when this is over, I'll still have enough money for a thousand lifetimes, but as long as you live—" the star patted the top of Harding's head as if he were a lapdog "—people will look down on you. You should get those teeth fixed, buddy."

Embarrassed, Harding kept his cool while the star was globally chastised online and on news shows. Harding's reporting led to a federal investigation. Several people were charged, convicted and jailed and the star who had demeaned Harding narrowly missed being charged and going to prison for his role in the corruption scheme.

"I knew some of the investigators on that one," Tanner said. "You stood your ground with egocentric stars." He handed Harding a mug of coffee that had a bulldog insignia on it. "You've sure gotten around over the years. How long you been back in L.A.?"

"A few months."

Harding stared into his coffee for a few seconds.

Tanner let a moment pass before saying, "Let's get started."

He led Harding down the hall to an empty squad room.

"This is my partner, Harvey Zurn."

Zurn was in his late fifties and had the warmth of a ball-peen hammer. Harding offered his hand and Zurn crushed it in his. His dark eyes burned into Harding over a thick dark moustache. The room's blinds were drawn, dimming the light. Updates on a handful of murders written in a felt-tip pen ran across the board on one wall. Faces of the dead stared down from photographs. A laptop sat on a table, a large screen hung over the far wall.

"As I was saying earlier, we discovered some disturbing elements in several homicides and we want to reach out to the public, through a story by you," Tanner said.

"What did you find?"

"I'll get to that. We're dealing with five specific unsolved homicides throughout greater Los Angeles, going back six to ten years. Find a seat. I'll give you an overview." Tanner settled at the laptop. "The first victim..."

A key clicked and the screen filled with the title One over a clear color photo taken in a wooded area. The corpse of a naked white woman rested on the tall grass, with her hands bound behind her back and a cord stretching from there to wrap around her neck. A clear plastic bag covered her head.

"Leeza Meadows. Age twenty-one. A birdwatcher found her body November 9, 2003, at the edge of Santa Clarita. She had been sexually assaulted, among other things, as you can see here."

The screen filled with an enlarged photo of her head. Harding stared, blinked a few times then started making notes as Tanner continued.

"She was last seen leaving her job at the Misty Nights Bar & Grill. Leeza never went anywhere without her cell phone. It was not found at the scene. Two weeks after her body was discovered, someone used Leeza's cell phone to call her home. Her father answered. The caller never spoke but her father insisted someone was on the line, refusing to answer his questions. Investigators determined the call was made from downtown L.A., but that's as far as they got. No other calls were ever made on the phone, which is still missing along with a second item."

"Which is?"

"We're not saying. That item is holdback, a key fact known only to a few investigators and the killer."

"Do you suspect it was the killer who called?"

"That's one theory," Zurn said.

Tanner's laptop displayed another victim's image, labeled Two, which showed a woman's naked torso, on its back, in a shallow grave.

"August 11, 2004, during some construction work for a new subdivision in Topanga, a grader flattening the ground unearthed the body of Esther Fatima Lopez, age twenty-nine. She had been sexually assaulted and her throat had been slashed. She'd worked for an escort agency."

A new photo titled Three showing a winding nature trail appeared on the screen. The image changed to a small hillside and the naked corpse of a white female, semiburied under branches.

"On June 3, 2005, in Lakewood's Monte Verde Park, a grade-nine science class on a field trip found the body of Monique Louise Wilson, a thirty-year-old accountant from Artesia. She'd been sexually assaulted and strangled with her own panties."

Slide Four showed an old factory and its storage area, followed by a slide of a steel drum containing a woman's corpse.

"On April 16, 2006, in San Dimas, two teenage boys

flying a radio-controlled airplane that crashed into the barrels near this abandoned fruit-packing plant discovered the body of Fay Lynne Millwood, age twenty-seven. She was an aspiring actress who'd been working in a bar in Burbank. She had been sexually assaulted. Family members confirmed her remains through tattoos and surgical scars."

The fifth photograph was of a ranch-style bungalow, with children's bicycles, balls and toys scattered across the front yard. The next image featured a kitchen, cereal boxes and empty bowls on the table, a cluttered family bulletin board.

Then the screen changed to an image of horror. In the bedroom, a naked woman in a spread-eagled position on a blood-drenched bed, each arm and leg tied to each corner. The walls cascaded with blood.

"On February 10, 2007, a neighbor discovered the body of Bonnie Catherine Bradford, age thirty-four, in her home in Temple City. Bradford was a script writer and a divorced mother of an eight-year-old son and six-year-old daughter. She had been sexually assaulted and stabbed more than fifty times according to the autopsy report."

Tanner shut down the laptop.

"The L.A. County Sheriff's Department handles more than a thousand homicides a year," he said. "I won't go into discussion on our clearance rate other than to say it's a fact that a lot of murders go cold. But no homicide is closed until the investigation is resolved.

"For years these five cases remained unsolved and unconnected among the hundreds of other cold cases. Recently, in reviewing the Bradford murder, we discovered a piece of critical evidence that had been overlooked—a cryptic message left at the scene by the killer."

"What did it say?" Harding asked while taking notes.

"We're not going to reveal that. It's holdback," Zurn said.

"What? You call me down here and hint at a big exclusive—"

"Easy, Mark," Tanner said. "No one has this story. Listen, after we had the overlooked evidence analyzed, we found that it was irrefutably linked to these five cases with a solid common factor."

"What could be the common factor among—" he flipped through his pages "—a waitress, a hooker, an accountant, an actress and a screenwriter? Did these victims know each other? Belong to the same book club?"

"Nothing like that. They're linked by the physical evidence we found."

"DNA?"

"We're not prepared to go into details, but we realize that this killer left us a message," Tanner said. "He wanted us to know what he'd done, that he's responsible for these five murders across L.A. He's very smart."

"Are there more victims?"

"We used the information we'd found and ran it through local, state and national databases, ViCAP and others. So far, nothing's surfaced to suggest other murders are linked to these five, but we can't rule out the possibility. The evidence ties the five together, five murders in a string that began ten years ago and stopped cold five years ago with the Bradford case in Temple City."

"Any theories on why they stopped?"

"The killer is dead," Zurn said. "Or in prison, or moved on."

Tanner resumed. "In any event we think these serial murders have ended and that the case is solvable."

"Really? You believe that?"

"We're forming a task force with the LAPD, the FBI and other major police agencies," Tanner said. "We're going to follow every lead or clue to find the killer and clear these cases. We're asking anyone anywhere who has information on any of these homicides to contact us."

Before they wrapped up, Harding asked Tanner several more questions. Tanner gave him a file of information and photos along with the offer to help him reach relatives of victims, or to call him with any questions.

"The tenth anniversary of the first homicide is coming up," Tanner said. "The profilers said an anniversary story may jog someone's memory or yield a lead."

"You're using me to reach out to the killer, aren't you?"

"We want him to know that while it took a little time, we got his message and now we're sending him one."

"Which is?"

"We may not be as intelligent as he is, but we'll do everything in our power to find him."

12

San Marino, California

The morning after the accident, Claire woke before her alarm and reached toward Robert's side of the bed.

It was empty.

She lifted her head and looked at their bathroom. The door was open. The light was off. Maybe he couldn't sleep? His body clock was always out of whack because he often flew across several time zones.

But his last trip had been entirely in Pacific time.

It didn't really matter, she thought, he was always up at all hours prowling around like a cat.

It was 5:50 a.m.

She got out of bed, tired but cheerful from yesterday's good news as she pulled on her robe and started for the kitchen to make coffee. Padding through their Spanish-style home, she noticed that the door to Robert's office was closed. Light spilled from the bottom. She raised her hand to the doorknob but froze when she heard Robert's voice. It was low and she only picked up bits of the conversation.

"No, I don't want to do that… Are you listening, Cynthia… No…"

Cynthia? Claire puzzled. *Is he talking to his ex-wife? What's going on?*

Robert was coming to the door. Claire left for the kitchen expecting to hear him behind her.

She didn't.

She shrugged it all off, attributing any qualms to her early-morning grogginess. She made coffee, then went to their front step to collect the *Los Angeles Times,* the *Pasadena Star-News* and *USA TODAY.* Despite her pleas to save trees, Robert had insisted on the subscriptions. He was a news junkie.

She scanned the *Times,* finding a story on the accident inside under the headline Miracle Rescue in Fiery Freeway Crash. There was a dramatic photo of a car in flames taken from the video a motorist had recorded with his phone camera. Accompanying the story was a small picture of Robert at the hospital with the caption Hero Pilot Robert Bowen Saved Mother and Baby. They had seen TV news reports of the accident and rescue last night. Their phone rang with congratulatory calls from friends and interview requests from reporters.

Claire was proud of him.

After her first cup of morning coffee, a bagel with peaches, and daydreaming about a nursery, she got into the shower. She tried taking inventory of the day ahead, but as the steam clouds rose around her, Claire was carried back through time, back to her deepest wound. Her Grand Canyon of pain…

…Her father is gripping the handgun, pointing it to the ceiling, keeping it out of reach from her mother's frantic fingers as they battle for it at the top of the stairs. In her other arm, Claire's mother holds Luke, Claire's baby brother.

Claire hurries to them, pounds her doll Miss Rags at her father's legs.

"Stop it, Daddy!"

His gambling and drinking had cost him his trucker's license. Her mother's part-time teaching job pays little, bills are piling up. Collectors are calling. He stinks of alcohol, mirrors have been broken, furniture has been smashed, he's raging again.

"I'm gonna kill all of you fuckers for dragging me down!"

"No, Daddy!"

Luke is crying.

"Claire, get out of the house! Go next door! Call the police!" Her mother yells but the gun explodes with the first shot, then Claire sees the barrel slowly turning toward her mother. As her mother fights him, Claire's father falls backward grabbing her mother and Luke, taking them with him as all three fall down the staircase to a sickening crash on the landing.

"No!"

Claire rushes to the aftermath. The gun slides across the floor, her father moans, not moving, her mother is on her stomach, one arm is turned all wrong and Luke's tiny leg sticks out from under her as she groans. "Claire, take Luke and run for help! Now!"

Claire takes her baby brother into her arms. "Please, Luke! It's going to be okay!" A bright red ribbon of blood oozes from his ear. He does not move. His eyes are open wide. "Please, Luke!" Claire is in the street and flinches at the first shot; turns and sees the muzzle flashes of two more bloom in the window.

At eight years old, Claire was the sole survivor.

Her family was dead, her mother and her father.

Her baby brother had died in her arms.

Claire's world had ended.

Her aunt and uncle in St. Paul adopted her. Their love helped her mend and start a new life. Claire's counseling sessions with therapists never erased her scars but they'd helped her heal. Over the years she gravitated toward psychology and by the time she was in high school, she'd decided that she would become a psychologist.

While she went to college, Claire worked at clinics and crisis lines, helping ease other people's pain. One night, while doing graduate work at the University of Minnesota, her car battery died. The tow-truck driver who came to her aid was Cliff Rivard, a former engineering student, who'd also studied business before starting his own towing company. He had seven trucks, a dozen employees and was doing well. Born in Duluth, Cliff was smart, funny and a Vikings fan. He was also easy on the eyes. Claire was attracted to him; they began seeing each other. Deep under Cliff's handsome, rough exterior, Claire found a sweet center and before long she fell in love.

Two years later, after Claire got her PhD, they got married.

With the help of her mentor from the U of M, Dr. Martha Berman, a respected psychologist in neuroscience and stress, Claire became a licensed psychologist and found an entry-level position at a small practice in downtown Minneapolis. During this time she'd discovered that Cliff's sweetness was hardening, that he often lost his temper with his drivers, cursing them, punching a desk or wall whenever something went wrong. At first she'd attributed it to the rugged nature of his business, given that they routinely dealt with fatal traffic accidents where they saw mangled corpses and body parts. Claire had tried to get Cliff to talk about his job, his stress and his temper, but he always refused.

Nearly three years after they were married, Claire was unable to get pregnant. She saw doctors and specialists, went through several examinations, procedures and had a laparoscopy.

Then came the day when one of her doctors, the one with the Swiss accent who'd kept her waiting forever in his office, entered with a file folder. He'd looked at her, removed his glasses and ran his hand over his face.

"I'm afraid the news is not good, Claire."

Her heart had stopped as she caught her breath, only half hearing as he'd said that she had endometriosis and a range of other complications, leaving her with primary infertility.

"I'm afraid that the chances of you having a baby are less than five per cent and should you get pregnant, you would likely not carry to term."

Alone in the car she'd slammed her palms against the steering wheel and sobbed before driving home to tell Cliff.

He had been stunned.

"What do you mean no kids, Claire?"

They'd grieved as they grappled with the realization that they could not have children. They'd kept trying and Claire had gotten pregnant but miscarried. She got pregnant again. And again, she miscarried. They'd considered expensive fertility clinics, using a surrogate or adopting but couldn't agree on what to do, which made matters tense between them.

Cliff had started drinking more than the usual couple of beers after work.

Eventually, their private agony leaked to their circles. Word had gotten back to Claire that some of Cliff's relatives had urged him to divorce her and marry a woman who could bear him children. When Claire had raised it with Cliff, it led to an argument that ended with him putting his fist through a wall.

Claire later saw that as the point when the seed of Cliff's resentment toward her had been planted. Although he'd never said it, she'd seen it in his eyes. Her infertility had made her less of a woman to him. At that same time, Cliff's company had lost several contracts to bigger competitors. He'd had to lay off four drivers while debts on his fleet mounted.

His business was failing.

Cliff tried to save it, but nothing he did could stop what was happening. In a short time he'd lost everything he'd built. And when the dust settled there was only Cliff with one old tow truck. Claire had known that Cliff's identity was entwined with his company. It was how he'd defined himself, and the loss, coupled with the anguish of never having children with her, was overwhelming.

At times, Claire would wake up in the middle of the night wondering if she would ever be a mother. She'd prayed for a miracle as the strain on their marriage increased.

Cliff had lashed out at her.

He drank more, argued more, belittled her, demanded to know about every place she went, every penny she spent. In one instance when she had come home after lunch with college friends, he shoved her against a wall. Her head cracked a framed oil painting of mountains that had been a wedding gift she cherished.

Claire had begged him to stop drinking and talk to

a counselor. She'd offered to go with him to seek counseling together.

He'd refused.

One night after leaving a bar for a service call, he'd crashed his truck into a tree. No one was hurt, but Cliff had been arrested, charged and jailed for driving under the influence and punching a cop at the scene. Cliff lost his license, his truck and insurance. After posting his bail, Claire had demanded he get help but he refused and kept drinking, flying into a rage when she tried to rid their house of alcohol.

"It's your fault. You've ruined everything!" He'd screamed at her before knocking her to the floor. "You bitch, you're useless to me!"

It had been the final straw.

Claire moved out that night. She'd done all she could, but accepted that Cliff was a violent, abusive man. Like her father. Men like that blamed others for their misfortune and used their fists to take out their anger on those who loved them.

I will not end up like my mother.

A few days later, before Claire flew to Los Angeles to attend a conference, she'd called Cliff and told him she wanted a divorce.

Ice-cold silence.

Then he'd hung up without breathing a word to her.

When her return flight touched down in Minneapolis, Claire spotted Cliff in Arrivals at the luggage carousel and grew uneasy. He must've lied to her office to get her flight information.

"We need to talk, Claire, please."

He'd smelled of alcohol.

"No, it's too late for that. You're drunk, Cliff, go home."

"Don't do this to us. I messed up, I'm sorry. I'll get help, whatever you want. Just come home."

Her heart ached, she was torn, but she knew, as a psychologist, as a survivor and as an abused woman, what she needed to do.

"It's over, Cliff." She'd fought her tears. "I'm so sorry, but it's over."

He'd stood stone still, glaring at her, breathing hard, his jaw muscles throbbing. With sudden fury he slammed her against a column. Claire screamed as he mashed his forearm under her chin, pinning her by her throat.

"Stop, Cliff, please!" Claire rasped.

"What happened to us is all your fault, you useless fucking bitch!"

He raised his fist to strike her when a hand seized it, overpowering Cliff, wrenching his arm behind his back until he groaned in pain. Claire's savior was a few inches taller than Cliff, strong and in uniform.

Keys jangled as two more people arrived, security officers who'd rushed to them and put Cliff in handcuffs. A small crowd gathered. Everything blurred. Her skin prickled with fear and shame. In the confusion that followed, someone—a police officer—took a brief statement from Claire, asked if she wanted to press charges.

No, she'd said then, she didn't know, she needed time to think.

Waiting patiently nearby was the man who'd saved her: Captain Robert Bowen, the pilot of Claire's plane from Los Angeles. He was concerned about her, so before leaving she'd agreed to have coffee with him in the airport once she'd finished with the police. After they'd found a booth, Claire regained her composure, thanked him, told him how embarrassed she was, explaining how she and Cliff were divorcing and it was a traumatic time.

"I understand," he'd said. "I'm recently divorced myself."

He'd seemed calm, confident and kind. As Claire had searched his dark brown eyes, she'd found a measure of pained sorrow, as if he perceived a great sadness no one else could see.

"If you ever want to talk about anything, Claire, let me know," he said before they exchanged emails.

She'd kept in touch with Robert.

In moving from the wreckage of her marriage, Claire had devoted herself to her work, gaining more experience. All the while she'd email or phone Robert, who'd helped her through her worst days. Whenever he was in Minneapolis, they'd meet for dinner downtown or sometimes just coffee at the airport.

Robert was working on finding the ideal corporate piloting position in L.A. and leaving the demanding life of a commercial airline pilot that had played a large part in ending his marriage—*"my wife couldn't handle me being away so much."* It would give him the chance to spend more time at his cabin, fishing, he'd joked.

When Claire's divorce was final, she'd found more reasons to fly to Los Angeles to be with Robert. She knew things between them were moving fast, but being with him was the best therapy, she smiled to herself.

About a year after her divorce from Cliff, Claire and Robert were walking on the beach near Malibu, when he'd stopped and looked long and hard into her eyes.

"I want to build a new life, but I can't do it without

you." He'd dropped to one knee and took her hand. "Will you marry me, Claire?"

Her heart had soared and tears filled her eyes.

"Yes, but there's something you should know. I may not be able to have children, but I don't ever want to give up trying. I want you to know what life with me could entail."

He'd taken a long time to respond, but when he had, her love for him deepened. He did not want to break it off or back out. And unlike Cliff, Robert never made her feel like she was less of a woman, or that her infertility was her fault.

"I'll do whatever it takes," Robert had said. "We're in this together, Claire."

They got married in Mexico in a small, sunset wedding on the beach. Then they flew to Europe for a honeymoon in Paris and London, ending with a week at Robert's secluded cabin out at Big Bear.

Claire moved to Los Angeles to live with Robert.

She got her license with the State. Soon, with the advice and support of her friend Dr. Berman, who'd since joined the department of psychology at the University of Nevada in Las Vegas, Claire established her practice in San Marino, specializing in victims of abuse.

Now, as she stepped from the shower, Claire counted her blessings.

It had been a long road to the happiness she'd found. She was married to a good man and her dream to start a family was stronger than ever.

She put on her makeup and dressed, then went to her small home office down the hall to collect her files and her USB flash drive that contained encrypted copies of confidential electronic patient records. She always copied them to the small storage device.

Funny, it was not near her laptop where she'd left it. She looked around, opened a drawer—there it was.

I don't remember putting it there.

She sighed, exasperated with herself. For the past couple of months she'd misplaced it a few times.

She found Robert in the kitchen reading one of the newspapers and eating cornflakes. She gave him a kiss and a hug.

"How's my Freeway Hero doing today?"

"All good. I have to go in today."

"Why? I thought you were off for the next few days."

"Jenkins called from the company, he saw the news and reminded me that the company doc has to check me out, clear me for flying. Got to keep everything in line with the FAA."

"You feel fine, right?"

"I'm good."

"How about we go out for that dinner, tonight? Celebrate our family news, your heroics and whatever ensues?"

He hesitated for several moments as if his attention had taken him elsewhere before he returned.

"Yes, it's a date."

"Are you sure you're feeling okay?"

"Yes, just had a little trouble sleeping, a little revved up from everything."

Claire looked at him, taking stock. She was certain he was grappling with something, but decided this was not the time to press him on what she'd overheard, or anything else.

"All right." She smiled.

Before kissing him again she snatched her keys from the counter. She headed for her car knowing that Robert was keeping something from her.

13

San Marino, California

Claire's office was in a one-story medical building at Garfield Avenue and Huntington Drive on San Marino's west side, close to South Pasadena and Alhambra.

It was shaded by fragrant eucalyptus trees and tucked behind lush holly hedges and blazing violet azaleas. The awnings offered seclusion from the busy street.

Because of yesterday's drama, Claire had canceled all of her appointments for that day. Today, she had to catch up. It was early and her first patient had not yet arrived.

Alice Pearson, her assistant, was making coffee. The big-hearted fifty-nine-year-old had come with the office when Claire took over the suite from Leo Schwartz, a psychologist who'd retired. Alice was a die-hard fan of the *L.A. Lakers.* A framed photo of her courtside and beaming beside Jack Nicholson, another die-hard fan, sat on her desk. She had a copy at her home and a smaller one in her wallet.

When Alice saw Claire, she gave her a hug.

"Oh, Claire, I'm so happy everyone's okay. That husband of yours— *Wow!*"

"I'm glad no one was hurt badly."

"How's Robert doing?"

"He's pretty cool about it all. He's my mild-mannered Clark Kent. So how do things look for today?"

"A full slate." Alice passed her the agenda and patient list.

Claire went to her office, fired up her computer, inserted her flash drive and transferred the notes she'd updated at home two nights earlier. Sipping coffee, she reviewed files for nearly an hour before meeting her patients.

There was Dorothy, a fifty-three-year-old bank teller, whom Claire had been helping for nearly a year following the death of her violent husband. Then there was Vanessa, a forty-eight-year-old graphic artist, whose husband was addicted to cocaine and abused her. Her other patients included April, a thirty-six-year-old former high school teacher who wanted to leave her husband. And Madison, a thirty-one-year-old hairstylist, whose husband, a limo driver, was abusive, jealous and controlling.

That was how Claire's morning and early afternoon had gone.

She ate lunch at her desk while working on her notes. All of her cases were different but they shared common factors. In many ways abused women were like hostages whose experiences were symptomatic of the Stockholm syndrome.

Seeing no way out, no alternative relationship, they bonded with the loving side of their captor-abuser, the part they'd fallen in love with, the part to which they had given their heart. They grew dependent on the spouse or partner to provide emotional comfort after an incident, usually during his repentant period. This would also be when the victims downplayed the violence and fell into denial.

Claire knew that no abusive relationship was violent all the time, but there were identifiable patterns and cycles in most of them—long stretches of calm, normal everyday living that were usually punctuated with an inciting event that led to a period of increasing tension culminating in the explosion.

With each patient Claire was on guard for danger signs.

Safety was paramount.

Many times she'd wanted to call police, wanted them to intervene in a relationship. But she could never lose sight of her ethical, therapeutic and legal obligations. Patient confidentiality was critical. Intervening was a heart-wrenching challenge. Often abusers had no clue their partner was seeing a psychologist. So there was always a risk of exacerbating a situation.

A range of agencies and outreach services was available to help victims of domestic violence, and Claire always ensured her patients were aware of them. Usually, she made arrangements on their behalf. She'd never had a patient die at the hands of her abuser but she knew therapists who had.

If pushed, Claire would stop at nothing to protect her patients.

Three graves in a Minnesota cemetery reminded her of what happened when no one intervened. Claire paused for a moment to bear that in mind before preparing for her last patient of the afternoon.

Amber was a twenty-eight-year-old office assistant. After initiating a divorce from her husband, Eric, a thirty-nine-year-old security tech, she'd moved out of their Long Beach apartment to Alhambra. She was now house-sitting for friends of friends who wanted to help her start over after the breakup of her marriage. They'd even helped her get a clerical job at the Huntington Library.

Claire consulted Amber's file again. The abuse in the relationship was extremely violent. Eric had come close to going to jail. Amber had sworn out a restraining order against him, a no-contact order. She had been Claire's patient for several months. They had regular sessions but Amber had pleaded to have her next session moved up as soon as possible.

"Patient reports being anxious, feels like she's being watched," the file note said. Claire flipped to the file on Eric's information. It contained his photo with a copy of the restraining order. Her eyes found the note, "Employed at installing residential/commercial security systems." Claire considered these factors as Amber sat down in her office.

Amber was wearing a dark pencil skirt and white top. She'd come directly from her job at the Huntington Library. She updated Claire on her divorce, Eric's failure to show up at the last court hearing, the restraining order and the news that he was moving.

"Okay, Amber," Claire said, "when you called, you said you feel like you're being watched. This is a new aspect in your case. Is that why you're here today? Why did you feel the need to move up your session?"

"This is going to sound stupid."

"It's all right. Take a breath and take your time."

As Amber twisted a tissue in her hands Claire noticed her new nails, bright red with tiny bright pink stripes, something Eric would never have approved of.

They symbolized the progress Amber was making in rebuilding her life.

"It's going to sound weird," Amber said.

"It's all right. Just tell me."

"It's hard to describe, but one night, just a few nights ago, I felt 'a presence' in the house."

"A presence?"

"Yes, like something, or someone, was in the house."

"You live alone, no roommates, no pets. You're still house-sitting in Alhambra?"

"Yes. So I went around the house checking windows and doors. I didn't see anything. I went to bed, but as I drifted off I felt someone was watching me."

"Can you describe this presence?"

"No."

"Did you see anything, touch anything, smell or feel anything?"

"No."

"Did you find any signs or evidence that someone, or something, a bird, a cat, a mouse was in the house?"

"No, nothing."

"And the house has a security alarm system?"

"Yes, the owners I'm house-sitting for said it was one of the best."

"Have you been having any strange dreams lately?"

"No. Not really."

"Are you taking any new prescriptions or over-the-counter medications?"

"No."

"Are you afraid?"

"Yes, it scares me."

"What do you think it was?"

"Well, my first thought of course is that it was Eric.

If anyone would know how to disarm and bypass a security system, he would."

"Do you think he's capable of this kind of behavior?"

"I don't know," Amber said. "The divorce is proceeding. Maybe he's having trouble accepting it, but this is so strange, I don't think he'd do something like this."

"I see."

"Then I thought that maybe I was just imagining the whole thing."

"Did you call police, or tell anyone?"

"No, not so far. You're the only one I've told."

"I see. There are a few possible explanations."

"Like I'm losing my mind."

"No," Claire reassured. "It could be a manifestation of your fear of Eric. That you are sensing this presence could be a reaction to your fear of Eric surfacing in your new life, because he was such a presence in the life you've left behind."

"That could be it."

"Every relationship is unique and the time it takes to heal varies," Claire said. "You've taken several brave, life-changing steps. You're undergoing a lot of pressure. This ongoing fear is real and to be expected. And given Eric's violent past, and his profession, and the fact you're ending your marriage to him, your fear that he is somehow stalking you is understandable."

"So it's all psychological? There's no man hiding in my home?"

"Let's hope not," Claire said. "But we won't take any chances by dismissing or underestimating the potential risk of danger, okay?"

Amber nodded.

"Remember we talked about an emergency plan, what to do if Eric ever tried to contact you?" Claire said.

"Yes."

"Here's what I suggest you do as soon as we're done here. Call the security alarm company and ask them to send someone over to double-check the system at the house. Don't go in the house. Meet them outside your home. And call the police, tell them your situation, tell them to look up Eric's restraining order and ask them to check your house, too. Taking these precautions will help restore your peace of mind."

"Okay."

"Then I want you to consider moving in with a friend for a few days."

"I will."

"Does this help?"

"It does. Thank you so much, Claire."

After Amber left, Claire poured a glass of ice water from her pitcher and updated various patient files before copying the day's work to her flash drive to take home.

As it loaded, Claire began texting Robert.

It had been a long day, the muscles in the back of her lower neck and shoulders were rock-hard. But the stress couldn't prevent her from smiling at the bright personal news on the baby front. Tonight would be a good night for that celebratory dinner—

"No!"

Claire's head suddenly snapped to her office window.

Someone outside sounded panicked.

Claire left her desk. Through the curtain she'd seen Amber in the parking lot, contending with a man who had her backed up against a car.

14

San Marino, California

Amber had unlocked her car in the parking lot and reached for the handle.

A hand shot out from behind her, stopping the driver's door from opening. Amber whirled around, her skin prickled as she recognized the man with a steel-vise grip on her door.

"Eric! What're you doing here? You're not supposed to contact me!"

"I only want you to listen to what I have to say. I need to talk, Amber."

"No! There's a court order! Let go of my door!"

"Baby, please."

"Have you been following me?"

He didn't answer.

"Eric, let go of my door!"

He continued holding it.

Amber cast glances to the street, then the building, hoping someone, anyone, would come by. He was six foot two to her five foot three and he weighed about two hundred thirty pounds. His biceps bulged as he moved closer. She caught her breath.

"The judge extended the restraining order and fined you for not showing up in court," she said. "Didn't your lawyer tell you?"

"I know."

"Then just leave me alone and we can let this go."

"We've got too many judges and lawyers between us."

"Don't do this, don't make things worse."

"You're still my wife."

His big hand clamped Amber's shoulder and he backed her against her car. Her heart was thundering. She couldn't escape, couldn't get into her purse for her phone.

"Eric, let me go or I swear to God I'll scream."

"Calm down, please. I need to talk to you without lawyers. That's all."

"No, we have to move on with our separate lives."

"No, no, baby, don't give up on us." Eyes brimming, he'd softened his tone, presenting the tender side of him she'd once loved. "Baby, I know I've got problems. I hurt you, I know, I'm so goddammed sorry."

"Stop it, Eric."

"No, just listen. I don't expect you to forgive me. That's not what I'm asking. I'm begging you to stop the divorce. Come back to me. Give me another chance. Let's start over. I've got a new job with my brother in Sacramento and I'm getting help. We can make it better than it was before."

Fighting tears, Amber shook her head slowly.

"Baby, I promise, I give you my sacred vow I'll change."

She kept shaking her head.

"Please, baby," Eric sniffled. "Please."

"No."

"No?"

"Eric, I've heard this before. What we had is gone. I can't be with you."

"What are you saying?"

"We can never, ever go back."

All the blood drained from his face.

His voice dropped to a whisper.

"But without you, I've got nothing, Amber." His grip on her shoulder tightened. "I've got nothing left in this world to lose."

"You have to let me go."

"I can't."

Amber struggled to break free, thinking she could run into the office building or down the street, or into traffic. Eric's eyes narrowed until something inside them snapped. He seized her shoulders and shook her with such force her head whiplashed.

"Do you think I'm going to let this happen? You want me to beat some fucking sense into you?"

"No! Please, you're hurting me."

"Let her go!"

They both turned to Claire, who was standing in the parking lot a few feet away. She had one hand deep inside her shoulder bag. The other gripped the strap, braced for action.

"Who the fuck are you?" Eric maintained his hold on Amber.

Claire did not identify herself.

"This is none of your fucking business," Eric said. "So fuck off, bitch."

"It is my business," Claire said. "I've alerted police that you're in violation of a protection order. They're on their way. Take your hands off of her and step away."

Eric turned back to Amber, his breath tearing in and out of his lungs.

"She's your fucking shrink, isn't she? She's the one putting ideas in your head, turning you against me, getting between man and wife!" Eric pulled Amber forward, then crushed her hard against the car. "I'm going to give her the same goddamned medicine!"

As he pulled Amber forward to slam her a second time, something hissed and a liquid stream splashed into his eyes. He doubled over screaming and cupping his hands to his face.

"Oh, you fucking, whoring goddamned bitch! You are fucking dead!"

Claire stood over him, gripping her can of pepper spray, ready to douse Eric again. Amber got into her car, locked the door and sobbed as they heard the sound of an approaching siren.

Eric sat on the pavement, writhing.

"Fuck! My eyes are burning! Fuck!"

A marked patrol car, its lights flashing and siren yelping to silence, braked in the parking lot and two uniformed officers with the San Marino Police Department took control.

Moments later, an ambulance arrived. Paramedics checked on Amber.

It was over in minutes.

The police officers handcuffed Eric and placed him in the backseat of their car. One of the officers dealt with Eric, checking his ID and processing it with the dispatcher. The second officer, D. Freeman, according to her name tag, spoke with Claire then Amber, taking initial statements while paramedics examined Amber and Eric.

"He'll go before a judge for violation of his protection order," Freeman said. "Most likely he'll be charged. He'll get jail time, but will likely be out in days."

"Under the circumstances, I think we have to get Amber into a women's shelter," Claire said. "We also suspect he's been stalking her and may have illegally entered her residence. We need you to check her home."

"Okay, once we process him, we'll meet you there."

The paramedics said Amber had suffered some neck strain and might feel some swelling and tenderness later. If it became painful, she should go to a hospital, they advised while making a summary report.

"Are you comfortable with everything, Amber?" Claire asked. "Want us to call anyone?"

After tearful nods Amber said, "I'll call my girlfriend."

Officer Freemen finished noting their concerns then returned to the car. Claire and Amber could see Eric seething in the backseat. As it rolled away, he turned to them and his tearstained, inflamed gaze found Claire's, telegraphing a raw, savage hate for her.

She did not flinch.

15

Santa Clarita, California

The address was in a residential section of the city that sat in a valley bordered by low, dry hills just north of San Fernando.

The area was once an expanse of rural emptiness, home to tranquil ranches and farms before it had surrendered to suburban sprawl—vast coral-stucco neighborhoods of schools, parks, big box stores and shopping centers.

Robert Bowen needed to see the home, a compulsion that had reached out from a dream. *Have I not been here before?* He was uncertain what he was searching for, only that he would know when he found it, he thought as he drove north from Van Nuys.

Earlier that morning, Allen Pace, who had been the team physician for the Dodgers before becoming Execu-Glide's corporate doctor, gave him a going-over. Blood pressure, heart, breathing, eyes, reflexes, the usual.

"All your vitals are fine. You're good to take your next trip, Bob. I'll fill out the form. Everything's normal."

If you only knew, Bowen gazed at the driveways

rolling by as he counted down house numbers, *if you only knew.*

Last night, when Bowen couldn't sleep, he was suddenly battling the urge to talk to Cynthia as he contended with another "episode." Then other torments emerged and he'd found himself online looking for this specific address. When he got it he was surprised and pleased to learn that it was for sale. It gave him the cover he needed to see it.

To get even closer.

And there it is.

He parked across the street, glanced at the for-sale sign. The ranch-style house was sky-blue stucco with wood trim. It had a curved driveway, sweeping front lawn and tidy landscaping. The clank of tools floated from the side yard.

Bowen got out and walked along the lush lawn toward the sound of hammering. A man, crouched near a garden bed, had just driven a nail into a piece of loosened trim. When Bowen's shadow fell over him, he looked up, hammer in hand.

"Can I help you?" the man asked.

"Hi, I saw the sign. Is the house still for sale?"

"It is."

"Are you the owner?"

"I am."

"I'm interested in it. Would it be possible to have a quick tour? My wife and I are looking for a house in Santa Clarita."

The man stood. He was in his late fifties and wore jeans and a flannel shirt over a faded T-shirt. His brush cut gave him the air of a retired soldier. His black eyes gleamed as they assessed Bowen.

"The agent handles that, everything's supposed to go through her."

"Well, I was in the neighborhood looking at another property," Bowen said. "I'm not sure how long it will be before I'm back this way."

The man twirled the hammer in his big, tanned hand as he thought.

"All right, seeing that you're here, I suppose I could show you around."

They entered the house through the front door. The living room was spacious with hardwood floors and a brick fireplace.

"You can burn gas or wood." The man passed Bowen a listing sheet from the coffee table, after he'd set his hammer down. "I'm asking four-seventy-five. Taxes are just under five a year. It's a three-bedroom. It's all there on the page. Don't worry about your shoes. We'll go this way."

"I'm sorry. I didn't catch your name?" Bowen asked.

"Meadows, Louis Meadows."

"And what's your line of work, if you don't mind me asking?"

"I retired from the navy. I was a cook on the *Abraham Lincoln*."

Although the place was pleasant, there was an underlying sadness and a trace of Old Spice. The house had an eat-in kitchen, ample tiled counter space, a dishwasher, a double sink with a sprayer and garbage disposal.

"The kitchen's new."

Bowen nodded approvingly, glanced around with an ear cocked for anyone else in the house.

"My wife had it redone last year just before she passed away."

"I'm sorry to hear that. My condolences."

"It was cancer. She never got to enjoy the renovation."

The dining room had a dark wood table and matching china hutch. Bowen wondered about the last time it was used. The bathroom was tidy. The master bedroom was neat. On the night table he saw a copy of *From Here to Eternity* and an old edition of *Jane's Fighting Ships.* He also saw framed photos of two women. One of them was in her fifties. The other resembled her and was in her early twenties.

They moved to a second smaller bedroom with a desk and two-drawer steel file cabinet. A U.S. flag and map, with colored pushpins piercing various countries, covered a wall.

"This could be a guest room. I use it as a study," Meadows said.

They moved down the hall to a room with a closed door.

"That's the third bedroom. It's bigger than the second one."

Keeping his hands in his pockets, Meadows stared at the door in mild trepidation.

"Is this your daughter's room?"

Meadows shot him a look, as if Bowen had read his mind.

"Sorry," Bowen said. "I saw the photograph in the other room and I'd just assumed."

"Yes." Meadows made no move to show the room.

"Guess we don't want to disturb her," Bowen said. "I understand."

But Bowen knew.

He damned well knew as he concentrated on the pain in Meadows's face the way a patron absorbs the aftermath of it in a work of art, like Michelangelo's *Pietà.* Bowen drank in Meadows's pain, as he'd done with the fear of the woman he'd pulled from the car accident.

"No," Meadows said. "My daughter's not there."

"Is she away at college?"

Twisting the knife in the wound.

"No."

"May I see the room?"

Meadows hesitated as if waiting for the will to open the door.

"Yes."

The room was cooler and smelled musty. Sunlight had caught the fine dust particles that were sent churning into the air when the door opened. On the wall, he saw a poster of Meryl Streep and a framed watercolor of flowers. He noticed the bulletin board with a calendar. Notes with hours under the word *work* were penned in for some dates.

The walls were an opaque bluish-green. The single bed was made with a white comforter. A stuffed bear was the lone occupant. There was a white desk with a laptop, a jar full of paper money and change, labeled Tips. The closet was open and empty save for a tower of cardboard boxes, sagging from age and marked in felt-tip pen with Leeza's Things.

The room was a tomb to the life that had resided here.

"That's a good-sized closet," Bowen said, turning to his guide.

Meadows was oblivious. His eyes were going around the room as if he were seeing something from another time. He nodded slowly, took one last forlorn inventory before leading Bowen out and closing the door.

They moved to the laundry room—"All the appliances are included"—then to the family room. It opened to the patio and a view of the hills. They stepped back outside and Meadows leaned against his picnic table and folded his arms across his chest.

"It's a good house. It's a good neighborhood, a quiet family neighborhood," he said as he contemplated the horizon. "Sorry, the agent's better at showing the place. I'm not much of a people person."

"No, I imposed," Bowen said. "May I ask why you're selling?"

"I'm moving into a condo in San Diego, to be near my niece."

"I guess with your wife gone and your daughter moved out, it's more house than you need?"

Meadows looked at Bowen.

"She didn't move out."

Another twist of the knife.

"Sorry, but you said… I guess I got confused."

Meadows rubbed the tension in the back of his neck as if this conversation were hurting him.

"My daughter was murdered."

"Oh, no. I am so very sorry. I didn't mean to— I'm sorry."

Meadows kept his eyes on the horizon.

"It's coming up on ten years. They never caught the guy who did it."

"Please, you don't have to talk about it."

Meadows just stared at the horizon as if he were talking to it.

"The pain never leaves you. Sometimes I can feel her, see her and hear her voice. I think about where she'd be now in her life—married with her own children, our grandchildren. And not a day goes by that I don't ache to know who killed her."

Bowen looked at him, feeling a surreal wave roll over them.

"And what would you say to him if you had the chance?"

Meadows's head swung to Bowen.

"Plenty, I can damn well guarantee you."

"What would you say?"

Meadows turned back to the hills.

"Did she suffer? Did she cry out? Did she fight back? Because I sure as hell know she would. What were her last words? Then I would ask the son of a bitch why he did it. Why did he do the things he did to her? Then I would ask God to make certain he burns for all time." Meadows let a long moment pass while he blinked at the sky. "Listen, I apologize for going on like that."

"No, it's okay."

They were interrupted when Meadows's home phone rang.

"Excuse me," he said, and stepped into the house to answer it. Alone on the patio Bowen heard his muffled voice. "Yes… Who?… Reporter?… All right, but you caught me at a bad time. Can I call right back?"

Meadows returned bringing an apology with him for the call and indicating the tour had ended.

"I guess that's about all I can tell you about the house," he told Bowen. "The agent's contact information is on the sheet I gave you. So if you're serious about an offer, get in touch with her."

Meadows escorted Bowen to the door where they shook hands. Electrified by the touch, Bowen found Meadows's eyes and for an instant kept his hold firm.

"Thank you for this," Bowen said. "You don't know how much I appreciate what you've done."

When he returned to his car, Bowen got behind the steering wheel and buckled up. Before he started the engine, he let his head fall back against the headrest and shut his eyes.

His heart was pounding.

16

Malibu, California

Later that evening, Claire and Robert were sitting at a patio table at a cliff-top restaurant in Malibu.

It was a long drive up along the Pacific Coast Highway but it gave them a majestic view of Point Dume's bluffs to the north, and the Queen's Necklace to the south. They breathed in the salty ocean air as the waves tumbled over the beach below and breezes caressed Claire's hair.

Robert had the filet mignon. Claire had the salmon with butter sauce. They shared half a bottle of wine and the waiter, an actor with dyed blond streaks in his chestnut hair, topped their glasses as the sun set.

On the drive out they'd talked about the likelihood of becoming parents and what room would make a good nursery; schools, college and careers—"He'll be a pro quarterback," "She'll be a surgeon"—before they laughed it off. Now Robert looked tired and had become a little inattentive during dinner, Claire thought as she looked back on the day.

"So your appointment with the company doctor went well?"

"Yeah, he cleared me for my next trip."

"And how are you feeling since the accident?"

"I'm fine."

"Is there anything on your mind you want to talk about?"

He smiled at her.

"I thought you were off the clock."

She smiled back.

"Claire," he said. "I'm fine. Tell me about your day."

"My day? Let me see. What can I tell you within the perimeters of what's legal and ethical? Well. It was very busy catching up with the backlog. And the partner of one of my patients violated his restraining order and assaulted her in our parking lot."

"Gee-zus."

"Yup, I had to pepper-spray him. Police took him away."

"Was she hurt?"

"No, not physically. She was shaken up by it all."

"And you?"

"Me? I'm all right."

"That guy's an asshole."

"That sort of thing happens from time to time." She sipped some wine, unable to wash away that niggling feeling she'd had ever since the morning. "I noticed you were up early today and when I walked by your office, it sounded like you were on the phone to somebody. Who were you talking to?"

"Oh, you're checking up on me," he teased, grinning.

"You betcha, buddy. You're a local hero."

"I couldn't sleep. I went in there to catch up on emails when I got one from a reporter in New York. I don't know how the press gets our information. She wanted me for a network show, insisted I phone her. I called her back and said no, I didn't want to make any more of this thing."

Claire looked at him.

And was her name Cynthia? Claire thought, immediately scolding herself for being silly, irrational. How long had it been since Robert even mentioned his ex-wife? As far as Claire knew he'd had no contact with her, just as she'd had no contact with Cliff. Her unease arose from the fact that recently Robert had become withdrawn. Claire had to decide if she trusted that he was not involved in a secret relationship with his ex-wife. She looked out at the coast for an answer.

"Claire?"

"So what did you do the rest of the day after your appointment?"

"Well, Detective, I puttered in the garage waiting for you. Bcforc that, I drovc around, thinking I might go to the cabin for a few days to decompress before the next trip."

"Sounds good. While we're on the subject of thc cabin…I was thinking, maybe we should consider selling it to start a college fund. You know I love it but I don't get the chance to go up that often. What do you think?"

"Sell the cabin for a college fund? Whoa. Aren't we getting ahead of things?"

"But on the drive out here, you said you were open to the idea."

"You're serious about this?"

"I'm definitely serious about it. Are we not on the same page here? This is all about our dream to start a family."

The air tensed.

"Robert, we start the treatment in a couple of weeks. Think of all we've been through up to this point. You *do* want us to have a baby, right?"

"Of course I do."

"What is it with you?" Claire caught herself and lowered her voice. "Lately you've been preoccupied."

"I guess I was a little more rattled by the crash than I realized."

"No, it's more than that. This started weeks ago before the crash. Ever since I first found Dr. LaRoy, you've been withdrawn. I get the feeling that you're keeping something from me. What's going on?"

"I've been concerned by the rumors that the company might be making cuts. Then along comes the crash. Today when I was driving around, I could not stop thinking about what would have happened if I never pulled the woman and her baby from the wreck. I see images of them burning up. All of it has me a bit on edge."

Claire looked into her wineglass and turned it slowly in circles.

What he'd said was reasonable and made sense, yet she wasn't entirely convinced. Still, she didn't want to push the issue.

"You're anxious and you've got some post-traumatic stress going," she said. "But I'm your wife. You have to talk to me about these things." She reached for his hand. "I guess I still have a little fight in me from my encounter today." Her fingers rolled over his wedding band, turning it playfully before she kissed his cheek. "Want to go home and see what we can do to relieve our stress?"

They drove amid the glittering streams of freeway traffic and the lights of L.A.

When they arrived at their home in San Marino, Robert complained that his neck muscles had stiffened. He started a hot shower to relieve his tension and invited Claire to join him as he stepped into the bathroom.

"Invitation accepted," she said, removing her jewelry, then her clothes.

She entered the shower, welcoming the hot water and his hands all over her body. They moved to the bedroom where they made love. Afterward, Claire snuggled against Robert. Too wound up to sleep, she remembered a concern and got out of bed.

Claire still hadn't been assured that Amber Pratt had been placed in a shelter and wanted to check her laptop for any messages there. She'd slipped on her robe, and while padding to her office, noticed something as she passed Robert's office.

The door stood open a crack. Something was on the floor. She entered and picked up a small photograph.

Robert was smiling with his arm around a pretty woman.

The note in Robert's handwriting on the back said "With Cyn in the mountains. Happier times."

Claire had never seen this before. It looked as if it had fallen from a framed painting that was ever so slightly askew, as though it might've been hidden behind it.

She left it there, then walked out of the room.

What the hell is going on with him?

17

Downey, California

"Aren't you getting tired of that book?" Joe Tanner, on the sofa, asked Samantha as she handed him *Green Eggs and Ham* and her brush.

"Dad, I told you it's my all-time favorite book in the whole world. Sam-I-Am. Sam! Me!"

"All right, smarty-pants, turn around." Tanner laughed.

Samantha had just come from her bath wearing her robe, slippers and smelling of soap. She stood for the ritual combing of her hair and dramatic "ouches" whenever he'd hit a tangle.

Then came story time. After the book it was bedtime, but Sam stalled.

"You know, Dad, if you wanted to have a girlfriend, it would be all right."

"Oh, it would? And what brought this on?"

"I was talking with Aunt Kim. She was asking me what I thought if you got a new girlfriend and stuff."

"Aunt Kim brought it up, did she?"

"We have lots of girl talks. Anyway, she said I should let you know that we think it would be all right, especially if you're feeling lonely."

"I tell you what—" Tanner stopped when his phone vibrated. He pulled it from his pocket and read a text from Mark Harding, the reporter.

Working on the story. Need to talk to you now about the case.

Tanner texted that he would call Harding shortly.

"Sorry, hon. I'll tell you what. I'll keep all this girlfriend business in mind. Now you get yourself ready for bed, pronto."

After Sam brushed her teeth, got into her pajamas and said her prayers, Tanner tucked her in with a kiss. Then he went to his study and called the number Harding had left.

"It's Tanner. What's up?"

"Thanks. Listen. I'm getting pushed. We've got to have more on the killer's signature."

"No, I can't do that because it's something only a few detectives and the killer know."

"My editors in New York are pressing me to give readers more detail on why you guys think the five old murders are connected."

"Like I said, a common thread surfaced one month ago."

"With the Bradford murder?"

"Yes, in reviewing the files we discovered an overlooked piece of evidence, a cryptic message left at the scene by the killer."

"Was it a note? What did it say? Was it a recording, a picture? Can you give me a summary?"

"No, Mark. You're an experienced reporter. You know we'll do everything to ensure the integrity of our investigation. I already told you, and you can quote me, the killer wanted us to know that he's responsible for these five murders across L.A. He's very intelligent."

"Yeah, I got all that. So you won't budge on the message?"

"I can't."

"I'll let New York know."

"The link to the five murders has never been made public before."

"Right. Thanks for the info on the relatives. We talked to them all and got photos."

"Be sure to put in your story that anybody with information should call us. But, and this is important, we think the killer's dead or in prison."

"Right, Joe, I know you're playing me."

"Yes, but you're getting a scoop. When will it run and where will it go?"

"In a couple of days. It'll go to every newsroom in the country and to all of our international subscribers around the world. They'll have the option to use it. Joe, if you get a lead from my story, I want exclusivity on it."

"I'll consider that but it depends on what, if anything, comes of this."

"Thanks, gotta go."

The call ended.

Tanner let his phone drop to his desk and massaged his temples. Getting this story out was critical for all kinds of reasons. Harding's challenge pulled him back to the handprint with the killer's message.

Yes, the cases were linked, but no one outside the investigation knew the details.

Tanner unlocked his desk, took out a bulging accordion file holder. Again, he went to Charlene Podden's full lab report on the handprint and reread it.

Her analysis showed that the tips of each finger had been rolled onto the paper in a "fingerprint process." The substance used for making the prints was human blood, but the blood used was not always the same. The left thumb impression belonged to Bonnie Bradford and was made using her blood, which was O positive.

None of the other prints belonged to Bradford. One of the remaining four prints was made in O positive blood, two were made with A positive and one was made in B positive blood.

Tanner and Zurn had gone full bore on running the four remaining mystery prints, submitting them to ViCAP, the FBI's Violent Criminal Apprehension Program database of violent crimes, and IAFIS, the national fingerprint and criminal history system, and every regional, state and local computer repository available to them. Within days they had hits on all four and each of them pointed to an unsolved cold case within L.A. County.

The print of the left index finger belonged to Fay Lynne Millwood, 27, A positive blood. Next they identified the print from the left middle finger of Monique Louise Wilson, 30, B positive blood. The next fingerprint was from the left ring finger of Esther Fatima Lopez, 29, A positive blood. The left baby fingerprint belonged to Leeza Meadows, 21, O positive blood. The five murders were the work of one killer.

Sitting alone in his home office, Tanner stared at a page containing the haunting handprint. Five families had been destroyed by the monster who'd made it.

Tanner glanced at Becky's framed picture. He knew

what it was like to lose a part of your life, to have the earth under your feet crumble.

His thoughts went back to the handprint and the killer.

He couldn't stop her killer, but this guy was different.

You better not be dead, because we're coming for you.

18

San Marino, California

I'm probably overreacting, Claire thought as she drove to her office with lingering unease over Robert.

It had been two days since she'd come upon the snapshot of his ex-wife. Yet she'd never voiced a word about it to him, because she'd rationalized every suspicion. Their ex-spouses had been part of their lives. She had photos of Cliff somewhere. If one happened to go astray, was that a big deal? Not really. So why make the picture an issue?

Let it go.

And as far as Robert's preoccupation went, his reasons were sound; he was anxious over rumored layoffs, and he was having a few aftershocks from the accident. He had a lot on his mind. They both did, what with parenthood on the horizon.

As for her part, Claire thought, wheeling into her space in her office parking lot, she was still a bit pumped after facing down a violent ex here some forty-eight hours ago. She gave the immediate area a quick scan as her remote key lock chirped twice.

Upon arriving inside the office, Claire greeted Alice,

then settled into her routine and prepared for her first patient of the day.

Amber Pratt.

After Claire reviewed the new aspects of Amber's file, Alice sent her in.

Amber sat on the cushioned sofa chair opposite Claire and twisted a tissue in her hands. This was her first session since her estranged partner had assaulted her and she'd moved into a shelter.

"I'm sure you've given your situation a lot of consideration," Claire said.

"I want to move back to the house," Amber said.

"You feel you're ready?"

"I'm ready. The police and the security company checked it. They told my lawyer that they couldn't find any signs that anyone broke in or anything."

"That's good."

"And that stuff about me worrying there was a man in the closet must've been like you said, me being paranoid about Eric."

"Amber, you need to keep in mind what happened here."

Claire flipped through the file folder on her lap containing updates she'd received from the court and the police.

"Officer Freeman said Eric learned you were my patient and got our office address through a courthouse screwup. His lawyer gave him copies of records that somehow included information your lawyer filed with the court. Then Eric violated the court order by stalking you here because he wanted to convince you to go back to him."

"Yes, but my lawyer assured me that Eric does not

know my Alhambra address and will respect the restraining order."

"Do you believe that, after what's happened? Amber, Eric got out of jail yesterday morning."

Amber said nothing.

"You're aware that he's no longer in custody?"

"Yes, I know. His brother posted his bail, twenty thousand dollars."

"How docs all of this sit with you?"

Amber twisted the tissue then said, "The shelter is a long way across L.A."

"It was the nearest one with available space," Claire said. "And you're safe there."

"Yes, but I've missed work because of this. I've only been working there a few months. I tell them I'm sick. I don't want everyone knowing my situation, because I need my job."

"What about Eric? What are your thoughts, given what he did?"

"This is so hard."

"I know."

"We were in love. He was my life, when he was kind he—" Amber let a few moments pass. "I know that after his brother bailed him out, he took Eric back to Sacramento with him right away to start his new job."

"How do you know he's now in Sacramento?"

"I called Eric's cousin Sharon, who lives there. If I have one friend in his family, it's Sharon. Anyway, she told me Eric is now in Sacramento."

Claire slid her silver cross back and forth on her necklace chain while weighing mattcrs.

"Taking everything into consideration, a case could be made for you to return to your home," Claire said.

"I always advocate that you should not let your abusive partner control your life. The main thing I'm trying to help you with is to break free of his grip, to take back your life."

"But it's more complicated now."

For the first time Claire noticed Amber was also holding a folded sheet of paper in her hand.

"Oh, God, this is so hard," Amber said. "After what happened, Eric wrote me this letter. His cousin scanned it and sent it to me."

"This could be a violation of the no contact order," Claire said.

"Sharon said Eric will file it with the court through his lawyer. You can keep this copy."

Amber passed it to Claire. It was a one-page letter, handwritten in clear, tiny, cursive script. Eric was apologetic, ashamed, remorseful and loving. He said he was getting help and begged Amber to come back to him, so they could start a new life together.

Claire had seen this type of entreaty before—acts of contrition, urgent pleas for forgiveness and undeserved grace. It's what Eric had tried in the parking lot, only this time he wasn't using his fists.

"I don't know what to do," Amber said. "I still love him and part of me wants to give him a second chance. Part of me still believes that with help he'll get better and we could start over in Sacramento and have a real life together."

Claire tucked the letter into the file folder.

Amber looked at her, tears filling her eyes.

"Tell me what to do."

"I can't tell you what to do, but I can tell you what to consider."

"Okay."

"I understand that the temptation to go back is strong. You hope that this time you can really make it work."

"Yes."

"Amber, you have to remember why you left and how difficult it was to leave. Remember we talked about the cycle, the pattern with Eric, as it is with most abusive partners." She nodded to the file with the letter. "There is the loving, makeup honeymoon period. Afterward all will seem normal, until pressures will ultimately trigger an inciting incident of some sort. It will set him off. There will be a time of mounting tension before he loses it again and explodes. This has been Eric's pattern."

"But I noticed that since we've been apart, he has changed."

Claire sat forward and stared into Amber's eyes.

"No."

Amber said nothing.

"Look what happened two days ago in the parking lot. Amber, it is the perfect example of what he does when he's under pressure. Your divorce is proceeding. He knows he is losing you. How does he make his case? By using violence, by violating a court order, stalking you, and then threatening you and me."

Amber buried her face in her hands.

"He's trying to lure you back, but a change of zip code is no guarantee that you would not be stepping back into the same abusive pattern. While some abusers who get effective help do improve, studies show many don't and in fact fall back into their old patterns."

Claire passed Amber a tissue box.

"You are strong. Think of how far you've come. You're building self-esteem, becoming confident and a new self-image is emerging. You've regained faith in yourself and now you need to hold on to it. Experiencing old and new fears is normal. You're tempted to go back to him because you're telling yourself you are going back to the man you fell in love with, not the monster that lives inside him. You have seen how that relationship can hurt you. Amber, it might even kill you, as it has in so many other cases."

"I know," she whispered.

"You are on the most difficult journey of your life. It's not easy, but you're a survivor. There's a whole new life waiting for you. So, again, think of how far you have come and all the reasons you left. I believe you already know in your heart what you need to do."

"Thank you, Claire."

Amber took a moment with the tissues to regain her composure, and then they talked about dates for her next session.

"I need some fresh air, so I'll walk out to the lot with you," Claire said.

Amber welcomed Claire's company and when she got into her car, she dropped the window and smiled.

"Thank you for helping me." She reached out and took Claire's hand, squeezing it hard. "I know I can get through this."

Claire gave a small wave as Amber pulled onto Huntington and disappeared into traffic. Maybe Claire was still jittery from the recent attack in this very spot. Or maybe she was not convinced that Eric was in Sacramento. But as she looked up and down the street, she was unable to subdue the nagging sensation someone was watching her.

19

Los Angeles, California

That night Mark Harding stared down at the lights of L.A. from Mulholland Drive.

He'd come here to reflect after filing his serial killer feature to the ANPA's world headquarters in New York.

It was a strong story and would get good pickup, he thought, while driving along the twisting, turning ridgeline that straddled the Hollywood Hills and Santa Monica Mountains. Mulholland wound by celebrity mansions hidden behind security gates, hedges and jagged canyon nooks. On the north side you could see the San Fernando Valley. To the south you got breathtaking views of the metropolis, its twinkling city grid stretching to the horizon.

Was the killer still out there?

Five women had been murdered, but his feature didn't explain how their deaths were linked, other than Tanner's vague reference to a cryptic message. It frustrated Harding that Tanner had refused to give him details on the killer's signature. He parked at a lookout point, got out and leaned against his car to ponder the view. The sweeping vista suited him. He preferred it to sitting alone in his apartment on the east side.

Harding's building was advertised as clean and quiet. And it was, provided you didn't count the beer cans bobbing in the pool, the overflowing trash bins in the parking lot, the yipping poodles or the hammer and thud of car speakers and LAPD choppers.

Tonight, after working late at the bureau to finish his story, he didn't go to his empty apartment. He went to a burger place to eat and think before taking a drive.

He'd worked hard on this story. Magdalena, the bureau chief, had cut him loose to go full tilt on it and over the past few days, Harding had talked to five grieving families. Meeting times and schedules had him pinballing all over greater L.A. In each case he'd called ahead to allow them to brace for what was coming. He was relieved when he'd learned that Tanner had already alerted them to expect a reporter's call.

In all of Harding's years as a reporter, talking to the parents of a murdered child, or the loved ones of someone who'd died tragically, was a part of the job he never stopped hating. Meeting the bereaved relatives and friends of murder victims face-to-face, even years after the fact, ripped open wounds that never would heal.

You saw it behind their eyes—something was broken.

Still, they'd all opened their doors to him and to Jodi-Lee Ruiz, a recent grad from UCLA, who was the bureau's interning photographer. Harding had asked Magda to assign her to work with him.

"She's close to the age of some of the victims," Harding had said. "She'd be a psychological bridge to the families."

Magda had agreed.

Jodi-Lee followed Harding's subtle cues. The first interview was in Santa Clarita—the case of twenty-one-year-old Leeza Meadows. Her father, Louis, took to Jodi-Lee. He showed them his daughter's bedroom where he talked about receiving the strange phone call from someone using Leeza's cell phone shortly after she was murdered.

"The police could never prove it was the killer but in my gut, I know it was him." Louis recalled the last time he'd seen Leeza. Then he answered Harding's question about the music box on the dresser.

"It was one of the last things she touched," Louis said.

Harding nodded to Jodi-Lee, who raised her camera and took Louis Meadows's photo as he brushed his fingers tenderly on the music box.

Later, Louis flipped through an album of photos of Leeza, proud of how pretty she was. The pictures contrasted with the crime scene images burned into Harding's mind of Leeza, leaving him to wonder privately if her father had ever seen those pictures.

"I just hope your story helps find the animal who killed my daughter and the other women," Louis said. "It won't bring Leeza or any of them back, but it might give me answers. And I hope to hell I stay on this earth long enough to see the son of a bitch go into the ground."

Harding and Jodi-Lee then went to Torrance to talk to Carmen Lopez, a retired janitor who lived with Sonny, her Shih Tzu, in a mobile home in Horizon View Hamlet. Her twenty-nine-year-old daughter Esther's body had been unearthed in Topanga in 2004. At the time of her murder, Esther had been working for an escort agency.

"It was drugs that ruined her life," Carmen said with Sonny on her lap. "My daughter wanted to be a teacher and was taking college courses when her husband was killed overseas. He was a soldier. After his death, Esther fell apart, turned to drugs and lost her way." Carmen stroked her dog. "Now, to learn that she was murdered by someone who has killed so many others— I pray police find him and bring him to justice before he hurts any more girls."

Next, they drove to Santa Ana in Orange County, where they met with Lana Gibson, a county administrator, whose younger sister, Monique Louise Wilson, was found murdered in Lakewood. Students on a junior-high science field trip had discovered her body in a park.

"Mon was engaged to be married. Her accounting firm wanted her to help run their new office in Sydney, Australia. She was thirty with her whole life ahead of her. I miss her so much," Gibson said, fingering a bracelet that had belonged to her sister. Jodi-Lee took a few frames. "And now we learn that the monster responsible for taking her life has killed so many other women and that he could still be out there?"

Harding and Jodi-Lee traveled to Santa Monica and the home of Will Parson, a security official at one of the big studios. The headless corpse of his fiancée, Fay Lynne Millwood, had been found stuffed into a barrel in San Dimas. She had been an actress and part-time bartender.

"Fay worked so hard and was starting to get bigger parts in pictures," Parson said. "When she was killed, she was up for a small role in a Brad Pitt, George Clooney project." Parson stared at nothing and shook his head. "People don't understand what this does to you. We were planning our wedding when she was taken from me. I wish I had had five minutes alone with this guy. No, five seconds."

After talking to Parson in Santa Monica, they went to Thousand Oaks to see Ross Corbett about Bonnie Catherine Bradford.

"We've been through a lot of counseling together," Corbett said, "and it's helped." He'd agreed to let Jimmy and Jessie talk to Harding and be photographed. "We're doing this," Corbett said, "because police think a compassionate story might yield another new break arising from the killer's message in the case."

This stopped Harding.

None of the other families had said anything about "another new break" relating to the killer's message. All that the others knew from police was that five cold case murders were now linked. Harding wanted to know exactly what the message said.

"Ross, what did you mean by 'another new break arising from the killer's message'?" Harding asked. "What does that message say?"

Corbett backpedaled and changed the subject, but later Harding pushed him on it.

"Look," Corbett said, "the detectives asked us not to say anything, so forget anything I said."

"Really?"

"Yes, but that's all I'm saying, I don't want to jeopardize anything."

Harding absorbed the revelation and now, as he stared down at Los Angeles, he exhaled slowly. Obviously there was more at stake for the families, but having had the emotional fallout of five murders filter through him had taken a toll and he was exhausted.

His cell phone rang. The number was blocked. He answered.

"Mark, this is Joe Tanner. Did your story run yet?"

"It's going out tonight."

"I got a call from Ross Corbett. He said you were pressing him hard to learn more about the killer's message."

"That's my job, Joe."

"I know. Zurn and I have discussed things with our lieutenant and captain."

"What did you talk over? You called me on this story?"

"We're prepared to give you a little more on the message to use in the story. We think it might help. Is there time to get it in?"

"New York's doing a final edit now." Harding did a quick mental calculation of New York's deadlines and time zone differences. "We'd have to hurry."

"Got a pen and paper?"

Harding pulled a notepad and pen from his pocket.

"Yup."

"Your story must emphasize that we think the killer is dead."

"It does."

"He calls himself the Dark Wind Killer, or goes by DWK."

"The Dark Wind Killer—what's the significance?"

"We're not releasing that, but there's more."

"Go ahead."

"He said, 'I'm just getting started.'"

20

San Marino, California

Robert Bowen stopped eating his breakfast midbite.

On the front page of the *Los Angeles Times,* below the fold across six columns read the headline Serial Killer's Message Discovered 10 Years after First Slaying, over the subhead Suspect Vowed Return, But After 5 L.A.-Area Murders, Detectives Now Believe The Dark Wind Killer is Dead.

The byline was Mark Harding, AllNews Press Agency.

Bowen shoved his plate of scrambled eggs aside, spread the paper on the kitchen table and pored over every detail. The article spilled from the front page to page two.

His scalp prickled as the faces of the five dead women stared back at him from the photos and profiles of the feature. It was keyed to the ten-year anniversary of the first victim, Leeza Meadows, and newly discovered evidence by investigators.

A locater map pinpointed the crime scenes. Relatives of the victims blathered about their anguish, justice and vengeance.

Bowen's jaw clenched as he read.

> "The suspect is very intelligent," said Joe Tanner, an L.A. County Sheriff's cold case detective heading the multi-agency taskforce that was formed to clear the homicides. "We've received his message. As to why he stopped in 2007, we can only speculate that he relocated, or went to prison, or stopped out of fear that he'd slip up. Our most likely scenario is that he's dead."

Tanner would not reveal contents of the "cryptic communication" left by the suspect, who'd identified himself as the Dark Wind Killer. Tanner appealed to anyone with information on the case to contact the L.A. County Sheriff's Cold Case Unit.

Investigators would not explain why so much time had passed before the discovery of the new evidence linking the murders of an accountant, a screenwriter, a waitress, an actress and an escort. The women didn't know each other or share any connections. The article summarized the grisly details of how the women were killed.

Bowen's body tingled as he reread every word, every sentence and every paragraph.

He looked closely at the women.

As he remembered each one, waves of sensual gratification rolled through him along with alarm. The urges he'd battled all of his life had begun, by degrees, to possess him again, stirring him to serve the monstrosity that lived within him.

The other being.

The urges rose in the blackest reaches of his existence and swirled through him with a force he'd come to call the Dark Wind.

Sitting at his kitchen table, Bowen felt as if a spike had suddenly been driven into his brain. He fell into a vague dream state, barely conscious of himself as he grappled with the other being. He fought to suppress it as he stared into the eyes of the dead women, confronting his horror, the revulsion and disgust over what he had done.

But the monster inside refused to be denied.

The police are mocking me, saying I'm dead. How could they not revere his five masterpieces and doubt his return?

But Bowen did not want this. Claire was his salvation. He had a new life, a good life. He had buried the monster deep inside himself.

No, I'm living a lie; Claire will destroy the being that I am. She told me she couldn't have children. Things changed when she pursued her intention to have a baby, to change me, to control me, put me in a cage.

That was not my life. Living like this never was my real life.

No one would ever understand what I am: a supreme creature with needs that are all-consuming. There was so much yet to achieve. I was on the brink of dispatching that woman and her cub in the car wreck. It would have been a perfect crime. Why did I stop?

It would have been wrong, that's why Bowen stopped.

There's no right or wrong for what I am.

Yes, there was. Bowen had seen it in the face of the father of number one. That's why he went to him, to search for a moral answer.

No, I'm deceiving myself. There's no wrong. No morality. No conscience. No remorse. I cannot deny what

I am. Look at the truth. I've already started work on new projects; started hunting again.

Amber.

I got into her bedroom and near enough to drink in her breath.

But Bowen had stopped, not only because Amber had stirred but because he'd caught himself standing over her, a reflection in a mirror of his hideous mask and the reason he wore it—to convince himself that he was not the other being. Bowen was not the vile monster in the mirror, and to prove it he'd abandoned the Amber project with every intention of destroying the other being once and for all.

Bowen's head ached. The being demanded he finish what he'd started because the stars were aligning.

The clock was ticking.

Bowen sat motionless staring at the paper. He saw nothing, heard nothing but the pounding of his heart.

"Are you all right?" Claire entered the kitchen, preparing to leave for work. "Who were you talking to? You sounded angry."

Running a hand over his face he went to the counter to freshen his coffee and nodded to the cordless phone on the kitchen table.

"A telemarketer called."

For a moment Claire gave him a look that bordered on doubt.

"Really, I never heard the phone ring?"

"Maybe you were in the shower or drying your hair?"

She resumed putting on her earrings. "What was the call about?"

"He was trying to sell me financial planning services and would not take no for an answer. He started to piss me off." Robert sipped some coffee. "I'm thinking about leaving this morning for the cabin. Get in some fishing. Maybe spend the night or two, before my next trip."

"I think that's a good idea, given all that's happened."

"And what about you, what've you got going today besides work?"

"Not too much, lunch with Julie, to catch up, gossip, girl stuff."

"Have fun."

Claire collected her bag, kissed Robert goodbye, then nodded to the newspaper on her way out.

"I read that horrible story," she said. "Thank God that's over with. I hope the creep is dead."

Robert watched through the window as Claire drove off, her words echoing in his mind.

21

Los Angeles, California

"There you are. Oh, my God, you must be walking on air!"

Claire's friend Julie Glidden got up from the table in Café Pinot and hugged her.

"Hey, stranger, it's been a while," Claire said.

"Sure has. You look fabulous."

"So do you, I love your new cut."

"I thought I'd try something casual." Julie flashed her beauty-queen smile, made an exaggerated sweep of her new angled bangs. "Speaking of new, when you told me the baby news on the phone, I thought, *wow!* And then that mild-mannered pilot husband of yours does his superhero impression. It's all coming together for you."

"I've been lucky."

"No, it's karma," Julie said. "The wheel is turning. It's been a long, rocky road from Minnesota to where you are now."

"When you put it that way, I can't argue."

"No, you can't." Julie patted Claire's hand. "It's so good to see you. What's new?"

Right off, Claire told her about having to save a patient from her estranged husband who'd assaulted her in the parking lot.

"I want you for my bodyguard." Julie grinned.

Over menus, drinks and lunch, the two friends caught up.

They'd been college roommates at the University of Minnesota. Back then, Julie was studying law and after graduating, she'd moved to California, continued her studies and passed the state bar exam. She'd taken junior positions at several law firms before she'd landed a job with the California Attorney General's Office investigating fraud, which bored her.

Three years ago, after beating breast cancer, Julie realized life was too short to not do what you want to do. She loved investigative work. So, she left the AG's office, got her private investigator's license and found a job with a big private detective agency.

She moved into a bungalow in Woodland Hills with her life partner, Phillipa, a set designer. They had no kids but wanted one, a subject that always came up whenever Julie and Claire got together.

"Phil wants to adopt a baby from China."

"And what do you want?"

"I want to adopt, too."

"I thought you were looking into surrogacy or a donor for Phil?"

"Yes, we did, but I think we're ready to take the China option."

"Sounds like you're playing chess."

"I know that didn't come out right. But just think, Claire, if it all worked out at the same time for us, we'd have birthday parties to schlep our brats to." Julie laughed. "I'd love that."

After they finished their salads they took their time with a dessert menu before giving in and deciding to share the apple tarte Tatin with ice cream.

"Okay, so you start treatment in a few weeks," Julie said. "The doc promises you'll be pregnant in no time. Have you and Robert got a lot of romantic dinners planned?"

Claire gave her a smile that faded a little too soon.

"Seriously," Julie said. "How's Robert with all of this? He must be ecstatic."

Claire hesitated long enough to change the mood.

"He's excited."

Julie's eyes narrowed as she stared at her friend.

"What is it, Claire?"

Claire searched the downtown skyline for an answer.

In the quiet of their table, the surrounding chink of cutlery, the restaurant's din became overwhelming. As Claire contended with her unease, she tried to wave it off.

"It's stupid."

Julie leaned forward and lowered her voice.

"Tell me, what's wrong?"

A nervous laugh escaped Claire. Here she was, the professional, licensed to help people with their problems, yet helpless in the face of her own. "I don't know. I'm a little troubled about Robert these days."

"What do you mean?"

"He's been withdrawn, pensive."

"Because of the baby news? Maybe he's nervous. You know, it is a milestone kind of thing."

"No. It started weeks ago. It's like he's keeping something from me."

"Like what? What do you mean?"

Claire shook her head.

"What?" Julie asked.

"It's silly."

"Try telling me what you're thinking."

"The other day at home I overheard him when he was in his office on the phone. I think he was talking to Cynthia, his ex-wife."

"So?"

"He never ever talks about her or his life with her. That little incident concerns me. I know he was up very early that morning—he could've been up all night talking to her."

"What were they talking about?"

"I don't know."

"You said you 'think' he was talking to his ex-wife. Do you know for sure he was talking to her?"

"No. That's just it. It happened right after the crash and when I asked him about it he said he was talking to a reporter who'd emailed him about the crash and asked him to call."

"Okay, so, then it was a reporter. He was the big hero, so that makes sense, doesn't it?"

"Yes, but not long after that I found a photograph on the floor of his office. It was like it had been dropped or fell out of something. It was a picture of Robert with his arm around Cynthia, with 'happier times' written on the back."

"Did you raise the photo with him?"

"No, I left it exactly where I'd found it. I have old photos of Cliff somewhere. But I don't know about this. It's making me a little anxious."

"So what are you saying? He still has feelings for

her? He's having phone sex or an affair? He's lying to you? What?"

"Maybe. Yes. No. I'm not sure. I don't know."

"Don't you keep in touch with Cliff?"

"No. Not at all. I just hear things through the old school grapevine that he remarried, has two kids. That's it."

Julie bit her bottom lip as she thought for several moments.

"Want me to do some digging for you?"

"On Cliff?"

"Robert."

"Gosh, no. Spy on him? No."

"No, I'm not talking about surveillance."

"What are we talking about?"

"A few things, I could start small."

"I don't know, Julie."

"Look, you want to know if he was talking to Cynthia, right?"

"No. I should just ask him what's going on."

"You did and he told you, didn't he?"

"Yes and I asked him about his pensiveness the other night at dinner."

"And?"

"He said he was a little shaken by the crash, going through a little post-traumatic stress. And he said he was preoccupied with rumors that his company might be making cuts."

"And does it end there? Are you satisfied he's told you the truth?"

"That's just it. I don't know."

"Look, you're about to have a baby with this man.

You owe it to yourself, and to your future, to deal with this nagging suspicion."

"Hypothetically, what would you do?"

"I could find out who he called, or who called him. Give me all of his numbers, your numbers, the dates and times you think he was talking to Cynthia and I'll look into it for you."

"I don't know about this. I don't want him to think I don't trust him— I'm just not..."

"Claire, it's what I do. He'll never know."

22

Greater Los Angeles, California

The freeway rushed under Robert Bowen's SUV as he headed east on the 210 toward the mountains.

Before leaving L.A., he'd taken care of a few matters. It was now late afternoon but traffic was still good. The *Los Angeles Times* article was folded in his bag.

He needed to think.

Problems were rising around him. Everything was at stake. The police were hunting for him. Claire was determined to bring a baby into their lives; and the darkness within him—the force he thought he'd conquered—was back full bore and fighting him for control.

As his wheels ate up the highway, his mind swirled with a million concerns. He loved Claire. He'd worked hard to build what he had with her. He could not lose it. He wanted to be a father—wanted a normal life.

But the monster inside him was relentless. For as long as he could remember he'd struggled against it. At times he was convinced he'd put it to rest. Then he would see a woman, the right type of woman, one that would give him a metaphysical vibration. He'd become enthralled by her smile, her look, her everything.

It would arouse him and the monster would take control.

He would stalk her, study her, and obsess about her until a spark would ignite a glorious, all-consuming inferno, leaving him to question his fate as a force from hell.

Will I ever escape this curse?

How much longer can I exist as two beings?

He searched the distant mountains for the answers, letting the hypnotic rhythm of the road carry him back through his life to his earliest memories.

Pain.

He's staring at a naked lightbulb burning bright against dark flashes as the leather belt slices through the air, whip-snapping over and over.

Each lash bites into his tender skin.

He is four, maybe five, years old. Wedged into a corner, he tries to shield the blows but his foster mother grips both of his tiny hands in hers and with alcohol-laced grunting, she continues beating him.

"Don't ever piss in your goddamn bed again! Do you hear me? You're lucky to be alive! You're a filthy little worm!"

He'd been told that he was orphaned as a baby after his parents had been killed in a car crash. He'd been placed with social services and moved from home to home.

At age six or seven, he was placed in yet another foster home. His foster mother, who'd lied to social services in order to get her check, was an unstable, manipulative drug addict. Whenever she was working her shift at some dive bar, she left him alone with her boyfriend:

an ex-con who watched pornographic movies in front of him.

At that time, he felt the stirrings of another force within him, one that compelled him to spy on his foster mother as she undressed, showered or had sex with her criminal lover. One summer afternoon when she was on the apartment balcony tanning in a bikini, she caught him staring at her cleavage and slapped his face so hard he bled.

He glances out the window at the vapor trail of a jet cutting across the sky. At that moment he wishes he were flying above the earth, above the pain and humiliation this bad woman is inflicting on him.

He also wishes he were smashing her head with a hammer.

Eventually, he was passed to another home where his foster mother was an ex-prison guard who looked more like a man than a woman. She had a teenage foster daughter. One day, he was alone in the house with her. She was in her room putting on makeup, drinking beer and smoking pot. She saw him in her mirror, watching.

"Stop staring at me, you little asshole!" She pauses for a second before her eyes glint with an idea. "Come here, it's time you learned the truth."

She takes him to their foster mother's bedroom, goes into a dresser drawer and produces a photocopy of an old news clipping.

"You can read, right, moron?"

The short news article reports that:

> *A newborn baby boy was found in a Dumpster at an abandoned northeast apartment complex, according to police. A homeless man searching for*

cans in one of the large trash bins near the old Stone Mill building found the infant in a bloody blanket...

"This story is in your file. It's about you, garbage boy. And you know what I heard? Back then, they called you the throwaway baby. They never found your whore mother and all the families that tried to adopt you brought you back because you're a freak."

At that moment he struggled to comprehend that his fate was more than being unwanted and unloved.

I am nobody. I came from nowhere. I was never meant to be.

He'd come to realize that he was utterly alone in this world. His isolation deepened, giving shape to the second being growing inside him, the one that was taking control.

He was not alone. The other being was with him and together they were better than all of them. They would make them, and everyone like them, pay. One day, everyone in the world would know and fear his name.

He retreated to his dream of becoming a pilot. He lost himself in books, spending hours alone in the library reading about aviation, aviation history and aviation engineering. He read entire sets of encyclopedias, classic literature and textbooks on science, everything he could find, gaining knowledge while strengthening his determination to escape his misery.

During this time, as he grew into his teens, he'd continued passing through a succession of homes. Nearly all of the cities and towns he'd lived in blurred by like the suburbs along the freeway.

His time with one family changed him forever.

In one small town, his foster father was a barely educated, self-pitying man whose job was to destroy life. He took him to his workplace.

"You ain't ever seen nothing like this."

The old man worked in the slaughterhouse at the edge of town, where he was "the killer." He spit on the ground, as if to dare you to challenge him. "Because that's what I do for a living."

The stench from the barns was choking. The mooing, the clang of chains and rattle of metal gates was deafening. The cattle were prodded along the chutes one by one toward the death pen where his foster father waited. When the animal was positioned, he fired a penetrating steel shaft from a bolt gun point-blank into its head.

Crack.

The animal collapsed dead.

The side of the pen opened, a chain was affixed to its leg. It was hoisted and hung from an overhead conveyor and cut so all the blood drained from its carcass. It was then moved farther through the process.

"Right now, I am God," his foster father said, standing there in his rubber apron and gloves as blood swirled around his boots. "I control life and death."

He passed the gun to him and nodded to the pen.

"Go on, you give it a try."

His heart beat faster.

He felt the weight and seductive power of the stick-like device in his hand. Amid the stinking chaos of the slamming steel pen, the mooing, clanging chains and snorting, the frightened animal lifted its head to him, its nostrils flaring.

As he raised the gun and pressed it against its skull, he met its eyes.

They were flashing with wild fear.

He felt nothing for the animal. Instead, he imagined its eyes to be those of every one of his abusers and he squeezed the trigger.

At the moment of death, his heart raced, his breathing quickened and he experienced a sensually cathartic release.

The other being inside him raged triumphantly.

He remained motionless for several moments, as if he'd fallen into a trance. As he watched the carcass being hoisted, he smelled the hot blood splashing onto the floor and his body rippled with waves of pleasure.

"I want to do it again."

He became good at killing.

Several months after he'd polished his skill as a detached killer, he'd moved into another home. As he adjusted to a new foster father, he continued dreaming of becoming a pilot. Throughout his youth, to escape his upbringing, he'd worked. He got jobs, pumping gas, washing dishes, stocking shelves and landscaping, whatever he could find.

He saved every penny he earned, often hiding it from his foster families. But whenever he could, he sought jobs at the local airport where he would learn everything he could about flying from ground crews, mechanics and pilots. Soon he set out on his own, working while putting himself through college and, later, flight school.

It was not easy.

In addition to the grind of physical jobs, the monster grew stronger and more demanding. At times it took control, dominating every thought until he was certain he'd go insane. There were frightening instances when he'd blacked out and couldn't recall the previous hours or remember where he went or what he did. The other being demanded he give in to its overpowering urges to replicate the ecstasy of the slaughterhouse with a woman. He battled to satisfy the hunger that was devouring him from the inside. He watched porno movies, visited strip clubs, paid for prostitutes.

In private moments, after joking around with some of the men he worked with, he'd come to realize what he already knew: his desires weren't normal. Afraid that they could get out of hand, he sought counseling and was prescribed relaxation tapes and medication.

He tried it for several months before giving up.

Nothing worked.

It was as if his brain were on fire.

Nothing fulfilled him. The more the monster demanded a controlled kill, the more he fantasized about taking live action with a real woman, forcing him to hunt until he found a target.

She worked at a bookstore in a local mall where he bought books about planes. He studied her for weeks. She had a lovely figure, beautiful eyes. She gave off the vibe that fed his desire to take her.

He'd learned everything he could about her; where she lived, where she bought her groceries and where she took yoga classes. He learned that on nights after she closed the store and made a deposit at one of the mall's banks, she walked alone in the parking lot to her car, a green Honda. He knew the route she drove home. Knew the ruse he would use.

He began preparing.

He'd dug a grave in a dense woods twenty miles from town where he would dispose of her body. He'd scouted a room in an abandoned factory where he would tie her up and possess her, possibly for days if he wanted, all while recording their sessions.

Everything was set.

But on the night he was to launch his mission, she didn't walk to her car. Her boyfriend had arrived and walked her to his. He backed off and aborted the project.

It was too risky.

The monster thrashing inside him became enraged. He fought to subdue the beast. He summoned every iota of sanity to battle the dark urges, praying he could suppress them or outgrow them, hoping that they would ultimately fade away.

It took a great effort, but he concentrated on his job and his goal. He soon got his pilot's license, then a job as a flight instructor, all the while working toward further qualifications. In time, he flew small charters, then cargo jets before ultimately flying across the U.S. and around the globe for a big commercial airline.

He was devoted to his career.

He stayed single, dated flight attendants and lived in cities around the world.

But in all that time, the monster would not rest.

With each passing month, each year, its craving intensified, creating fantasies as it presented him with plans for missions, insisting that together they possessed more intelligence than any other killer before him.

What they would achieve would surpass anything in history.

And no one would ever know.

Unless they wanted them to.

They could claim their glory, like Jack the Ripper and the Zodiac Killer, and turn their work into art. Ultimately, the monster won. They launched a major undertaking of multiple projects. It was flawless.

Robert glanced at his bag in the passenger seat holding the article.

Five perfect kills.

But he could not bear the burden of his curse. He ached to be free of this evil, to live a normal life, an upstanding, virtuous life and when he found Cynthia, he'd been convinced she was his salvation.

He'd been so happy when they married.

He'd restrained the beast inside him. Maybe he'd even laid it to rest.

But his grueling job as a pilot, the days and nights away, his struggles with temptations and his past had caused irreparable damage. He was sorry about how it ended with Cynthia.

The disaster had forced him to take stock.

Again he searched for redemption, driven by the need to rebuild himself as a moral man and a compassionate human being.

Is that possible, given what I am?

After his marriage ended he had taken steps to leave the demanding world of a commercial airline pilot. He had been in the process of lining up a charter pilot job in L.A. when he met Claire.

Claire would always believe that he rescued her from her violent spouse that day at the Minneapolis airport, but Robert knew the truth: she'd saved him. She was a force of light in his life, a light that would grow even brighter with a child. With Claire, he was living in grace.

But the monster had returned.

He could feel its hot breath on him as he got closer to the mountains where he'd come to bury his demon.

As he drove along the narrow road that cut through the dense forest, his jaw clenched with one thought.

Only one of us is coming back.

23

San Bernardino Mountains, California

Long after Robert Bowen had left the freeway for the smaller byways that led to Big Bear Lake, he turned onto a gravel access road that forked from the highway, curving along the north shore.

Stones popcorned against the undercarriage before he reached the jutting granite rock that marked the way to his property.

He stopped.

Dust clouds enveloped his SUV. The entrance was all but concealed by shrubs, which swallowed his vehicle as he rolled onto the earthen pathway. Like an enormous snake, the path coiled into a forest so dense with towering cedar, pine and sequoia trees, they blotted out the light.

He crept along the undulating trail, awakening branches that scraped and tugged at his SUV in protest, or warning. For he had entered another realm, a secret world cut off from the life he knew with Claire in L.A. This was his place of solitude and truth, where he would confront his other self. He'd gone a short distance under a canopy of shadows and light before arriving at his cabin.

It had been built with hand-hewn logs in the 1920s and, in the 1970s, it had been upgraded with basic electricity and plumbing. Keeping with ritual, Bowen first walked the perimeter, inspecting the building and the property for any signs of vandals, attempted burglaries or damage by animals.

He didn't find any.

He owned a large piece of land. The other tracts on either side were empty. As Bowen took in the tranquil pine-scented air and sweeping views of the lake and mountains, enjoying the isolation, he rejected the idea of selling the place.

He went inside.

There were two spacious bedrooms, a kitchen-living area, bathroom and a utility room. He went into each one and opened the windows, letting in the crisp breezes. Then he went to the SUV and hauled in a box of groceries and his bags.

The cabin didn't have a phone. The nearest landline was at the gas station a few miles away. More cell phone towers had recently been built and wireless service to the region was improving, but it was still far from perfect. Dropped calls and bad connections were the norm. He fired up his laptop. Then he unfolded the newspaper and again studied the article on *The Dark Wind Killer.*

A sudden shiver knifed through him, his head began thudding. The faces of the dead women haunted him, excited him with tortured longings.

The monster was present and flailing in his cage.

Was Bowen ready?

Yes. He was going to bury the thing. He wanted a life with Claire.

No, he didn't. He had to accept the truth. Look at the five of them. It was a masterpiece. Remember the power?

Yes, he remembered.

Remember the ecstasy?

He ran his tongue over his lips, it had been off the charts.

He had to admit he wanted to do it again, needed to do it again.

No. He'd stopped. He had a life.

That was a lie. He'd already started a new project.

No, he stopped. It proved he was finished.

It proves nothing! You go back and finish what you've started! Look at her again! Look at how flawless it was! Go on! Do it now! You know you want to look!

Bowen licked his lips. His hand trembled a little when he plugged a USB flash drive into his laptop.

A video played, from the perspective of a head cam. It began with a house at night, a large ranch home, then jumped to its alarm system being disarmed, and then the lock of a side door expertly defeated with burglar's tools.

The interior was tastefully decorated, the home was empty. The footage faded to black, then resumed with Amber Pratt preparing a bath, getting ready for bed. It then jumped to her fast asleep.

The camera pulled in on her pretty face. Then it cut to a naked man standing over her, reflected in the mirror. His face was a hideous mask of thick white makeup. His mouth, a blood-red, smeared frown. His black hollow eyes accentuated horror and agony.

Watching Amber now in the ambient light while she slept caused him to moan aloud in his cabin.

She was so beautiful. She was perfect.

Amber had triggered a vibration.

She had rekindled his dark urges and resurrected the monster. Ever since that day when he first saw her several months ago leaving Claire's office, he ached to have her. Amber: The twenty-eight-year-old secretary, vulnerable and living alone in that big house in Alhambra.

Some nights he'd awake with his head splitting with so much pain he'd black out again. Once he woke with bloodstains on his clothes and no memory of how he'd got them. He'd tossed his bloodied pants and shirt in a Dumpster and took bleach to his car and cleaned it.

Now, sitting in the cabin, Bowen jolted from his trancelike state.

He had a life with Claire.

He had abandoned his project to take Amber.

No, he wanted her. It was true.

He wanted his torment to end.

Bowen slammed his laptop shut, went to the bathroom, yanked off his clothes and started to shower. He'd set the water so hot it nearly scalded him in his attempt to purge himself of the other being through a reverse baptism. He clawed at his skin, nearly scrubbing it raw.

Why was he cursed?

As steam clouds rose around him, his mind raced back to the slaughterhouse and the words of his foster father after he'd taught him the art of death.

"When you kill, you cross a line. There's no feeling like it in this world. It's mighty powerful, what they call primal, it gets into your system, gets hold of you and you can't ever beat it, or stop it. I love it, truth be told." He winks and spits on the ground. "And you will, too."

Now, as needles of hot water stung him, Bowen recalled Louis Meadows's wish for his daughter's killer.

"I would ask God to make certain he burns for all time."

Aghast at his depravity, Bowen continued washing to no avail as he slipped closer to the edge of an inferno.

What about the fact that he fought to let Amber live? What about the fact that he rescued that mother and her baby from the car wreck? Didn't these good actions wash away the evil?

Nothing would ever undo his monstrous acts.

Bowen's head was splitting. He gripped it in his hands, leaned back against the shower and slid to the floor as the truth tore at him.

He was condemned to a dual existence.

Nothing would free him. No one could save him. He had to accept what he was.

He could not accept it and live.

He left the shower without dressing and rushed to the utility room, rummaging in a supply box for a long piece of yellow nylon rope. He fashioned a noose, dragged a chair from the kitchen and flung it over a crossbeam where he tied it off.

What are you doing?

He climbed onto the chair and slid the rope over his head.

It all ends here, now.

You must not do that!

"Fuck you!"

He tightened the noose on his neck. His pulse raced and he gritted his teeth. As he braced to kick out the chair he glanced at his laptop and in that instant thought of how they would find him.

He thought of Claire. He caught his breath. Then he thought of nothing.

Numb with fear and confusion he removed the rope from around his neck, sat on the floor, naked and defeated.

He sat that way, motionless, numb, not thinking, for a long time.

Night had fallen by the time he stood and went to the utility room. He got on his hands and knees and worked his finger carefully around a loosened floorboard, pressing one end until its edge rose, allowing him to lift it out cleanly. Then he removed three more next to it revealing a storage space.

It contained a number of old CDs and textbooks on trades. One was subtitled *All That Every Locksmith Needs to Know about Every Type of Lock and Security System*. There were cell phones, cameras, keys for private storage units, cash and scores of official-looking IDs and a number of passports. As well, there were several small sealed plastic storage tubs, each about the size of a shoe box. Each tub had a name on it.

He set them on the kitchen table.

Each container held various articles, including women's bras and panties, drawings, maps, photographs.

His trophies.

He selected items and placed them on the table: Esther's bra, Fay's panties, and photos of Monique at the mall when he was hunting her and Bonnie in the moment before she died.

Suddenly he closed his eyes, returning to the moments of his artistry; how at the precise moment, as life ebbed from each woman, he'd touched her finger to her blood and rolled it with tenderness in its position on the special page he'd carried with him to each project.

His work in progress.

He'd been so careful, wearing surgical gloves, giving time for the blood to dry on the page, exercising such gentle craftsmanship in creating the artwork that would represent the five perfect kills—the masterpiece—he was determined to bestow upon the world. The beauty, no, the glory of it, still gave him shivers, which he enjoyed until he drifted from his reverie back to the kitchen table.

Each tub also contained a doll corresponding with each woman. Lovingly, he ran his fingers over them, as he came to realize that he was losing his grip on himself. Slowly, the way a snake devours a rat, he was being swallowed whole by the evil that lived inside him.

He accepted that.

He reached into his bag for a small travel kit, returned to the bathroom and began applying his macabre makeup.

"I am the Dark Wind," he said to the mirror when he finished.

He returned to the kitchen, sat in the darkness and worked at his laptop, his screen lighting his grotesque face.

One of his videos showed images of Claire. She looked beautiful as she stood at the edge of her office parking lot, the breezes caressing her hair. Another showed her asleep in her bed, a gloved hand hovering, nearly trembling almost touching her skin.

Watching the recording he licked his lips.

Blood hammered through his veins.

24

San Marino, California

Claire set a frozen chicken entrée in her microwave oven and keyed the time on the touch pad.

As the fan whooshed and the carousel turned, her unease about Robert began whirling again in the back of her mind. She dismissed it, went to her bedroom, pulled her hair into a ponytail, washed off her makeup and changed into her T-shirt and sweats.

It had been a busy day.

She'd had a late afternoon appointment with Dr. LaRoy, and fighting the rush-hour traffic from his office had been intense. It was just as well that Robert was away at the cabin, she'd use her time alone to decompress.

I need to assess things.

She nestled into her sofa, flipped on the TV, deciding to watch *Casablanca* already in progress. The Nazis sang while she ate dinner. By the time she'd finished, her attention had drifted from the movie to her own matters.

Dr. LaRoy was preparing to start her on a new protocol for the experimental treatment. It would mean that he soon would commence giving her a series of injections coordinated with her cycle. She could expect an impact on her hormones, he said, but assured her it would not be as severe as what she'd experienced in the past.

In her struggle to have a baby, Claire had undergone various treatments for IUI and IVF involving the rigors of self-injection and the PMS-like hell ride that came with it.

Bring it on, she thought. She'd do whatever it took to have a family.

Except give up.

She set her plate aside and picked up the maternity magazine she'd bought while downtown with Julie. The features about nurseries and clothes and glowing moms and dads pulled Claire back to happy but achingly brief memories of her childhood.

She's a little girl in a park running into her mother's open arms, seeing her smile, breathing in her soapy fragrance and feeling the warm love of her embrace. Another flash and she is in a huge hospital chair holding her brand-new baby brother, who felt like an angel. Then the whole family, even her father, happy at the beach in the sun.

Now Claire imagined herself pregnant and having a healthy baby. But when she tried to envision herself and Robert as parents, Claire's dream stalled over her nagging anxiety about the way he'd been acting lately.

Does he still have feelings for his ex-wife? Am I being unreasonable or silly?

She chided herself. Again she returned to the same excuses: Robert was still rattled by the crash, enduring some post-traumatic stress, all mixed with lay-off rumors and possible fatherhood.

If that's the case, then why won't my misgivings go away?

Because in her heart she knew something was just not right. Julie had made a good argument. After Claire had asked Robert about the phone call and his brooding, she was not convinced his answers explained everything.

Claire felt frustrated and needed to talk to someone.

A little therapy for the therapist, she thought, reaching for her phone and dialing the Nevada number for her longtime mentor, Martha Berman. They'd stayed in touch and Martha was up to speed with much of Claire's life. Maybe the esteemed Dr. Berman could give her some advice, Claire hoped as the line was answered.

"Hello, Martha, it's Claire in California."

"Well, hello, Claire."

"Did I catch you at a bad time?"

"Not at all, dear."

After pleasantries and small talk, Claire related her worries to the senior psychologist.

"Maybe Robert's just not ready to be a dad, Claire, or he's anxious about it."

"What about the possibility that he may still be in love with his first wife?"

"Always a possibility, but from what you've told me you don't have any proof of that, do you?"

"No, it could be a result of my own anxiety."

"That's right. One thing you should consider, given that you are about to bring a baby into your marriage, now is not the time to let any doubts about your relationship fester."

"Yes, I know. Thank you, Martha."

"Call me anytime you want to talk."

After hanging up, Claire went into her home office,

turned on her laptop and logged in to their account for their landline and cell phones.

Their phone company's new online billing service showed charges only for outgoing long-distance calls on the landline, but for their cell phones, it displayed all outgoing and incoming calls, downloads and texts.

Claire studied the information history on charges for calls made after the crash, when she'd overheard Robert's early morning call. From what she saw, nothing showed that would be a New York call on his cell phone.

Maybe he'd used the landline?

If he did, she wouldn't see it until the bill arrived.

She continued studying Robert's call and text history. Plenty of calls and texts to her, a lot from media following the crash, a lot from all over L.A., from his trips made in the San Francisco Bay Area, Seattle and Vancouver, Canada.

As she scrolled through his calls to his office, auto dealer, sports tickets, guy things, she was uncertain what she was looking for. There were toll-free numbers, online banking and credit card calls; and a sprinkling of numbers she didn't recognize.

This is nuts. I don't know what I'm doing. I should forget it.

No, she had to resolve this.

Claire picked up her cordless phone and called Julie's cell phone.

"Hey, it's me."

"Hey there, Claire."

"I want to do it. I want you to look into the phone numbers. He'll never know, right?"

"He'll never know."

"Okay, you've already got our numbers, what else do you need?"

"Your carrier, your phone company."

Claire gave it to Julie.

"Also, what is his ex-wife's last name?"

Claire thought.

"I don't know."

"Where does she live?"

Again, Claire didn't have any idea.

"Never mind," Julie said. "It's okay. Give me some time. I've got some urgent stuff I need to take care of, so I'll get back to you."

After Claire hung up, she found herself in Robert's office, thinking. A hint of his cologne mixed with the leathery smell of his office chair. He was neat and orderly. Nothing was out of place. She glanced at the spot on the floor where she'd found the photo of Robert and Cynthia.

He'd obviously put it back.

As she traced her fingers over his mahogany desk it dawned on Claire how little she knew about Robert's first wife and his marriage.

25

Los Angeles, California

Mark Harding arrived at the L.A. bureau at 6:00 a.m., hours before any of the other ANPA staffers. He took the elevator to the twenty-fifth floor, swiped his security card at the office door and started working at his desk.

He'd been coming in early ever since writing his feature on the Dark Wind Killer because he was desperate to land another exclusive with a follow-up.

When he broke the story, it had received major play in newspapers across L.A. and Southern California. But beyond that, pickup by news outlets that subscribed to the news service was spotty for print. *The Chicago Tribune, The Boston Globe* and *The Washington Post* were some of the big metros that ran the feature, while most online sites carried an abridged version.

Feeding on the angle of the killer's vow to return, L.A.'s TV and radio news crowd had followed Harding's five victim profiles. They'd also interviewed the relatives, criminology experts and the lead investigator.

"Is the killer still out there?" one TV reporter had asked Tanner.

"We can't rule that out, but we think he's dead," Tanner had said to the camera. "We invite anyone with information on this case to contact us."

L.A.'s press kept the story alive for a few days before it faded.

Now, nearly two weeks later, nothing new had surfaced. The story was all but forgotten and Magda had been quick to resume burying him with dull stories of limited interest about the entertainment industry.

It pissed him off.

Harding refused to abandon his story and came in on his own time to secretly work on it, trying everything he could think of. He monitored all social network traffic for any leads. He stayed in touch with the victims' families, asking if police had privately indicated any breaks in the case. He used the time zone difference to call his cop sources across the country, thinking, hoping some had friends on the task force Tanner was leading. In the early hours he texted Tanner directly, or called him.

"Nothing so far," Tanner said each time. "I'll let you know if anything significant surfaces."

Each morning Harding unfolded a map of L.A. on his desk, then set out all of his notes and the documents that he'd collected in his growing file on the case. Like a miner panning for gold he searched for the nugget of information that would advance the story.

He was so tired.

This morning, after working straight for nearly two hours, he stood at the window and looked at the city.

Somebody out there has to know something.

But he was at a loss at what to do next. All of his efforts had been futile so far. He started to doubt himself.

"What are you doing, Mark?"

He turned to see Magdalena Pierce standing at his desk, taking stock of all of his material on the Dark Wind Killer.

He glanced around, realizing that while ruminating he'd failed to notice others were now settling into the office before he had time to put his research away.

"What's this?" she asked.

"I was just reviewing notes." Harding started collecting papers.

Magda stopped him, setting her expensive-looking coffee mug—a gift from some aging European movie star—on Harding's desk smack in the middle of his notes, as if driving a stake through them.

"I thought I told you, Mark, this—" she nodded her chin to his work as if it offended her "—is a one-hit wonder."

"I don't agree."

At that moment, across the small office at the reception desk, Allison Porter was well into the morning practice of handling the day's mail. Even though it was an online world, people still used the post office, she thought. She was going through bills, junk mail, solicitations, news releases, résumés and other items when she came to a white business envelope.

It was addressed in handwritten block letters to NEWS DEPARTMENT, ALLNEWS PRESS AGENCY—LOS ANGELES, and continued with the proper address and zip code.

But it was the return address that gave Allison pause.

In smaller block letters it read MY TORMENT, then IN THE BOWELS OF HELL.

The envelope had a bit of thickness to it. There was

more than paper inside. The bureau received the occasional rant from fringe groups or nut jobs but this one was weird, kind of creepy, Allison thought, slipping the letter opener under the flap.

Back at his desk Harding tried to make his case.

"I think we need to follow this story closely, or someone else like the AP, Reuters or the *L.A. Times* will take it away from us."

Magda remained indifferent. Her designer jewelry was chiming as she scrawled a note on a page of one of his notepads, a habit of hers that annoyed him, tearing the fragment and handing it to him.

"There's nothing to follow until something breaks, meanwhile—"

"But that's the point, we should be dig—"

"We need to stay on the stories that yield dividends. This guy—" a polished nail tapped the number "—is an old source of mine and he's just heard that there's going to be a massive shake-up at one of the big studios. Several executives are leaving to form a competing company."

"You're serious?" Harding stared at her. "You think that is what the vast majority of people want to read about?"

"Everybody loves the movies."

"A monster killing women, versus overpaid people switching chairs."

"Please follow my instructions, Mark."

In that instant he tried to fathom why New York had not fired her, or maybe they were giving her enough rope. He was on the verge of really telling her off when—

"Oh, my God!"

Allison's scream yanked their attention to the reception desk.

26

Los Angeles, California

Mark Harding was first to arrive at reception.

Allison was standing, gaping with shock, and drawing back from the letter and its contents. Harding saw the sheet of paper and the salutation.

To Mark Harding

He caught his breath, his pulse quickened. The instant he read the first line a sense of knowing erupted in the pit of his stomach. Without touching the letter, he leaned closer. Each word hit him hard as he read:

To Mark Harding: Reporter for the AllNews Press Agency.

This is DWK speaking.

Thank you for your recent interest in my work. It has been a long time and I was beginning to think that the brilliant minds of L.A. law enforcement would never appreciate the meaning of the beautiful gift I'd left them.

Your article awakened the evil inside me.

No one can save me. No one can stop me. No

ONE CAN UNDERSTAND MY PAIN, MY TORMENT AND THE UNPARALLELED AGONY AND ECSTASY OF MY EXISTENCE.

I LIVE A NORMAL EVERYDAY LIFE AMONG YOU. BUT I AM NOT LIKE YOU, OR ANY OTHER HUMAN BEING. I LOOK DOWN ON THE MORTALS OF THIS WORLD—SO WEAK, SO VULNERABLE, AS I PREPARE TO FULFILL MY DESTINY.

THEY CALLED ME A WORM. THEY TOLD ME I WAS NEVER MEANT TO BE. THEY TORTURED ME, TAUGHT ME TO KILL UNTIL I COULD NO LONGER EXIST WITHOUT KILLING.

TO AUTHENTICATE MY REALITY I HAVE ENCLOSED AN EXAMPLE OF MY WORK THAT WILL REMOVE ALL DOUBT.

IT WILL ENABLE YOU TO "SEE" THE LIGHT.

I AM REACHING OUT FROM THE DARKNESS TO WARN THE WORLD THAT I HAVE KEPT MY WORD.

I AM BACK TO CLAIM THE REVERENCE AND THE WONDER THAT I AM OWED.

I HAVE ALREADY EMBARKED ON MY NEXT CREATION.

I WILL SOON UNLEASH FEAR UNLIKE ANYTHING THE WORLD HAS EVER KNOWN FROM JTR AND ZK, MY LESSER PREDECESSORS.

I DECIDE WHO LIVES AND WHO DIES.

I AM THE OTHER SIDE OF THE WIND.

YOURS IN BLOOD,
DWK

All the saliva in Harding's mouth evaporated.

"What are JTR and ZK?" Allison asked.

"Likely Jack the Ripper and the Zodiac Killer from San Francisco," Harding said.

"It's a hoax." Magda had read over his shoulder. "It has to be a hoax."

Ignoring her, Harding saw that two other pages were folded under the letter and he turned to Allison.

"Do you have tweezers, or something?"

Flustered, she seized her bag under the desk, went through her manicure set and thrust small tweezers at him. Using them to grip a corner, Harding carefully moved the one-page letter off the next page.

The second page was neatly divided by two crisp, color photos of the head and shoulders of a naked woman in her twenties. In the first picture she was bound in wide-eyed terror. In the second she was dead.

"Jesus Christ!" Nick Obrisk, one of the bureau's soon-to-retire staff writers, said. "That is un-freaking-believable."

Under that page there was a third page. Taped to it was the California driver's license for Leeza Meadows, aged twenty-one, of Santa Clarita.

"Is this for real, Mark?" Obrisk said.

"I think so. Leeza Meadows was the first of the five victims. Tanner said two items were missing from her bag where she was found. One was her cell phone. Police never made public what the second item was. I think this is it, Leeza's California driver's license."

"Who's Tanner?" Magda asked.

Harding and Obrisk looked at her. She'd just confirmed she didn't read the work of the people she supervised.

"He's the detective leading the DWK task force. He's in my story."

"Of course," she said. "It slipped my mind."

"That's a helluva thing you got there," Obrisk said. "What are you going to do?"

"We need to record this." Harding scanned the bureau. "Where's Jodi-Lee?"

"She's buying a yogurt downstairs. She should be back by now," Allison said. "Mark can we just get this stuff off of my desk?"

"Hang on. Nobody touches anything." Harding spotted Jodi-Lee Ruiz at the door, waved her over and told her what had happened.

"Holy crap." She set down her yogurt and juice and slipped off her camera bag. She pulled out a camera and changed the lens as Harding gave her directions.

"We need photographs of Allison's desk with the pages, showing exactly how the letter was received. Then close-ups of each page so we'll have our own copies, the envelope, the license, everything."

While Jodi-Lee's camera clicked with shot after shot, Harding saw Magda pull out her cell phone.

"I'm calling New York. Mark, I want you to knock out a quick, exclusive item about the killer writing to us," she said. "Can you put it together in an hour?"

"What?" Harding was incredulous at her 180-degree turn on the story. "Hold up, we need to call the task force first."

"Why? Screw them. This is a huge story."

"No, let me talk to Tanner first."

"Burn him. We need this exclusive."

"What? I'm not going to burn him. Are you nuts?"

"I don't understand why you need to go to the cops with this. The killer wrote to us, it's our property."

"We need them to confirm that this is from the killer. We'd look pretty stupid if we got taken in by a hoax."

Magda's face flushed. It was clear to everyone that she lacked the experience to handle breaking news of this magnitude. Struggling to replace embarrassment with authority, she put her phone away and glared at Harding.

"Fine." She glanced at the wall clock before walking away. "I'll give you three hours. Then I want a story."

27

Los Angeles, California

Tanner checked his phone for messages while watching L.A.'s sprawl roll by his window as Zurn exceeded the speed limit on the 10.

Twenty minutes earlier, Tanner had been at his desk reviewing an old file when Mark Harding called his cell phone.

"We just got a letter that you need to see. It's from the Dark Wind Killer."

"The killer wrote to you?"

"He's responding to our story."

"What does it say?" Tanner had opened his notebook and poised his pen.

"He's going to kill again, and he included Leeza Meadows's driver's license and a photo of her bound and alive and a photo of her dead."

Tanner's gut had spasmed.

While he'd told Harding about the cell phone, only the killer would have knowledge about Leeza's driver's license. Investigators had never released that fact.

In the silence that followed, he wedged his phone between his ear and shoulder while he searched the documents on his desk.

"Do you still have the license and photos?"

"Yes, at our bureau. We just got it."

"You're there now?"

"Yes."

"Don't leave. Don't move or touch the material, and don't let anyone who touched any of it leave. We're on our way."

Before they'd left, Tanner had alerted his lieutenant to the break in the case. The lieutenant then advised the captain and a series of actions began. Calls were made to prepare to expedite a warrant in case the news agency refused to volunteer the letter. A request went to the FBI to dispatch its Evidence Response Team to collect and process the material. The FBI's Los Angeles division was about four miles west of the ANPA's bureau. Special Agent Brad Knox led a small team of agents and other specialists. They joined Tanner and Zurn, filling the ANPA's small reception area where Harding met them.

"Okay," Harding told Tanner and Knox, "we kept the letter on Allison's desk, right over here where she was opening the mail."

"We'll need to talk to everyone who's handled it," Knox said.

"Excuse me," Magda interrupted as she emerged from her office. The sight of the investigators, some wearing sidearms and T-shirts saying FBI Evidence Response Team, and carrying equipment cases, made her jittery. "I'm Magdalena Pierce. I'm in charge of this bureau. What're you doing?"

"They need to process the letter," Harding told her after quick introductions and displays of IDs.

"Not without a warrant. That letter is ANPA property," Magda said.

"Ma'am, if I may," Knox said. "You're correct. It is your property and we can get a warrant. But we're hoping you'll volunteer it to us. It would speed up the process for everyone. Otherwise, getting a warrant will just keep us here that much longer."

She hesitated for a moment.

"Let me call our headquarters in New York."

Magda left and Harding caught up with her in her office.

"If we volunteer the letter we can make a case for exclusivity," he said.

"I want to get a story out ASAP."

"So do I, but do you want to be first, or do you want to be right?"

She stared at him and then glanced at the investigators waiting down the hall.

"We already own this story," he said. "We have to play this right."

"Let me call New York."

Harding returned to the group and took Tanner aside. From down the hall they watched Magda through the office glass walls while she spoke to the ANPA's world headquarters.

"You used us with that first story, didn't you?" Harding said to Tanner.

"We gave you an exclusive, Mark."

"You never once believed the killer was dead. You used our story to goad him to reveal himself. You know more about him."

Tanner remained silent. His face betrayed nothing.

"Look, Joe, I'm trying to get you the letter now. Work

with me. How about you give us a copy of the message the killer left you?"

"I can't." He glanced over his shoulder. "See Agent Knox and my partner there, on the phone? They're working on the warrant. We're going to get that letter, Mark."

Magda stepped from her office and waved Knox, Tanner and Harding inside and pressed a button to activate her speakerphone.

"I've got Sebastian Strother, ANPA executive news editor, on speaker with Herschel Abramowitz, ANPA legal. Gentlemen," Magda said. "And joining us in my office, we have Agent Brad Knox of the L.A. FBI and Detective Joe Tanner, L.A. County Sheriff's office, with Mark Harding."

"Thank you," Strother said. "Magdalena's briefed us and we have a few questions. We're aware that with a warrant that is likely forthcoming, you'll obtain the letter, so the ANPA turning it over to you for analysis is a foregone conclusion."

"That's correct," Knox said.

"Have you received any other calls from any other news outlets indicating receipt of communication from the alleged killer, in the wake of our first report on the case?"

Knox and Tanner exchanged glances.

"None," Tanner said.

"All right" Strother said. "You will not need a warrant. The AllNews Press Agency will provide you the letter on the condition we have copies of its contents and with the understanding that the task force will alert us to the surfacing of any other communication from the killer in time for us to produce a story. We'll give you five hours for analysis."

"We'll need forty-eight to confirm its authenticity and process it fully."

Strother muted his line for several seconds.

"We'll agree to those terms provided you maintain cooperation with the ANPA for the duration of the analysis and the duration of the investigation."

"Agreed," Tanner said.

The FBI specialists set to work. Allison Porter was questioned about receipt of the letter. Had she made any new folds or notes on it? Had she marked it? Where did she touch it? Was she the only person in the office to touch it directly? Would she volunteer a set of elimination fingerprints?

The investigators also questioned the people who managed the building about mail delivery and who would have handled the letter. They alerted the U.S. Postal Inspection Service. The FBI people photographed and provided copies of the letter to Tanner and the ANPA as promised. Finally, they collected the original envelope and its contents in protective cellophane bags so they could be taken to the lab for further analysis.

It took a few hours.

"We'll be in touch," Tanner told Harding before leaving.

In the car, on their return trip to their homicide bureau in Commerce, Tanner studied his color copies of the letter. The quality was so good they looked original.

"What do you think, Joe?" Zurn asked him. "Is it our guy?"

"I don't know for sure."

"If it is, it's going to scare a lot of people."

"If it is, this could be our only shot at him."

28

San Marino, California

The piercing whine of the high-speed table saw filled Robert Bowen's garage as he carefully moved a sheet of three-quarter-inch plywood along the pencil line.

Another perfect piece.

Bowen enjoyed the smell of fresh-cut lumber as he brushed away sawdust. He was pleased his work was proceeding well. Since returning home a few days ago from the cabin, then a trip flying executives to Dallas, Denver and Phoenix, he had a number of tasks to take care of, in addition to the several chores he'd promised to do for Claire.

Maybe when he completed them it would change her frame of mind. She'd become a bit cooler toward him over the past few weeks, a little standoffish. At times it was if she were looking at him differently while trying to mask it. Maybe her moodiness was a side effect of her new treatment? Whatever it was, he was too busy to give it much thought.

He set the new piece aside and prepared to cut another. When that was done, he measured and cut two more pieces, this time using the pine. He positioned them all with others on his worktable, reached for his power drill and fastened the sections in place with screws.

Soon the wooden sections evolved into a sturdy oblong box with latticework between the ribbing. He stretched his measuring tape to check its dimensions: two feet wide, six feet long and two feet deep.

It would do nicely.

The rattle of aluminum at the approach to the open door of his garage distracted him from his work.

"Gosh, Bob, what're you building there, a coffin?"

Gabe Taylor, the Bowens' neighbor, had Bowen's metal extension ladder on his shoulder. Taylor was a retired lawyer. He and his wife, Margie, sang in their church choir.

"I saw your gate open and garage door up and thought, Bob's home," Taylor grunted as he and Bowen successfully replaced the ladder on the wall hooks. "Thanks again for rushing over with your ladder to help me last week with that window problem. Good neighbors are such a blessing. Margie's making you one of her blue-ribbon apple pies."

"She doesn't have to go to all that trouble, Gabe."

"She's happy to do it."

The older, heavier man padded his brow with the back of his arm and exhaled as he looked over the box.

"She enjoys it, and now that you're our famous local hero, it gives her bragging rights with the alto section. So, what's this you're making?"

"It's a planter box. I've been catching up on a few chores for Claire. She wanted two for the patio."

"I see. It looks like a fine job. I won't keep you from your important work. Thanks again." Gabe extended his hand and shook Bowen's. As he left he said, "Margie will be by later with the pie."

"Tell her thanks, Gabe."

Bowen got himself a glass of cold lemonade from the kitchen before he resumed measuring and cutting, which took him into the late afternoon. He was still working when Claire's Toyota rolled into the driveway.

He was putting the finishing touches on the second planter box when she kissed his cheek. She looked good in her cream suit, he thought.

"I see you finally got around to my planter boxes," she observed, running her hand over the sanded parts of the fragrant wood.

"Just have to stain them. I'm thinking of making a few extras."

"I'm impressed. I can't wait to load them up with flowers."

"How did your day go?" he asked.

"Fine. Very busy."

The cordless house phone started ringing. It was on the bench next to Claire and she answered. Bowen only heard her side of the short conversation.

"Hello?… Yes… Yes, it is… Well, of course, Mr. Montero, I remember you from the hospital. Yes… My goodness, how thoughtful." Claire threw a glance to him. "Thursday? At seven-thirty? I'll check with Robert… Really? How wonderful. Yes, I'll check with him and we'll get back to you.… Yes, yes, thanks again."

Claire hung up.

"That was Ruben Montero, the husband of the woman and baby from the car."

"So I gathered."

"His community association is having its annual banquet Thursday. They want us to come."

"Why?"

"When the crash happened, Ruben's wife, Maria, had been doing work for the association."

"I recall something about that."

"Well, the association board voted unanimously to make you the guest of honor and give you an award for your bravery."

He gave a little half smile. "I don't know, Claire."

"Don't be modest, Robert. Besides, Ruben sounds like a nice man and he said it would mean a lot to him, his family and friends. It'll be easy. We go to the dinner, you stand up and say thanks and everyone's happy."

He didn't respond. He was clearly thinking it over.

"What harm could it do, Robert? All part of being a local hero."

"All right. If you want to, sure."

Claire nodded, then shifted the subject.

"I've got a lot of work backed up that I want to get at after dinner. I'm going to take a shower," she said. "What do you say about ordering a pizza tonight?"

"Sure."

She went into the house, leaving him in the garage thinking, *there it is again—that ever-so-subtle coolness.*

He didn't have time to dwell on that.

He glanced under his work table. Hidden behind the small piles of scrap wood, concealed under the tarp, was a third oblong box.

This one had a sealable lid at the halfway point, creating a false bottom.

Whatever he was going to put under that lid would never escape.

29

San Marino, California

Claire stood in her bathrobe and stared into the mirror for nearly two minutes after her shower, brushing her hair while fighting tears.

She and Robert had made love last night but it was passionless and clinical, bordering on awful.

Something's wrong between us. Robert's changed. Something's different. Or is it me? Maybe I'm reacting to the new injections?

I have to stop this. It's nuts.

Look at the positives, she told herself while dressing. *I love Robert and I know he loves me. We're closer than ever to starting a family. Maybe I'm pregnant now. Why am I so uneasy about Robert?*

What has he done? Seriously, what has he done?

I have no proof he's done anything wrong. So I overheard a bit of a phone conversation out of context, found an old photo, so what? Maybe I misread his post-traumatic stress as something else? My qualms about him having feelings for his ex-wife are based on nothing concrete. I should push them aside.

The doorbell rang. Claire heard Robert pay the pizza

delivery kid. She savored the aroma as she went to the kitchen.

They passed the time eating and making small talk about her garden plans, while avoiding prickly subjects like the nursery or selling the cabin. They both had things to do that evening. Claire needed to review files. Robert had to go to the Van Nuys airport for a pilots' meeting about a new plane the company was acquiring.

"I might be out quite late," he said as they cleared the table.

Afterward, when Claire heard the side door open and close, Robert's departure left her with a pang of regret. He was a good-hearted man, who would risk his life for strangers. He'd always been kind and protective. Rather than analyzing him, Claire needed to focus on her patients.

After tidying up in the kitchen, she went to work in her home office, reviewing and updating her patient notes. All of her patients had worrisome cases, but the patient Claire felt the most concern for was Amber.

It had been about two weeks since Amber's estranged husband, Eric, had assaulted her and threatened Claire in the office parking lot. Amber had since resumed living alone in the house in Alhambra. But Claire was still wary of Eric, having experienced his wrath firsthand that day. As Claire reread Amber's file, she slid her small silver cross back and forth on her necklace chain.

Claire did not like the fact that after the attack Eric had violated the court's no-contact order by writing to Amber and pleading for reconciliation; something Amber had considered, despite Claire's advice to the contrary. Claire was concerned. Eric was a dangerous, manipulative man and Amber seemed to be weakening. Claire consulted the calendar. Amber's next session was coming up soon. Good, Claire thought, there were a number of areas they needed to address.

Claire's cell phone rang. The caller's number was blocked.

"Hey, Claire."

She'd recognized Julie's voice.

"Hey, there."

"Sorry, it's been ages," Julie said. "We've been swamped. So how are you?"

"Oh, you know, the same old—except I've just started the treatment."

"I see."

The silence that passed underscored where they'd left matters—with the understanding that Claire was going to wait on her treatment until Julie had taken care of Claire's request she check out Robert's phone history.

"I couldn't put it off," Claire said. "It's timed to my cycle and my doctor would've had questions, then there's the cost."

"It's okay, I know," Julie said. "Congratulations. My fingers are crossed for you. I called to let you know that I did not forget my assignment. I looked into the phone numbers like you asked."

"And?"

"I didn't find anything out of the ordinary. All pretty innocuous stuff, nothing tied to Cynthia that I could see."

A tiny wave of relief rippled through Claire.

"I guess this confirms that I was being silly."

"I did discover something."

"What do you mean?"

"In trying to find Cynthia's surname, I had a search done of California's divorce records. Nothing surfaced for her, nothing at all. In fact, there's no record of Robert Bowen's divorce in the State."

"Oh, well, that's not surprising. I think he was married in Montana, or someplace like that. Before we met he'd lived in a lot of different places."

"Yeah, I remembered you telling me. So, seeing this as a challenge I had a search done nationwide of all court records, thinking surely we'd find Robert and Cynthia's papers."

"And?"

"Nothing. It's quite the mystery, very odd. I was thinking that if you might be able to somehow get a bit more info, like where they were living at the time of the divorce, or where they were married then I could..."

Claire went deaf to what Julie was saying. She felt the earth shift under her, resurrecting her doubts. *How could this be? How could I be married to him and not know something so basic?*

"Claire? Did you hear me?"

"Sorry."

"You and Robert were married in Mexico, so you both had to supply divorce decrees, remember?"

"Yes."

"I'll work with our contacts in Mexico and see if I can get information on Cynthia from the documentation Robert would've provided the Mexican authorities, okay?"

Silence passed.

"Hello? Claire?"

"Yes, sorry."

"So, do you want me to keep looking into this?"

Claire's mouth had gone dry and she licked her lips and swallowed.

"Yes."

30

San Marino, California

Arriving at work the next morning, Claire saw two San Marino police cars in her parking lot.

Their revolving emergency lights were splashing red and blue throughout the neighborhood. Claire spotted a third police vehicle in the lot, an SUV with a caged rear interior. A ribbon of yellow tape stretched around the building. Uniformed officers were talking on the front sidewalk with staff from the offices of the dermatologist, optometrist and dentist that were also in her building.

Claire parked, grabbed her bags and got out.

Alice, her assistant, materialized and went to her at the same time as barking echoed from the rear of the building. An officer in tactical clothing hurried behind the taut clinking leash of a dog with its snout to the ground, tracking a scent leading away from the building and deep into the neighborhood.

Alice's face was creased with worry. "Someone broke into the office last night!"

"Oh, no!"

"I got here first thing this morning and saw broken glass on the floor at the back. The door frame was all splintered. They went through all the offices, trying to pry open filing cabinets and going through desks."

Police radio transmissions crackled. The women turned and Claire recognized Deena Freeman, one of the officers who'd responded when Amber's husband assaulted her in the parking lot.

Freeman said, "Ten-four," into her shoulder microphone, then walked over to Claire, while paging through her notebook.

"Officer Freeman, what more can you tell us?" Claire asked.

"It looks like they were going after Dr. Ramsallie's office."

"A dentist's office?"

"They went through every office, but it appears they were looking for cash, drugs and maybe gold used in fillings."

Dr. Ramsallie approached them, patting his tanned brow and thick moustache with a handkerchief.

"Please put in your report that for insurance purposes, we have very little gold on-site, just a few pebble-sized pieces for a few crowns, worth only a few hundred dollars. We order gold when we need it."

"Yes, sir," Freeman said. "We've noted that information."

"I took a closer look from the window. I think a few canisters of nitrous oxide are missing, but I need to go inside to inspect my supplies."

"Yes, sir, we have that. Please don't lift the tape and walk through the scene again. I ask you to bear with us. Our forensic people are on the way. Until they're done processing, we can't allow anyone inside."

"You must arrest these criminals. They must be punished."

"Yes, sir, we're working on it." As Freeman waited patiently, Dr. Ramsallie left her alone to continue her business with Claire.

"How long before we can go inside?" Claire asked. "I was expecting to see patients this morning. We'll have to scramble to reschedule."

"I know. Our crime scene people should be here at any moment. They've indicated that they'll have things wrapped up later today."

"Can't you let us in to get our hard-copy files so we can start calling patients, to tell them what happened?" Claire asked. "Some may be on their way. I need to reach them. Given our recent history in this parking lot, this situation makes me a little anxious."

"I know and I assure you that we're not discounting the complaint history of this address."

"So what are you doing about Amber?"

Freeman nodded. "I've requested Alhambra P.D. to check on Amber's welfare and alert her as a precaution."

"You're aware her estranged husband works at installing security systems?"

"We've requested Sacramento P.D. confirm Eric Larch's whereabouts for the last forty-eight hours. We want to ensure he's complied with his bail conditions and the terms of the restraining order. This is all being done as a priority this morning."

Claire found some comfort in the actions Freeman had taken.

"We're working on all aspects of the crime committed here," Freeman said. "Unfortunately, we can't let anyone inside right now, but you must have your files backed up?"

"Yes, we have to follow professional standards and procedures for securing our files. They're password protected and encrypted. We have an off-site hard drive and I have my USB with me. It also holds my files, but I'll call my husband to bring my laptop here ASAP. We don't live far. We'll work from that."

"Okay good, thc dctcctivcs will want to talk to you once we get a little more information from the scene."

Robert arrived with Claire's computer moments after the crime scene technicians had suited up, entered the office and started processing it. One of them worked outside photographing the building and neighborhood.

Robert watched with interest. From the distance he strained to see them working through the windows. "Do they have any suspects?"

"I don't know," Claire said. "They're thinking they were trying to get the gold from the dentist's office."

Robert never took his eyes off the investigators.

"I'd read about that trend, thieves stealing gold from dentists." He turned to Claire. "Are you okay? Is there anything else I can do? I was on my way to get some stain for your planter boxes, but I can stay here with you."

For a moment she'd forgotten her feelings of uncertainty about him. The crisis underscored that she could count on him when she needed him. "No, thank you. I'll call you later. I expect it'll be a long day. Thanks for rushing over with my computer."

Claire kissed his chcek.

After Robert left, Claire and Alice searched the files on Claire's laptop, then used Claire's cell phone to call

all of her patients to alert them to the burglary. They'd managed to reschedule morning sessions. To accommodate patients, Claire offered to provide evening appointments later in the week, as well.

For the next few hours the crime scene experts checked the alarm system and took photographs among their other work. The lead was Detective Cobb, who'd joined the San Marino P.D. after putting in twenty-five years with the LAPD. Cobb and his partner interviewed the tenants one by one. When he got to Claire, she summarized her concerns for him.

"Okay, they're done processing things," Cobb said afterward. "I'm taking you inside first to walk you through your office. Be sure to follow my steps."

The desks, walls, cabinets and keyboards were smeared with fingerprint powder—white chalky stuff on dark surfaces and black graphite dust on light surfaces.

"Whoever came in wore gloves," Cobb said. "They also smashed the security cameras. They were experienced. Let's see if they got into your files."

The cabinets, although damaged, seemed to have held. They were reinforced steel. But when Claire tried to log in to her computer, it took several attempts and several passwords, an indication that previous attempts had been made by the thieves.

"What do you think?" Claire asked Cobb.

"I think it's possible a former partner would benefit, say for custody or a divorce settlement, from gaining access to a confidential file."

"Is that what you think happened? I thought they were after Ramsallie's gold and laughing gas."

"You've recently had an enraged ex show up here."

Claire recalled Eric glaring at her from the back of the police car after the attack.

"Now we have a burglary," Cobb continued. "It could've been staged to disguise other intentions."

Claire stared at Cobb.

"It's just one theory," he said, shrugging. "But at this point, we can't rule anything out."

31

Commerce, California

Leeza Meadows had high cheekbones and eyes that sparkled with hope.

She was just twenty-one.

Tanner stared at the photocopy of her driver's license that he'd paper clipped inside the cover of his file folder for the task force meeting. Leeza was the youngest of the five victims. A few years out of high school, she was working at the Misty Nights Bar & Grill to put herself through college. Her eyes blazed with life, he thought, flipping through the other pictures in his file.

Terror consumed her in one of the photos that had been sent to the AllNews Press Agency. Again Tanner's gut tightened at the indignity. It had been nearly two days since Mark Harding had alerted them to the letter. In that time the task force had held several case status meetings.

It was now 9:00 p.m.

The ANPA had been calling Tanner every thirty minutes, demanding confirmation so they could run their story. Tanner was leading the group's last meeting before the task force would respond, aware that they'd already missed the agreed upon deadline with the news-wire service.

More than two dozen investigators from a spectrum of law enforcement agencies had taken seats around the table in a meeting room at the L.A. County Sheriff's Department.

"Let's get to this," Tanner said. "We've concluded that the letter and contents originated from the person responsible for Leeza Meadows's homicide and the four others."

"Hang on." Art Lang, a detective with the LAPD, was drawing circles on his case status sheet. "Are we ruling out the possibility that someone originally happened on the Meadows's scene, collected the items and sent the letter in response to the article as a hoax?"

Tanner acknowledged the theory.

"Our analysis shows that the photographs are authentic," Tanner said. "And they were taken before and after her death. Only the killer could've taken those images and only the killer would know about, and possess, her missing driver's license. Only the killer could've used her pinky print in the message the Cold Case Unit discovered in Temple City."

Lang let a moment pass before nodding, and Tanner continued.

"Unfortunately," Tanner said, "the material sent to the ANPA has yielded no suspect DNA or latent prints. Nothing so far. Our guy was careful."

Tanner turned to FBI Special Agent Brad Knox, who said that preliminary lab results showed the envelope was sealed with moisture activation of the manufacturer's adhesive. Examination was still in progress to determine the type of camera used to take the photographs of Leeza Meadows. The writing instrument used for the letter and envelope was a standard felt-tip medium-point marker. The paper was standard, white, twenty-pound recycled. We're still working on it."

Knox said the Behavioral Analysis Unit had found that the syntax of the block-lettered message was indicative of someone of above-average intelligence who craved attention and was likely in a highly regarded position of control.

"This is someone who enjoys being looked up to. This guy needs to have his ego fed," Knox said. "Can we get more time before the news agency prints its story?"

"The letter is their property," Tanner said. "If we take much longer, they'll do a story without us confirming it's from the killer. They'll say it's from someone claiming to be the killer and that we're investigating. We'd lose our chance for some control of the fallout of the story."

"Why did we go to the press with this?" Lang asked.

"When the evidence first surfaced we talked to retired detectives who'd handled the original five cases and we consulted with the FBI profilers. It was suggested we use an anniversary to draw the killer out, if he was still alive. We went to the wire service so we could reach across the country."

"It worked," Lang said. "We're going to panic Southern California. Every whack-job will be confessing to us. We'll have to set up for tips. This could get as huge as Son of Sam, the Zodiac Killer and the D.C. Sniper. It's going to draw intense scrutiny. We're going to be in the national spotlight once this breaks."

"Can we get them to hold back running the letter's entire contents?" Knox asked.

"Working on it," Tanner said, going around the table

for last questions. None came. "All right, then we're as ready as we're going to be."

Less than half an hour after the meeting ended, Tanner arrived home to a dark, empty house. Sam was spending another night with his sister. Kim had been great. When she realized that his long hours would lengthen further, she'd offered to take Sam for a few sleepovers. Sam loved going there, so it worked out fine, gave him time to concentrate on the case.

In the dim light of his kitchen he texted Mark Harding.

I'm ready to talk in the a.m. — my office.

Harding responded instantly.

9?

9 is good.

Tanner went to the fridge, took out a box with a few pieces of leftover pepperoni pizza. He ate a slice with a glass of water. When he finished, he was still too wired to sleep.

He grabbed his car keys and drove through the night, one thought hammering in his head.

This case is solvable. The asshole contacted us. It's our shot to grab him.

It wasn't long before Tanner found himself at the edge of Santa Clarita. A lot can happen in ten years, he thought, taking in the new subdivision that had risen in the vicinity of the first homicide.

But, like a hallowed patch of earth, the exact spot

where the killer had left Leeza Meadows's body, had not been touched. It was deep in a hilly sector that remained undeveloped.

Tanner parked.

Scanning the ground with his flashlight, he walked along a path that twisted into the wooded section where ten years earlier Leonard Nallis, the birdwatcher, had found her.

"At first I thought it was a mannequin, or some kind of sick joke," Nallis told Tanner, who was a deputy then working out of the Santa Clarita station.

Now Tanner thought it was strange how his life had gone full circle. He remembered being a young deputy, staring at Leeza's remains.

At that moment he'd yearned to be the lead investigator on that case. Now here he was. It was all on his shoulders. He'd gotten exactly what he wanted, but at what cost?

Tanner turned on his phone. The darkness glowed with the tiny light of his wife's video.

"I almost think I can beat this, I— If I don't beat this, just hug Sam today for me, okay."

Tanner swallowed hard.

He prayed to Becky's ghost to help him stop the Dark Wind Killer.

"Help me find him, Becky, before he does it again."

32

Alhambra, California

A few hours earlier and some forty miles south of where Detective Joe Tanner kept vigil at the first crime scene, Amber Pratt was in her kitchen slicing cucumbers for a salad.

She was preparing her dinner, having returned home from a full day at the Huntington Library. Taking in the strong, cool smell of the cucumber, it felt good to get back into her routine. These recent days had been among the hardest she'd ever faced, underscored by the nights she'd been forced to spend in a shelter because of Eric.

Why did he have to make everything so hard?

And if she wasn't already dealing with enough, Alice from Claire's office called her at the library that morning to tell her about the break-in.

Take it easy, Amber told herself. *The police don't think it has anything to do with Eric trying to find me. He's moved to Sacramento. Police think the burglars were going after the gold in the dentist's office, but said they would drop by later as a precaution. All routine, at least that's what Alice said. I just hope she's right.*

Amber touched the back of her knife hand to the tear

rolling down her cheek, but kept her composure. She had to get on with her life, that's all there was to it.

The doorbell rang.

She went to the front. Glimpsing the black-and-white Alhambra police car in the street, she opened her door to two uniformed police officers.

"Afternoon—" the older cop with silver hair glanced at his notebook "—Amber Pratt?"

"Yes."

"I'm Officer Ian Tate. This is my partner, Les Campbell. Our visit pertains to a standing protection order and recent charges against your estranged husband, Eric Larch, that took place at—" he flipped through the pages "—at the Simpkins professional building at Garfield Avenue and Huntington Drive in San Marino."

"Yes."

"There was a burglary at that location in San Marino. Because of the recent history of violence at that address with Eric Larch, of which you were the victim, San Marino P.D. requested we check on your welfare and the security of your residence. May we come in and take a look around?"

"Yes, thanks."

Their utility belts gave soft leathery squeaks, and Amber picked up the pleasant scent of cologne as she showed them into the house. Their muted police radios echoed as they tested the alarm system before going from room to room checking windows and doors.

Their presence made her feel safe. She offered them coffee or soda, but they declined. They had other calls waiting. While Tate, the older officer, went outside to check the property and exterior of the house, Campbell double-checked the security system contacts in the pantry, utility room and finally the kitchen, where Amber was flipping through a magazine for a recipe.

"This is a nice house, and you live alone here?" he said.

"I'm house-sitting for friends of friends. They've been so nice, helping me. It's been a tough time with the divorce, as I'm sure you know. I mean, it's why you're here."

He nodded sympathetically. Despite his nice smile, the young cop seemed shy, excusing himself as he walked around the kitchen island to check the windows.

"What about you?" Amber asked. "Do you live alone?"

"Yes, ma'am, all by my lonesome, unlike my partner. He and his wife have four daughters and a lot of worry."

"And you? Have you found the right girl, or guy, yet?" She'd attempted a little flirty joke. He looked at her before she realized her mistake. "I'm so sorry, that was rude."

"It's okay."

"I'm sort of on my own at work, I don't talk to many people. I'm so embarrassed, forgive me for prying."

"You're forgiven." He chuckled. "And no, I haven't found the right girl."

They both glanced up at the sound of a loud radio dispatch as Tate reentered the house from the back door, locking it behind him before coming to the kitchen.

"All right, ma'am, we're done here," Tate said. "Your residence is secure and we've received word from Sacramento P.D. that earlier this morning they confirmed Eric Larch was in Sacramento at work."

"That's reassuring. Thank you for coming."

Amber escorted them to the front door where both

gave her business cards. After dinner, she started cleaning up.

In a small, uncertain corner of her heart, part of her still considered going back to Eric. She unfolded his letter to her and reviewed his tiny, neat handwriting—the *I'm sorry*'s, his *shame,* his *remorse,* his effort to get counseling, his begging her to recall the tender times, their dreams, and his asking her to come back to him so they could start a new life together.

Think this through, she told herself.

She let the letter drop to the desktop and cupped her hands to her face.

When I think of why I married him, I'm so tempted to go back. We had beautiful dreams of our life together. Part of me still loves him and always will love him.

But Claire's right.

I have to remember why I left. I see that evil look on his face each time he hurts me. I saw it when he attacked me in the lot. Then he went after Claire. He'll never break out of his cycle.

Protection orders, attacks in public and police checks—it was no way to live. Was this a foundation for her future? The man she'd loved was gone and she had to move on.

She checked the time.

It was late. She had to be up early for work. She drew a hot bath to ease her tension and help her sleep and as she soaked in the tub, she seized on a warm, fleeting thought of Officer Campbell.

The spark of attraction was surprising.

Amber climbed out of the tub, drained it, toweled off and brushed her teeth. As she blow-dried her hair she smiled at the fact that she, Amber Pratt, had flirted.

Maybe I am coming out of my shell. Gaining some self-confidence? Maybe there's hope for me yet.

In her bedroom, Amber pulled on her nightshirt and started running a comb through her hair when she froze.

A soft *thud-thump* somewhere in the house.

What the heck is that? She went room to room, throwing on every light, checking every window, every door, every closet. Nothing was out of place, yet her instincts told her something was not right.

Unease pinged in her stomach. What if Eric did break into Claire's office and got this address? Remember what Officer Tate said. Sacramento police confirmed that Eric was in Sacramento at work.

But that was early this morning, which left him time to fly, even drive, to L.A.

This was just stupid. Amber couldn't stand it. She grabbed her cell phone and called Sharon. After three rings, the line was answered.

"Hello?" Sharon's husband answered.

"Kyle, it's Amber, could I speak to Sharon."

"Amber— Geez, yeah, hang on." It sounded as if he had a hand over the mouthpiece, but a muffled "It's Amber—how should I know what she—" leaked out before Sharon got on the line.

"Amber, honey, it's Sharon. What's going on?"

"I need you to help me."

"Of course, what do you need?"

"Is Eric in Sacramento right now?"

"What? Yes, he's working with Pete on some new places in Citrus Heights, I think. Kyle, Eric's working in Citrus? Yes, Citrus Heights. Why?"

"Is he still in Sacramento tonight?"

"Why? What's going on?"

"You know what's going on. You know everything that's going on in everybody's life."

There was a long pause.

"I thought you were on my side, Sharon."

"Amber, he really thought the letter would work to bring you back. I'm in the middle. I pray for both of you."

"Where is he right now?"

"I don't know exactly, but we heard that there was some sort of burglary in L.A. and the Sacramento police paid him a visit on the job site this morning, which really ticked him off."

"So where is he now?"

"I don't know. I guess he was so pissed that he told Pete that he wanted to take a long drive to take care of something."

Amber's hand flew to her mouth and her eyes went around the house.

"I'm calling the police."

"Wait!" Sharon's hand covered the phone, then she came back on. "Kyle said he stayed on the job and Pete and Marty took him to a bar after work to cool him off."

"Call Pete now. Get him on the phone. I need to know Eric's in Sacramento, or I'm calling the police. I know Kyle has Pete's cell number."

"All right, stay on the line I'll get Kyle to call them now. Then we'll put the phones on Speaker and turn them up."

After a few harried moments Amber heard Eric's brother, Pete, always the calm, smart, mature one of the two.

"Pete, it's Amber. Are you with Eric?"

"Yes, we're watching the game at the Nugget, he's right beside me."

"Put him on."

"Amber?" Eric said. "What is it? Sharon said you got my letter."

Satisfied she'd heard Eric, she said, "Everything's fine. Give the phone back to Pete."

"What? What about my letter, did you think—"

"Eric, put Pete back on, please."

"What is this? Why are you being such a—" Eric stopped himself.

"Such a what, Eric? What were you going to call me?"

A tense moment passed.

"Here's Pete," he said. "I don't know what she wants," Eric told his brother before Pete came back on. "What's going on, Amber?"

"Pete, I want you to pass your phone to the first female server you see. Just for one second."

"What?"

"Please."

"Are you okay?"

"Just do it, please."

More muffled sounds.

"Hi," a young cheery voice greeted, "this is Dixie."

"Dixie, what city are you in?"

"What? Is this some kind of contest? Are there cameras?"

"Please just answer."

"Sacramento."

"Thanks, you can give the phone back."

"Amber?" Pete came back on.

"Thank you, Pete, goodbye."

Sharon was on the line again.

"Amber, this is really unfair for you to put the Sacramento police onto Eric when he's trying to straighten his life out. He had nothing to do—"

"Thank you, Sharon, goodbye."

Amber hung up, trembling from the anger and fear pumping through her body. She sighed and put her head in her hands until it subsided.

I must be losing my mind.

Taking long, deep calming breaths she walked through the house again, checking doors, windows, closets, shutting off lights, trying to relax. She went to the kitchen and made cocoa. As she waited for the milk to warm she pondered Officer Campbell's card and smiled.

Everything's okay, I'm just on edge, she thought, heading to bed where she read the opening of *Madame Bovary* before her stress yielded to exhaustion and she gently drifted off.

Amber fell into a deep sleep that swirled with dreams of a pretty little home overlooking the ocean where her children played under a brilliant sun in the yard. She was smiling, calling them, lowering herself so they could run into her open arms, but they stopped short and looked up at something behind Amber.

A large shadow fell over them.

Amber's eyes flicked open. The sun gave way to darkness and the naked man standing beside her bed, staring down at her, his face a white, hideous mask of malevolence.

Amber's scream was silenced when he crushed a wide strip of duct tape over her mouth. A sudden blow to her head rattled her teeth in a pyrotechnic explosion of stars before everything went black.

33

Commerce, California

The forty-eight hours the AllNews Press Agency had given to the task force to examine the letter was up.

Mark Harding's phone had been vibrating all morning.

First Magda wanted an update, and then Sebastian Strother phoned Harding, demanding he deliver a story without police confirmation.

"We no longer need them. We've honored the agreement. They didn't. I don't trust them. They could be arranging a news conference," Strother said from headquarters in New York. "Our story will say that someone *claiming* to be the killer has written to us and the task force is analyzing materials the writer included."

"No, wait, we should give them a little more time," Harding responded. "I should have it all taken care of soon."

"Forty-five more minutes," Strother said.

The ANPA was losing patience and fearful of losing its exclusive, but Harding kept pleading for more time because confirmation that the real killer had surfaced and written to the ANPA would give them a world exclusive.

After forty-five minutes passed, Harding called again.

"A few more things to check. Sorry, I have to push back meeting you until ten-thirty," Tanner had told him on the phone.

It was now 10:37 a.m. and Harding was waiting alone in an empty meeting room at the Homicide bureau of the L.A. County Sheriff's Department. His stomach had tightened. If the letter, license, photos and the whole thing were not a hoax, then he'd have a story that could be counted with those of Jack the Ripper, Son of Sam, BTK and the Zodiac, infamous killers who'd written to the press to confess their crimes while committing them.

His phone vibrated with a text from Magda.

"Strother wants me to assign another reporter to write the story."

"Tell him I'm talking with the lead investigator now," Harding responded as Tanner entered the room with a file folder.

Casting a glum eye to Harding, Tanner sat as though a weight had forced him into the chair. There were no apologies and no exchange of niceties as the weary detective opened his folder. Tanner's body language and the room's funereal air screamed confirmation to Harding.

"It's him," Tanner started. "We've confirmed that the person responsible for the murders of the five women is the same person who wrote the letter you received."

"Have you told any other news outlets?"

"No."

"Are you planning on holding a news conference or issuing a news release?"

"No, not until after you run your story. We'll keep our end of the agreement."

"All right, I need to get a few comments from you before we put out a story."

"Hang on. I need something from you before you run with anything."

"We've already done everything you've asked. The letter and pictures are ours. We're going with a story as soon as possible."

"You have copies," Tanner said. "The driver's license belongs to Leeza's family and—" Tanner tapped the file "—we'll get court orders to keep the material as evidence. But that's not what I need to talk to you about."

"Can't this wait?" Harding stared at his vibrating phone. He had another message from Strother. "I'm facing a deadline."

"Look, Mark, I know I can't control what you write, but a little cooperation would go a long way to help us both."

"What're you talking about?"

"Would you publish the task force toll-free tip line we've set up?"

"I'll suggest it. Is that all?"

"No. I'm also asking you not to publish photos of the letter, or the full contents because we'll get cranks copying his style. We'll get flooded with false leads, false confessions and nut job copycats that will drain our resources, divert us from pursuing valid leads."

Tanner slid a page to Harding.

"Here's a version showing which areas of the letter we think you could quote from."

Harding studied the censored version. "No guarantees."

"It's our request, but ultimately it's your call."

"I'll see what I can do."

"I'm also asking you not to publish the crime scene photos for the same reason, but also out of consideration for the families of the victims."

"We'll likely crop them to remove the graphic elements."

"And finally, like last time, we've alerted the families of the victims that a story may be coming. They're expecting to hear from you," Tanner said.

"Good, is there anything else, because I have a request?"

"Go ahead."

"I want complete access to you and the task force from here on in."

"We'll continue to make ourselves available, conditional on work demands."

Harding then interviewed Tanner for the story, taking down his comments before concluding.

"Okay, we're good," Harding said. "I really have to go."

"Give me a heads-up when the story goes live."

Hurrying out of the office to his car, Harding called Magda from the parking lot.

"We have on-the-record confirmation that it's the real killer," Harding said. "Let Strother know that I'll deliver a story within an hour."

"Is the task force planning a news conference?"

"Not until after our story runs. People will be reacting to it."

"Good, I'll let Sebastian know. New York will send out an advisory on a world exclusive to all subscribers."

Harding drove farther along Rickenbacker Road to

the edge of a large warehouse and a small treed area with picnic tables that he'd spotted earlier. He parked near one, seized his laptop. Using one of the tables as a desk, he fired up his computer, went to the story he'd already started drafting, flipped through his notes and began plugging in Tanner's quotes.

Then he called Louis Meadows, Leeza's father.

As the line rang, it pulled Harding back to when he and Jodi-Lee Ruiz visited his Santa Clarita home. Images of them in her bedroom, of Louis flipping through the family album to photos of Leeza, streaked across his mind. Images of Louis caressing the music box on Leeza's dresser—*the last thing she touched*—tore at Harding.

"Hello?"

"Mr. Meadows?"

"Yes."

"Mark Harding, AllNews Press Agency."

"Yes."

"I apologize in advance, sir, for this very rude intrusion because I'm facing a deadline, but my call concerns an update on the investigation."

Harding paused for Meadows to absorb what was coming.

"Tanner told me you might be calling. I'm guessing that this is about the letter you got, from the killer?"

"Yes."

Harding elaborated on the nature of the story, then asked Meadows to comment. Meadows thought for a moment before speaking.

"I understand he sent you gruesome pictures."

"That's true."

"I hope you'll continue to treat my daughter's memory with dignity."

"We will, sir."

The older man cleared his throat.

"I'm encouraged by the latest break in the case. I pray that it leads to justice."

That was it. No elaboration.

Surprised by the abruptness, Harding thanked him, ended the call and inserted the quotes. He gave his story a quick proofread, then filed it to the ANPA, well within the time that he'd promised.

When he was done, he sat at the table, rereading it. Then he read through the first story he'd written on the case, comparing it with how subdued Meadows's reaction was just now.

In the earlier story Meadows had said, "I just hope your story helps find the animal who killed my daughter and the other women… I hope to hell I stay on this earth long enough to see the son of a bitch go into the ground."

Where was his outrage this time?

As Harding thought about it, realization slowly dawned on him.

Of course, Tanner had likely coached Meadows, warning him who he'd really be talking to when Harding called: the most important reader of all.

The killer.

34

San Marino, California

Ninety-minutes after his meeting with Tanner had ended Mark Harding broke the story for the AllNews Press Agency when it posted a condensed version on its website under the double-decker headline:

> Killer Linked to 5 Murdered Women Surfaces
> Vows More Deaths in Letter to Reporter—
> L.A. Police Confirm

Harding's story went up at 3:50 p.m. Eastern standard time. Links were tweeted and blogged. Network news outlets included the ANPA's exclusivc in their evening news broadcasts. Other news organizations ran the full story on their sites. Most newspapers, especially those in Southern California, cleared space for print editions.

The next morning, the *Pasadena Star-News* ran Harding's feature. The *Star-News* was a large daily that also covered South Pasadena, Monrovia, Arcadia, Alhambra and San Marino, where Robert Bowen got his copy from his doorstep.

When he saw the headline he froze.

Standing on his front landing, in sweatpants and a T-shirt, reading Harding's report in the morning sun, Bowen looked like any other neighbor in any other town catching up on the news.

He devoured the front page in seconds, then followed the story to an inside page. Again, as with Mark Harding's first article about the killings, there was a map and headshots of each of the women. Staring at their faces, memories swirled and Bowen relished a few intense moments. Then he went inside, excitement prickling his skin as he made coffee, sat at the kitchen table and read the story again, delighted by the passages that quoted the letter.

> "I am reaching out from the darkness to warn the world that I have kept my word…I am back…I will soon unleash fear unlike anything the world has ever known…I decide who lives and who dies…"

He went to his office, turned on his computer, got online and searched for the story. News sites everywhere ran the same story. All of them quoted his letter. He went back to the kitchen and made breakfast—scrambled eggs and hash browns. As he ate, he reread the story, dimly conscious of his surroundings, basking in what he'd achieved.

People around the world now knew and feared the Dark Wind Killer.

I've been exalted. I'm in control and I will claim my place in history, alongside Jack the Ripper and the Zodiac. They never caught them and they'll never catch me. You can't stop the wind. I'm on the path to glory.

As Bowen ate, he remembered the sweetest moments

of each mission, savoring how Esther had pleaded, actually prayed, *"Hail Mary full of grace..."* How Monique had begged, *"Please, don't let me die, oh, please!"* to the point that she was incoherent in the final moments. And Leeza's soft cries had been operatic as if arising from a requiem. Each one of the five was a piece of craftsmanship, inspiring him now to do his best work ever.

Bowen glanced at the microscopic bits of dirt under his clean fingernails, a reminder that he had projects in progress and needed to move his work along before his next trip. He sat in the morning quiet a long time, thinking before the light in the kitchen diffused.

Claire kissed his cheek.

"Good morning." She went to the fridge for a glass of orange juice. "Are you nervous about the hero's banquet tonight?"

"I'm no hero."

"Ruben Montero's community association thinks otherwise."

"I don't know about this, Claire—all this attention."

"Come on. Be gracious. It'll make Ruben happy, and we'll have a nice time." She smiled. "And thanks again for bringing my laptop to the break-in the other day. It was a big help."

"How are things going with that?"

She allowed a few seconds to pass, as if she had opened a door to a room of unsettled things.

"We managed to rejig the schedule, and I got a call from police last night when you were out. They checked on my patient who'd been assaulted by her partner, to be sure everything was okay. They said she was fine."

"You must be relieved."

"I'm concerned, given the situation." Claire got a muffin from the cupboard and sat at the table with him.

"How are police doing with the investigation?" he asked. "I thought they said the bad guys were going after gold fillings."

"The detective had theories that the burglary was disguised to look like that. He thought that maybe a vengeful ex might've been going after files in my office, especially since my patients have suffered abuse and attacks, you know."

Chewing on a piece of her muffin, she took a moment to shape her next question, aware that two new magazines about babies and pregnancies were on the far side of the table.

"Is there anything else you want to talk about?"

"I got another trip coming up, Chicago and Toronto."

"Okay." Claire broke off another piece of her muffin, swallowing her disappointment, her focus shifting through the glass patio doors to their backyard and two planter boxes by a mound of fresh earth next to one of her large flower beds.

"I see you're still working on my boxes. They look great, by the way. Is that what you were up doing last night? You were up late."

Bowen followed Claire's gaze to the yard.

"Yes, I want them to be just right."

"You're such a perfectionist. What time did you come to bed?"

"I don't remember. I have to take a new plane for the next trip, so I went out to Van Nuys to check it out."

"You drove to work in the middle of the night to look at a plane?"

"I couldn't sleep. You know how my job plays havoc with my body clock."

"Yes, it just seems unusual." Claire shrugged, then turned to the *Star-News* headline about the killer surfacing. She read a few paragraphs before tapping her finger to it. "Scary stuff."

She stood, cleaned up and kissed him. "Gotta go. Remember, Ruben called you a great hero, so just be yourself tonight."

Claire left, taking a parting glance at the newspaper then the backyard, thinking how the boxes looked like coffins next to a fresh grave. She held that grim observation briefly before shifting her attention to the day ahead.

35

San Marino, California

Claire drove to her office, contending with traffic and a million worries.

Focus on the positives and count your blessings, she told herself.

It had become her mantra.

Robert was a wonderful man, the man who'd rescued her from hell. He's a good husband, a caring and loving man. He was going to be a fantastic dad. She smiled to herself.

He paid attention to the little things.

She'd only casually mentioned how planter boxes would be nice for the yard and he set out to make them for her. He rushed to her aid when she needed her laptop. You could count on him. He'd saved the lives of two strangers, a mother and her baby, for which he was going to be publicly honored tonight as a hero.

Robert was perfect.

Wasn't he?

Claire came to a red light.

Wasn't he?

She pounded her palms on her steering wheel and bit back her tears.

Face the truth.

She was haunted by doubt and suspicion.

Does he really want a baby?

He's never asked me about the treatments, not really. He avoids the subject. He never wants to talk seriously about the future. He balked at the idea of selling the cabin for a college fund. And what about Cynthia?

The questions consumed Claire until a horn sounded.

The light had changed.

Claire resumed driving and grappling with her unease.

Maybe it's all me? I'm overreacting again to everything: the treatment, Robert's issues, Amber's assault in the parking lot, the burglary.

I'm just going through a rough time.

Claire began counseling herself. She knew she was compartmentalizing, putting up a wall of psychological self-defense. She didn't approach Robert directly because she wanted to avoid conflict with him, because deep down she was afraid she'd learn a truth she couldn't bear. She was rationalizing to maintain a consistent belief system—that while her relationship might not be perfect at this time, the positives outweighed the negatives and things were going to be fine.

Claire adjusted her grip on the wheel.

Let's leave it there for now.

At the office, matters had nearly returned to normal.

Claire got right to work at her desk, installing her flash drive to review her updated patient notes. Alice brought her fresh coffee, the day's patient list and a smile.

"Everything's back on track," Alice said. "You've got April and Madison this morning, then only Dorothy this afternoon. I'll make the appointment reminder calls for Vanessa and Amber. They're scheduled for tomorrow."

"Thanks, Alice."

"Oh, and the insurance guy is coming back today to drop off some papers. I'll handle that, if you're busy." Alice caught herself and concentrated on Claire. "Are you okay, dear?"

"Oh, sure, thanks. Just a bit tired," she lied.

"You've been through a lot lately. Want me to look ahead? Tomorrow looks light. I can shift things around so you can take a day."

"No, no," Claire said, appreciating the offer. "I've got Amber coming. I won't put any burden on my patients. Thanks, Alice. It was thoughtful."

Claire got on with her day.

Her first patient, April, the former teacher, had been making improvements. She'd left her abusive husband and taken their three children to live with a girlfriend in Thousand Oaks. It had not been easy, there was heartache at every turn, but April was fortifying her self-confidence and forging a new life for herself and her children.

It pleased Claire that her next patient, Madison, had made similar progress. The thirty-one-year-old hairstylist had taken steps to leave her controlling and abusive husband.

In the afternoon, Claire's session was with Dorothy, a fifty-three-year-old bank teller, who had been widowed for a year. Her husband had abused her throughout their marriage. Dorothy lived alone in a small house in East Pasadena where she was struggling with weak self-esteem and guilt. Her issues arose from her estrangement from her two adult daughters.

"They always blamed me for not leaving Gerry. They've even threatened to sue me in court for the abuse and anguish they'd suffered."

In today's session Dorothy presented a new issue.

"These last few nights I've been having trouble sleeping. Late at night I sense there's someone in my house—a man hiding in my house."

Claire took notes, concern slowing rising.

"Is there evidence of someone in your house? Did you call the police?"

"No, because I found nothing and thought I must be dreaming or imagining things and had better discuss this with you."

"Are you taking any new medication I should know about?"

"No."

"Are you facing new stresses at work, or new issues that cause you to worry?"

"I may be forced to retire early. The bank is downsizing."

Claire noted that and asked more questions, assessing Dorothy's responses until their time was up.

"Dorothy, this sensation of a presence in the house could be due to a number of factors—worry about your job, or the fact that Gerry was such a troubling part of your life for so long, or your strained relationship with your daughters. All of these fears and worries could combine to manifest themselves as a presence in your house at night."

Dorothy took some comfort in Claire's analysis.

"However," Claire said, "as you know, our building

was recently burglarized. So, I want to take precautions. With your permission, I'll have police check your house and note your address for patrols."

"Yes, I'd like that."

"I'll take care of it."

After Dorothy left, Claire returned to her desk, took out Officer Deena Freeman's card, called and advised her of Dorothy's situation.

"We'll look into it," Freeman said after confirming Dorothy's work and home addresses.

Satisfied she'd taken the right steps, Claire spent the rest of the afternoon reviewing patient notes. As she finished and prepared to leave for the day, her cell phone rang.

It was Julie.

"Hey, Claire, can you talk?"

"Yeah, what's going on?"

"Are you knocked up yet?"

"I've been wondering that myself."

"What? What're you saying?"

"No. I'm not pregnant yet. I'm just not sure how it'll go." Claire laughed at Julie's boldness. "I'm still going through the treatment phase."

"So it's going to take a while."

"It might. It could happen for us at any time. I'm not sure. The drugs kinda mess up my cycle."

"I see. Okay," Julie said, "I'll switch subjects. What did you find out?"

"What do you mean?"

"Remember? I'd asked you to get me more information about where Robert and Cynthia were living at the time of the divorce, or where they got married?"

"Oh, that."

"Yes, that. You wanted me to keep digging, remember?"

"Yes," Claire said.

"So, did you ask him? Or find anything more to help me?"

"No, we— I got sidetracked. There was a burglary at our building and—"

"What?"

"I should've told you. The police think the robbers were going after the gold the dentist uses for fillings, but there was damage showing someone tried to get into my files."

"That's a bit alarming, especially after you had that run-in with one of your patient's exes."

"Yeah, but the police have been very good about it. I wish I had something more to give you, but we're going to a banquet tonight."

"What banquet?"

"The man whose wife and baby Robert rescued—his community group is having a banquet and they want to honor Robert."

"That's nice, Claire, so why not ask him then?"

"Ask him what?"

"Where he was married and divorced. Work it into the conversation. Make it a joke or something. You'll figure it out."

"I suppose."

"Then with the right info, I can track Cynthia down and investigate whether or not he's had any contact with her—get the truth for you."

"I'd like that."

"Good, then *that* is your mission."

Driving home later Claire replayed her day, smiling

at Julie. She was the best kind of friend because she cut through the B.S. Claire would follow Julie's suggestion and extract some information from Robert about his first marriage.

Claire arrived home earlier than expected and used the extra time to check on her gardens in the front and back yards. Gardening was one of her joys and rather than hire professionals, she preferred to do it herself.

She hadn't had much time lately.

Claire kicked off her shoes and started toward the front of the house. Her rosebushes were doing well, as were her azaleas and rhododendrons. She was pleased as she went around the side of the house to the back.

This was their sanctuary, enclosed by towering hedges, shaded by mature sycamore and palms. The lawn was deep green and lush under her bare feet. Monarchs flitted to the bright red, white and pink blooms of her butterfly bushes. Her foxgloves were dazzling with a cascade of purple flowers. She loved how her Japanese plum tree was thriving, just like her pomegranates.

At the far corner of the yard she saw one of the planter boxes Robert had made and went to inspect it. The box glistened with new wood stain. It was filled neatly to the surface with dark rich soil and waited next to a mound of fresh earth.

Claire knelt down on the grass, ran her fingers along the smooth wood, wondering what she might plant inside. She was considering more roses when her heart skipped a beat.

The box vibrated subtly under her hand, with faint muffled scratching noises.

Something alive is in that box!

Claire shot back and bumped into someone.

"What is it, Claire?"

"Robert! Oh, my God! You scared me! There's something inside—something scratching to get out!"

He knelt down to inspect the far end.

Claire peeked over his shoulder and saw the bushy tail of a squirrel burrowing. Robert seized a small branch, gave it a gentle nudge and it scampered off.

"You should get ready for the banquet," he said, and stood. "You always need more time than me and we'll have to leave early. The traffic to Maywood could be tricky."

"Okay, thanks."

Claire collected her shoes and walked toward the house with a glance back at Robert, who'd gotten down on his knees again to work near that box.

36

Monterey Park, California

Mark Harding's story had ignited a firestorm.

Five miles east of downtown L.A., network satellite trucks and news cars from the city's media outlets had crammed into the parking lot of the L.A. County Sheriff's headquarters. The brass had called a press briefing, which was set to begin within five minutes.

This is our shot to speak directly to the killer, Tanner thought, waiting with other officials against one wall of the media conference room.

Earlier, throughout the morning, reporters had reacted to the ANPA's exclusive bombshell by relentlessly calling the department to demand interviews. Tanner and the task force had taken some of those calls that had distracted them from other work on the case. He'd come from Commerce to the Sherman Block building in Monterey Park to participate in the news conference.

Tanner surveyed the jungle of TV cameras and tripods as operators made final adjustments, estimating seventy newspeople in the room. Reporters gossiped, gabbed on cell phones, texted or made notes. Some of the TV journalists primped.

Next to the waiting podium, Tanner saw the board bearing enlarged color photos of the five murdered women and a map of Greater Los Angeles marked with where their bodies had been found. Tanner spotted Harding at the far edge of a row of chairs. They nodded to each other as Captain Martin Bronson of the sheriff's homicide bureau, went to the podium. He began with background on the five cold case homicides before summarizing the news—that the killer had written to Harding.

"We believe the person responsible for the deaths of the five victims is the same person who's contacted the AllNews Press Agency," Bronson said. "We're asking for anyone who may have any information relating to any aspect of this case to use our toll-free line to contact us or your local law enforcement agency. Now," Bronson said, "we'll take only a few questions."

The first hand to rise belonged to a reporter with KTKT News.

"Do you have any suspects?"

"We can't discuss that at this time," Bronson said.

"Nick Vellore, the *Daily News.* Captain, why did it take so many years to find evidence linking the Dark Wind Killer to these five murders?"

"That's explained in the background material we've provided you. Next."

"Jill Savagge, Associated Press. Will you release the killer's letter, or its contents?"

"I'm afraid we're holding that back to protect the case."

"You gave it to the ANPA," Savagge shot back.

"No, the killer did that."

"Mitch Fredrick, *L.A. Times*. Did you recover any DNA?"

"We're not going to discuss that at this time."

"Kate Hernandez, KMLA Action News. Captain, can you give us any indication as to why or how the killer chose these five women?"

"That's under investigation."

"Kyle Porter, *Ninety-Nine News Time*. Sir, how many tips have you received since the ANPA story about the letter ran across the country?"

"At this point, we've received two hundred seventy-four tips. The FBI is helping with those received outside of California. Our task force is drawing on resources throughout the city, county and state to process them."

"Rico Estrella, *MetroBeat*. In his letter the killer threatens to kill again. Are you not concerned that by issuing this information you are creating panic and giving him the attention he wants?"

"Let me assure you we've grappled with that and came to the conclusion that in order for us to keep the community safe, we need to keep it informed," Bronson said. "We advise people to exercise caution and common sense."

"Can you give examples of steps they should take?" Estrella asked.

"Ensure your home or apartment is properly locked and secure. Don't walk alone at night where you'd be vulnerable. Be wary of strangers."

"Should women be buying guns for protection? Maggie Fox, KSEN."

"We're not advocating that. But people have a right to take legal steps to protect themselves. Okay, one last question."

"Dan Jennings, KLKL. It's likely the killer will be watching this news conference. Captain, if you could talk to him, what would you say?"

Bronson thought for a moment before turning to Tanner.

"I'm going to let Detective Joe Tanner with the task force answer."

As Tanner took Bronson's place at the podium he cleared his throat. Tanner had discussed strategies on how to communicate to the killer with the task force and his supervisors.

In analyzing the letter, the earlier message, the crimes, the patterns and all the information they had so far, the FBI's profilers had determined that the killer was above average intelligence with an enormous ego.

"We invite you to contact us again," Tanner said. "You've demonstrated your intelligence, talent and skill at getting our attention, and the attention of the world. Contact us again, let us help you bring this to an end without any more people getting hurt. Please."

37

Maywood, California

"Looks like a lot of people are attending this thing," Robert said, scanning the vehicles in the lot, taking Claire's hand as they walked to the entrance of the Maywood Gardens Community Center. He looked good in his navy suit, she thought. She wore a green mock-wrap dress that draped nicely around her figure, finishing with a pin at her waist.

The stucco building sat between the chain-fenced yard of a transmission recycling shop and a line of small bungalows, circa World War Two. Music spilled from the hall as Claire struggled with Julie's urging to use this evening to draw more information from Robert about his life with his first wife. Claire was unsure how she would do it.

Inside, the crowded hall bunting and colored lights looped from the rafters and stretched the length of the main room. Music flowed from speakers suspended high on walls covered with blue and gold crepe-paper streamers. To one side there was a long table where servers navigated platters of food around people.

On the main floor, twenty round tables covered with

white tablecloths were arranged before a stage with a podium. It was flanked by tables adorned with flowers. Claire's eyes widened slightly at the backdrop's banner that read:

> Great Light and Hope Association Thanks Robert Bowen—A True American Hero!

"They're venerating you." Claire nudged Robert, who took it all in without speaking. After several seconds, she added, "Let's mingle and try to find Ruben."

As they worked their way through knots of conversations, people began recognizing Robert. Men slapped his back or shook his hand. When two pretty young women, their faces beaming, asked Robert to let them have their pictures taken with him, he obliged.

Claire was proud of her husband, but her smile yielded to a sudden ripple of unease at the manner in which Robert had inserted himself in the middle of the women. It was the way he'd slid his hands around their waists and pulled them closer to him. For an instant Claire thought he'd gone beyond a normal pose. He brushed against the line of propriety with a motion so smooth, Claire thought it revealing. It was as if he were accustomed to putting his hands on other women and the way his fingers spider-walked along their sides as he gently squeezed...

The way a shopper might check for quality.

It was so swift, so subtle, Claire wondered if she'd misread it.

"Claire! Robert! There you are!" Ruben Montero was battling his way to them, accompanied by several other people.

"You remember my wife, Maria. Thank God, you met!" Ruben hugged Robert. Then Maria stepped forward.

"My baby and I would not be here today, if not for you." Maria flung her arms around Robert, as well.

Acknowledging their gratitude, Robert introduced Claire before Ruben and his wife excused themselves.

"My apologies, we have a few last-minute details to take care of before we get started," Montero said. "We'll join you at the guest table in a moment." He turned to a man and woman waiting to meet Robert. "Let me introduce you to our senior board members, our president, Gloria Rosario, and our treasurer, Eddie Melendez."

"Welcome," Gloria said. "We're so happy you've come this evening."

"Thank you for being our guest of honor." Eddie shook Robert's hand. "Would you like something to drink?" He flagged one of the servers and ordered for the group.

"As a pilot, you must see a lot of the world," Eddie said.

"I have, but not as much now that I fly corporate charter," he said. "I'll be flying to India next month and I'm going to Toronto in a few days."

"Canada? I've never been there but I hear it's beautiful," Eddie said.

"It is. I lived there when I was first married," Robert said.

Canada? Claire threw a look to Robert, thinking it odd that he would mention any aspect of his time with Cynthia, especially socially. She couldn't recall him ever saying he'd lived in Canada. This was a revelation. Their drinks arrived, diverting her attention.

"So, Claire, are you Canadian?" Gloria, a retired school principal, asked.

"No, but close," Claire smiled. "I'm from Minnesota."

"Yes," Robert interjected. "I was referring to my first wife—" then he slid his arm around Claire "—that was before we met."

"And," Gloria asked Claire, "do you work outside the home?"

"I'm a psychologist.'

"A psychologist? That must be fascinating and challenging."

"Much like being a principal, I'm sure," Claire replied.

"Oh, goodness," Gloria said, waving the air. "Don't get me started." Gloria took refuge in her sangria. "Do you have children, Claire?"

The question resurrected a familiar hurt and Claire reached for her worn response.

"Not yet, but we hope to," she said, preparing for Gloria to do what most women did to her in this situation—secretly guess at her age and the time remaining on her biological clock. But Robert intervened.

"We're working on it. We love kids," he said.

The music stopped, a squeal of feedback pierced the air before the loudspeakers crackled.

"Welcome to Great Light's annual banquet!" a woman's voice said to cheers. "Now, if everyone would please take their seats. The kitchen staff tells me that everything's ready for us to begin."

After the food, the evening progressed with small speeches highlighting the charity's work to help the underprivileged people of the community. They touched on reports on donations, bake sales, carnivals, scholarships, awards and future goals. Then the agenda moved to recognition of donors and volunteers before it was Ruben Montero's turn at the podium.

"Friends, members of the board, it gives me great pleasure to tell you about our guest of honor, Robert Bowen."

Ruben unfolded a sheet of paper.

"But it'll be hard for me to get through this without choking up." Ruben cleared his throat, then recounted the events of the day and how Robert Bowen saved his family.

Then Ruben folded his sheet, blinked away his tears and turned to Bowen and patted his shoulder.

"Robert Bowen embodies the great light and hope that our organization represents and for that, it is our great, great pleasure to honor him tonight. Robert, please say a few words."

The room shook with applause that grew into a standing ovation as Ruben reached under the podium for a plaque to present Robert, who stood to join him as cameras flashed.

Robert began by thanking Ruben and the association.

"I really didn't expect this, nor do I think I deserve it but I accept this gracious honor." Robert passed his plaque to Claire before he resumed speaking. "In some small way each of us is called to help someone every day. We can be selfish when we get that call, or hardened by indifference, or paralyzed by fear. We must overcome the easy choice of doing nothing. You have to look inside yourself and determine how you will answer the call when faced with the temptation to turn your back, to let your heart go cold."

Robert paused, and, as some in the audience nodded

in agreement, he took in the crowd. A long moment passed and he remained silent. The air became uncomfortable, people coughed and shifted in their seats.

Ruben turned to his wife, then looked up at Robert as if wishing him to continue. Claire gently touched his arm and whispered, "Robert, are you okay?"

Without looking at her, he nodded, letting another moment pass before he resumed.

"Now each of us must ask, how will I answer the call to help? You must overcome the temptation to do nothing. We overcome it with action. That's how we defeat it, that is how we find our humanity. That is our great light and that is our hope. Thank you."

People rose to their feet again and clapped. Some cheered and whistled. The overpowering sound made the hall vibrate. Ruben and Maria embraced Robert, and as the applause continued, they were joined by their son, Alex. Then someone brought Bonita, their baby daughter, to the podium and Maria passed her to Robert. Robert held her in his arms, smiled and waved to the audience. Again, cameras flashed throughout the hall, some people crowded before the stage to take better pictures.

Standing next to Robert, seeing him holding Bonita during the deafening applause, Claire's heart swelled.

Her husband looked every bit the hero. *He was a hero,* and holding Bonita, he looked like a natural father.

How can I justify any misgivings about him?

Yet how could she dismiss them?

Should she ignore the way he'd held the young women or his unusual remarks about evil, and the look on his face during his long awkward pause?

He had been reveling in the silence, leaving Claire to wonder: *Where did he go in that moment?*

38

Los Angeles, California

Robert and Claire drove home in the afterglow of the banquet and as they got on to the freeway, he glanced at her.

"All in all that went pretty well, don't you think?" he asked.

"Yes, everyone was thrilled to have you there."

Claire's tone dropped the temperature and Robert looked at her again.

"What is it?"

As hard as she tried, Claire could not stop her concerns and troubling questions from gnawing at her.

"Are you happy you married me?" she asked.

"What?"

"Are you happy you married me?"

After a moment he took her hand and squeezed it in his.

"More than you'll ever know."

Claire withdrew her hand and stared straight ahead.

"Why are you keeping things from me, Robert?"

"What things? What are you talking about?"

"You never told me you'd lived in Canada with Cynthia."

"That's what this is about? Claire, I did tell you that Cindy—"

"*Cindy?* I've never heard you call her that before."

He exhaled and repositioned his grip on the wheel to remain calm.

"Claire, I did tell you that my first wife and I lived in Canada. I told you that when we first met."

"No, you didn't."

"I did, and I also told you most of my life with her was miserable and I don't like talking about it." Robert paused to soften his voice. "Claire, meeting you was the greatest thing—the best thing—that ever happened to me. You're everything I ever wanted."

She continued staring ahead at the freeway traffic.

"Do you want us to have a baby, Robert?"

"What?"

"Do you?"

"Yes, I do. What kind of question is that? What's troubling you?"

"I'm angry."

"At what?"

"Robert, I can't help but feel that lately you haven't been entirely honest with me. It's like you're keeping something from me."

"I don't understand where this is coming from."

"You say you want a baby, but ever since Dr. LaRoy started us on this new treatment you've barely showed any interest. When I talk about the future, you shut me down. And recently, when I walked by your office, I thought I overheard you talking to Cynthia on the phone."

"We went over that, I was talking to a reporter."

"I also saw a snapshot that had fallen from somewhere onto your office floor. It was a picture of you with 'Cindy' during happier times by the mountains, but I shrugged it off."

"What's this all about?"

"Are you still in love with Cynthia?"

"What? That's so ridiculous. Why would you even ask that? The answer is no. She's out of my life."

"What am I supposed to think, Robert?"

"I can't tell you what to think. But I'll tell you what I think. I think it's immature of you to eavesdrop and snoop in my office, but it's our house so snoop and eavesdrop all you like. I've always told you I don't like talking about my first marriage or my childhood. They were agonizing times for me."

"My childhood was no bed of roses."

"I know that, Claire."

"Getting people to talk about their pain is my job, Robert, in case you've forgotten."

"I'm not one of your patients," he said. "Tell me something, Claire. Why are you doing this? Why on this night?"

She didn't answer for several seconds.

"Robert, I didn't like the way you held those two young women who took their picture with you tonight. It was inappropriate."

Robert's jaw tightened and he said nothing.

"And that long pause you made during your acceptance speech was not only awkward, it was disturbing. What happened?"

A tense moment passed before Robert answered.

"Nothing happened. As for the women, I was posing for a photo. As for my speech, I was gathering my thoughts and pausing to make a point."

He looked away from her before continuing.

"What is this, Claire? Is it a hormonal thing because of the treatment? Or are you spooked after dealing with that asshole in the parking lot? What about the burglary at your office? Maybe you should talk to somebody?"

"Robert, you're deflecting my concerns and you're being cruel."

He shook his head bitterly.

"You've accused me of a million crimes and *I'm* being cruel. Claire, I've always been there for you and I always try to help. You're going through something. I don't understand it but I'll be there for you, because I love you and I vowed to stand by you."

Claire looked at him.

The headlights of oncoming traffic brightened the interior, creating a web of dark shadows on his face, and she answered him softly.

"It's like a different side of you is emerging. It worries me, Robert."

He stared into traffic and didn't speak another word for the rest of the evening. He slept on the sofa that night while Claire, alone in their bed, bit back tears until sleep finally came.

39

Downey and Commerce, California

"So, can I go, Dad?"

The question surprised Tanner.

His thoughts had been buried deep in the case as he drove Samantha to school. He glanced at her in the rearview mirror.

"Go where?"

"Dad! Are you listening? Lindsay's birthday party!"

"Oh, right, sorry, honey."

"Aunt Kim said she would take me on Saturday. And today, after she gets me at school, we're going to the mall to get Lindsay's present, *re-mem-burr?*"

"Yes, I do."

Tanner brought their car to a stop in the drop-off zone at school. He put his holstered gun in the glove compartment, got out and helped Sam with her backpack. In the seconds he looked into her little face, he caught a glimpse of Becky and his heart warmed. "Love you, Daddy."

"Love you, too."

After watching his daughter head into the school,

Tanner drove off with a load of guilt as he shoved any thoughts not connected to the case from his mind.

Ever since they'd found the gruesome fingerprint message, proving that one killer was responsible for five cold case homicides, Tanner needed to ensure he hadn't missed anything, or overlooked a new angle. The monster having surfaced brought them a step closer to the suspect, but the pressure on the new task force to make an arrest was mounting.

Will we stop him before he kills again?

Tanner arrived at the bureau and checked the time. He had half an hour before the next case status meeting. Inside, he got a fresh coffee and set to work at his desk, following the same routine. He looked for any new leads or breaks and resumed examining the files. As he reread them for the thousandth time, something was materializing—something in a corner of his mind that had niggled at him the other night. He'd been drifting between sleep and consciousness when an idea took shape, but he couldn't identify it.

What the hell was it?

Tanner was still concentrating on it when the status meeting began with FBI Special Agent Brad Knox saying that the task force had now received 323 tips from across the state and across the country. Police agencies everywhere were helping pursue each one. Even though most were vague, superficial or just plain weird, seasoned investigators knew that each one had to be cleared.

"Here's a sampling." Knox presented the summary. "This is from Anaheim. 'My neighbor talks to his dog and I overheard him confess to his Great Dane that he killed them girls.' Then we have this from Texas, 'A trucker in a bar in Fort Worth was bragging that he had all the information cops needed, but was waiting for them to post the right amount of reward money.' Then we have this, an anonymous call to Bakersfield P.D.—'This was channeled spiritually so receive it as you wish. The killer is Delbert Gill Gettysen, age forty-three, recently paroled from a prison in California after serving time for assaulting women. Gettysen told his parole officer that he was the Dark Wind Killer and was going to continue offing bitches."

Knox acknowledged that on the face of it, the tip was consistent with the pause from the time of the fifth victim to the killer's communication.

"We checked with parole and prison officials in California. Nothing surfaced for the name, variations of the name, the age, nothing. The call was from a public phone near a mall. Nearby security cameras were not working," Knox said. "And, I should add, we were already involved in reviewing the status and whereabouts of known offenders."

LAPD Detective Art Lang peered over his bifocals from his notes.

"Where are we with physical evidence, starting with the killer's letter to the reporter? We were awaiting further lab work?"

Eugene Rowe, a postal inspector with the U.S. Postal Inspection Service, had a status report.

"The envelope is a national federal eagle design, made exclusively and sold only by the U.S. Postal Service. Our forensic lab is working with the FBI lab. We're analyzing the ink used via solubility testing and thin layer chromatography to give us more information on the felt-tip pen that was used. Neither the envelope or the letter exhibited watermarks, hair, latent fingerprints or any trace DNA."

"So we've got nothing to run through CODIS," Lang said, referring to the FBI's national database, called the Combined DNA Index System. The network lets crime labs exchange and compare DNA profiles electronically, providing the ability to identify ties to crimes and convicted criminals.

"No, nothing so far," Rowe said, and returned to his page of notes.

"As we all know, the letter bore an Alhambra, California postmark. It doesn't mean our sender lives in Alhambra, but it's a focal point for next steps," Rowe said.

Tanner waited, tapping his pen against his pad, then turned to Knox.

"What do we have on our ViCAP submissions of the five cases in the wake of the letter and its contents?"

"Nothing," Knox replied, shaking his head. "But the profilers updated their further analysis of the cold cases and the letter. They peg the likelihood that our guy will kill again at seventy-five percent. And if he does, he'll gloat over it with a message to investigators and the press. He's gaining what he needs, worldwide attention."

Soft cursing rippled around the table as the meeting ended.

Tanner returned to his desk with images burning in his mind: Leeza Meadows, aged twenty-one, her body found by a birdwatcher at the edge of Santa Clarita. Tanner suddenly thought of Samantha and how he would feel if it were his daughter they'd found sexually assaulted, her naked body dumped. He knew the pain of losing his wife, but to lose your daughter—to evil, to darkness.

And this creep is still out there.

Time was slipping by them.

Why these five? Why did he select them?

Tanner echoed the question the reporter Mark Harding had asked: *"What did a waitress, a hooker, an accountant, an actress and a writer, all have in common with their killer?"*

Again, Tanner went back to the six-month rule. What had each woman done in the last six months of her life? Where had she gone? Who had she seen? What did she do? Was it something common in all five cases? He'd flipped through pages and pages of notes detectives had made in working with the family members and loved ones. Notes, journals and logs on routines, appointments and activities.

Then he cross-checked them through the database, searching for a common thread, almost willing one to appear.

Again, he found nothing.

All of the women had jobs, all had routines, friends, social circles that had been investigated extensively.

All had traveled in the last six months of their lives.

Traveled?

Tanner paused. Thinking.

Now that was an angle he hadn't pursued deeply.

Where did they travel? He reached for the files. *A charter group?* That would be a common factor. Flipping through the files, he saw that Bonnie Bradford had made a few trips to New York to talk to a literary agent. Monique Wilson had visited Chicago, Houston and Philadelphia so many times for her accounting firm, she got to know some of the airline crew, her sister had noted. Then there was Fay Lynne Millwood; she'd gone to Denver for a conference. Esther Fatima Lopez had gone to

Las Vegas and Atlantic City to work. Leeza Meadows had flown to Boston to visit a friend in college.

All had flown but not with a charter group. The common link couldn't be travel, Tanner thought as his phone rang. The distraction caused him to pass over the name of the airline listed in each file and the fact that at one time or another, each of the women had flown with the same airline.

40

San Marino, California

Claire, I'm sorry for what happened last night. I felt horrible. I came to realize that you're right, I've been ignoring you. Guess I'm still dealing with a little post-traumatic stress myself. The truth: it was Ruben's retelling of the event that made me lose track and pause. Suddenly, all I saw was an inferno. I was trapped in it and it terrified me. Do not doubt for one second that I want to start a family with you. You're my world, my life.

I need you more than you'll ever know.

Claire stopped reading the note Robert had left on the kitchen table to brush away a tear before finishing.

I couldn't sleep, so I worked a little on your planter boxes. The company texted me last night. One of our guys got sick so I had to go in early this morning to take his trip and then add it to mine. I tried not to wake you. I'll call you. I hate leaving like this.

Forgive me.

Love,

Robert

Claire sat down as if winded and cupped her face in her hands.

At this moment she loved him.

At this moment she hated him.

What's happening to us?

Claire looked through the glass of the patio doors to their backyard, her flower beds and the planter boxes. He'd moved them again. She half smiled at how he was so concerned about getting them just right for her. She loved them and he'd built more. They were beautiful.

We've both been through a lot lately. That's what's happened to us.

It was true, she admitted as she prepared a piece of whole-wheat toast with a peach for breakfast. But she had patients who needed her. She glanced at the time on the microwave. And she was running late.

In the shower, the hot water sharpened her concentration and she fell into the same old debate with herself over Robert that continued as she put on her makeup.

Why am I rationalizing every negative to convince myself that this is just a "rough patch" and everything's going to be fine? I'm such a stupid, stupid woman. Every one of my instincts is telling me, screaming at me, that something's terribly wrong between Robert and me.

Being honest about the problem was a start, she thought as she dressed, but she couldn't deal with it any further at the moment. She was late and had a ton of work waiting for her at the office. Amber was her first patient this morning and Claire was hopeful that she was building on her progress and decision not to return to Eric.

Adjusting her necklace, Claire entered her home office to collect her USB flash drive. Then she disconnected her phone from the charger and, as if on cue, it rang.

"Hey, Claire, it's me," Julie said.

"Hi."

"Did I get you at a bad time? Can you talk right now?"

"Sure, but I'm late and on my way out the door."

"So how'd it go last night?"

"Overall, it went really well, very emotional and touching, I was proud of him but there were some strange moments."

"Strange, how?"

"I don't know, he seemed kind of touchy-feely with a couple of young women who had their picture taken with him."

"What do you mean?" Julie asked.

"When he put his arms around them to pose, his hands just seemed to wander in a way that made me uneasy."

"What about the women? Did they mind?"

"They didn't care. If they did, they didn't show it."

"And he knew you were watching?"

"Yes."

"That is strange. Where was it again?"

"Maywood." Claire got into her car.

"Did you find out any more information for me?"

"I did, and that was one of the odd things. I didn't need to ask—it came up randomly in conversation. Robert said that he and Cynthia had lived in Canada when they were married."

"Canada? That explains why I couldn't find anything. You know where in Canada?"

"No, it was a surprise to me and it made me angry and we got into it on the way home. He said he'd told me when we first met, but I swear he didn't." Claire pushed the button on her remote garage door opener. The door rose with a groan, light flooded the garage and she started her car.

"Okay, Canada," Julie said. "That's helpful. Our agency has subs there."

"Subs?"

"Subcontractors. We have contacts to help us. I'll see what I can find out."

"Thanks, gotta go."

During her drive to work Claire tried to focus on her practice, but it was futile. She was anxious. When she stopped at a long red light her mind swirled with images that pulled her back to her childhood home and…

…Her mother's fingers desperately clawing at her father's hand that gripped the gun… Suddenly Claire is a woman slammed with fury against a column in the airport and Cliff is crushing his forearm against her throat… Cliff raises his fist to smash her face when Robert seizes it, saving her… Robert last night…"I've always been there for you…you don't know how lucky you are."

The light changed and Claire resumed driving to her office.

She was not too late when she arrived. Alice was on the phone, her face creased with concern. Without disturbing her, Claire got a coffee and left reception but her attention lingered on Alice, curious about her demeanor and why no one was seated in the lobby.

Amber should have been in the reception area by this time, Claire thought, settling in at her desk, turning her computer on and waiting for Alice to bring her the agenda and patient list. Claire took her first sip of coffee when she heard Alice hang up and enter with the day's list. Amber's name had been crossed off. Claire looked at her for an answer.

"She didn't confirm," Alice said. "I just tried reaching her at home and on her cell and work numbers."

"That's unusual. Amber never cancels without telling us."

"I know. What should we do?"

Claire tapped her pen to her chin.

"Let's play it safe." Claire got her wallet and a business card. "I'll give Officer Freeman a call and let her know, just as a precaution."

Claire got Freeman's voice mail and left a message, but it was enough to put her and Alice somewhat at ease as they carried on with the morning.

Throughout the day, Claire's concern grew as the Amber question remained unresolved. They'd heard nothing from her and, after a few hours with no response from Officer Freeman, Claire called San Marino P.D. She was put through to a duty sergeant and explained her unease.

"Freeman's on a course in San Diego, but let me look up that case file." Claire heard the sergeant typing on his keyboard, taking a moment to read the most recent summary. "All right, I'm up to speed. So basically given her circumstances and because she's missed an appointment, you're requesting we check on her welfare?"

"Right."

"Okay, that address is in Alhambra, I'll flag this with the Alhambra P.D., but I have to tell you, they've got a major apartment complex fire going. They've put a lot of traffic units on it. In fact, we're supporting with some of our units. So it might be a while."

In the back of her mind Claire clung to the hope that

Amber would return Alice's messages. At least the police had been alerted, Claire assured herself throughout the afternoon. After her last patient session of the day had ended, Claire gathered her things, instructed Alice to call her with any word on Amber, then headed home.

Claire got as far as the parking lot when she remembered she had to pick up a lamp. The antiques shop was in Alhambra and not far from her office. After paying for her lamp and putting it in her car, Claire's thoughts returned to Amber.

Since she was in Alhambra, she should go to Amber's house.

In the car she turned on her laptop and inserted her flash drive to review the file for Amber's address. Was she crossing an ethical line? Visiting patients outside of the office was frowned upon. Claire stared at the address.

Am I going too far?

She reached for her cell phone and tried Amber's numbers without reaching her.

Claire then tried the San Marino P.D. again and got a different sergeant this time. Like the previous one, he had to look up the status.

"No, apparently Alhambra P.D. did not get to it yet," the sergeant said, "but they indicate here that it's moved up the call list. I know they've had their hands full all day with the fire, and now they've had a bomb scare at a school. Meantime, maybe you could have a friend or relative check?"

Claire thanked the sergeant and hung up.

She had to make a decision.

Given everything that had happened with Amber's case: Eric's attack, the rage in his face, his attempt to drag Amber back into the relationship, the fact she was considering it—*and now I can't reach her*—it was time to do something.

Claire keyed Amber's address into her GPS, then started her car.

41

Alhambra, California

As Claire guided her Corolla onto Amber's street, reality eclipsed her reasoning for being there.

This could be a dumb thing to do.

Battling her growing embarrassment, Claire challenged her instincts, asking herself over and over with each house number she counted: Was coming here the right thing to do?

Yes, damn it, yes!

It was the only thing to do to allay the fears that were twisting in her stomach. Those images from the worst times of her life that had recently flashed in her mind were like harbingers. She knew what happened when people did nothing in the face of looming trouble.

My mother, brother and father died because no one got involved. I can't let this go. I can't ignore everything that's happened with Amber.

She stopped in front of Amber's address, shifted into Park, turned off the engine, got out and took a quick read of the house.

It was a sprawling ranch-style bungalow that sat back from the street on a large lot. The lush landscaping with shade trees and thriving flower beds gave the property the sedate air of a well-maintained park, she thought as she took the winding cobblestone walk. Noting the small yard sign for the security company she came to the door and rang the bell.

Claire remembered how Amber had said she was fortunate to be house-sitting for friends, the generous owners of such a beautiful home.

A long moment passed without a response.

She rang the bell again, then knocked, hard.

Nothing.

A neglected newspaper jutting from the mailbox offered her a glimpse of the headline about the Dark Wind Killer stalking L.A. The reality of a monster out there pricked at her anxiety.

Claire took out her cell phone and called Amber's number. She heard it ringing inside before it went to voice mail. Claire hung up, stepped carefully into the shrubs under the nearest window, pressed her face to the glass, cupped her hands near her eyes and looked into the house. She saw the dim forms of a sofa, a table, a chair, then heard a soft noise from inside.

Oh, no, I could have triggered the alarm system or something. Goodness, if someone reports me, I'll be arrested.

Claire stepped out of the shrub and pressed her ear to the door and held her breath.

She heard voices inside.

Someone's in there. Why won't they answer?

She knocked hard on the door but no one responded.

She went around to the side of the house, along the knee-high hedge that bordered the driveway where

Amber's small Chevy was parked. As she neared the back of the house she saw a metal gate with a lockbox.

"Hello!" she called.

Nothing. No dog, no movement of any sort.

She tested the latch, and to her surprise the steel door swung open. She walked along the patio stones and knocked on the back door. No response, yet she heard voices.

Someone's in there.

Once more, Claire peered through a window that gave her a clear view. She saw the tiled floor of the kitchen, the granite counters, wood cabinets, a cooktop, but no people. Yet she heard sounds and they were louder now. Frustrated, she knocked again and tried the door handle.

It was unlocked.

This is weird.

Claire inched inside, her eyes scanning the kitchen. The mild, pleasant smell of dish soap lingered.

"Hello, Amber! It's Claire Bowen!"

"...I wouldn't do that if I were you..." A man's deep voice stopped Claire's pulse for the seconds it took her to realize his voice and the voices she'd been hearing were coming from the radio on the kitchen counter. It was tuned to a talk radio show. *"...damn straight I'd tell those fat cats in Sacramento that I would not even consider a tax for..."*

Claire took a small breath.

The kitchen table was clear, the counters gleamed, the sink held one glass that had been rinsed. Otherwise, it was empty of dishes, and tea towels were hung neatly. Nothing seemed amiss as she moved to the living room.

"Hello, Amber, it's Claire Bowen. Are you home?"

On one end table the red light of a message machine

blinked like a panicked heart. Claire did not think it was her place to listen to Amber's messages.

Right, and here I am standing in the middle of her home.

Claire continued checking the rest of the house.

In the study, files were stacked neatly on the desk. Claire thought they looked like court and divorce records, causing her to wonder if Amber had been talking to Eric again.

The laundry room, pantry and family room were fine. The smaller bedrooms and bathrooms were empty with nothing out of the ordinary. The bed was also made in the largest bedroom, although it looked a bit sloppy, as if done in a rush. On the nightstand she saw a paperback copy of *Madame Bovary* and a business card for Officer Les Campbell of the Alhambra Police Department.

Maybe she went back to Eric? Lord, I hope not.

Claire went to the en suite bathroom. There was a toothbrush in its holder, clean dry towels on the rack. Claire returned to the bedroom and opened the large closet to clothes and a set of luggage on the floor.

It doesn't look as though she packed anything.

Maybe she's had an accident and is in a hospital? Or is lying unconscious somewhere?

Something's wrong here, I feel it.

Claire put her hands on her hips and exhaled, thinking. As she inventoried the room, she froze.

The sunlight drew her attention to something she hadn't noticed before on the gleaming hardwood floor. She got down on her hands and knees for a closer look, drawing her face to a trail of coin-sized circles that led from the bedroom down the hall.

They were bloodred.

"Oh, God."

Alarm rang in Claire's ears as she reached for her cell phone.

It took several attempts to call 9-1-1 because her hands were shaking.

42

Alhambra, California

"Would you like more water, Claire?"

Claire was lost in the numbing fog of her thoughts while sitting in the empty meeting room of Alhambra police headquarters.

Tammy Newberg, a uniformed officer with a perky ponytail, who looked more high school senior than cop, held a glass. Tammy had been with the wave of officers to come to Amber's house, and had been quite kind. "How are you holding up, Claire? We're trying to get a number for you to reach your husband. We understand his trip was unexpectedly extended in Canada and we're waiting to hear back. Is there anyone else we can call for you?"

A whirlwind had ensued in the few hours since Claire had told a 9-1-1 emergency dispatcher that Amber was missing and that she'd found blood on her bedroom floor. A young patrol officer, Claire had forgotten his name, was first to arrive. He'd kept Claire at the kitchen table while he inspected the rooms. Afterward, the officer reached for his radio and time blurred as he made more calls before taking Claire's initial statement, careful to ask her what she'd touched.

Events then blazed by as more police arrived, including Tammy, then Tate and Campbell, the officers who'd last had contact with Amber. All of them talked to the detectives and crime scene people. Claire had overhead one officer say, "Did you look under the sheets of the bed? There's more blood, a lot of blood."

Oh, God, she'd thought.

A detective caught Claire's reaction and she had then been taken outside to sit under the umbrella of the patio table. The investigators, focusing on Amber's history with her violent estranged husband, had advised her that they would need to take a fuller statement and obtain elimination fingerprints from Claire at Alhambra police headquarters.

A yellow plastic police line was stretched across the front of the house. Claire saw kids on bicycles and neighbors on the sidewalk. She'd read the concern etched in their faces as she was escorted into an unmarked police sedan. The car cut through the city, driving Claire deeper into a state of stunned haziness as one thought screamed over and over from the far reaches of her worried mind.

Where is Amber? Where is Amber?

Now ice cubes clinked in a glass and Claire sipped the water Tammy had poured for her.

"The guys shouldn't be much longer," Tammy said. "I got hold of your friend Julie. She's on her way."

Claire thanked her.

The door opened and the two detectives, Norm Seeton and Ed Belinski, entered, then positioned their chairs.

"Okay, Claire." Belinski undid his collar button and

loosened his tie. "Let's take it from the last time you saw Amber to where we are now."

Claire took a breath and let it go slowly before relating all that she knew about Amber. The detectives listened with sober, poker faces, saying little, asking an occasional question as Seeton took notes. When Claire finished she asked the detectives what they were doing to find Amber.

"We've circulated her photo and description across L.A., the county, the state and we've alerted the FBI," Belinski said.

"Is that it? What about Eric, her estranged husband?"

"Given the case history, his violation of the protection order and the assault, he's a person of interest. We've issued a BOLO for him."

"What's a BOLO?"

"For police units to be on the lookout for him and arrest him on sight."

"Why don't you just question him? He's in Sacramento?"

"He was up until two days ago. Seems no one knows where he is now. He's missed work and is in violation of his bail conditions for not reporting. He left Amber a message on her machine."

Guilt pricked at Claire for not doing something about Amber's revelation of the letter Eric had written—but that had been an ethical call.

Hadn't it?

"You have to find him." Claire stared at nothing. "What do you think happened?"

Belinski blinked as if deciding how far to go in answering.

"Amber hasn't reported for work for two days. Her

car's in her driveway. We're trying to reach her relatives in Orange County. For two days there's been no activity on Amber's cell phone, no activity on her bank or credit cards. It doesn't look good. We're still processing her residence. We've found a substantial amount of blood on the bed, but not enough to make it clear someone died there. The alarm system's been defeated. She's a missing person who may have come to harm."

"Do you think Eric took her?"

"Anything's possible. She could have hurt herself. She could have fled and could be hiding. Maybe she's been in an accident and is in a hospital. She could've been taken against her will. Everything seems to have stopped after her last phone call to her in-laws in Sacramento."

Claire covered her face, swallowed air and took a deep calming breath. The detectives gave her a moment before it was broken by the vibration of Seeton's phone.

"Your friend's here for you," he said.

As Claire collected herself and her bag, Belinski passed her his card.

"Call us if Amber contacts you. Or you come across any new information about her or Eric—anything."

Officer Newberg took Claire to the reception area where Julie consoled her with a hug before they walked to Julie's car.

It was dusk.

"I can't go home yet," Claire said. "Can we just drive?"

They drove across the city and north along the coast. Claire knew her friend had a lot of questions but appreciated Julie letting her have the quiet. When they passed Malibu, they stopped at a roadside diner where Julie ordered a salad. Claire wasn't hungry.

“I’m so sorry for what happened,” Julie said. “If there’s anything I can do to help, tell me.”

Claire thanked her.

“I feel it’s my fault. I should have done more. The signs were there. They were all there. Oh, God, I hope she’s alive.”

Claire stared out the window at the ocean, then reached for her bag. “I have to try reaching Robert again. I’m not sure where he is at the moment, Toronto or Chicago.”

As her cell rang, Claire looked at Julie.

Her friend’s concern appeared to have deepened, as if she had something significant to say but was holding back. Claire had forgotten that Julie had taken the new information she’d given to her about Robert and had resumed digging into his past.

The line broke and Claire heard Robert’s recorded voice, prompting her to leave a message.

“It’s me. Something terrible has happened. I need you, please come home as soon as you can.”

Claire hung up, exhaled and shifted her attention to Julie.

“What is it?” Claire asked.

Julie shook her head and gazed out the window.

“Nothing,” Julie said.

Claire knew that was a lie but didn’t push it. She was still struggling with Amber’s disappearance.

43

Los Angeles, California

Early morning traffic was light. Harding sipped his coffee as he drove to the news bureau, struggling with ideas for his next story. He needed to keep the ANPA out front.

But how?

It had been more than two days since he broke his exclusive on receiving the letter, which drew a lot of attention. Local TV talk shows covered the response and switchboards at radio call-in stations lit up. Throughout greater L.A. people were on edge over the Dark Wind Killer's threat to claim more victims.

Arriving at his building, Harding stepped from the elevator and into his office, determined to advance the story. His resolve was underscored by his first email of the morning. It was from Sebastian Strother at headquarters in New York.

> Mark: Need an unbeatable follow today before the competition takes this away from us. As you know, the pickup for your exclusive was huge across the country and around the world. Do not rest on laurels. SS

Harding downed the last of his coffee, tossed the cup into the trash and put in a call to Tanner, thinking maybe he could get an update on tips, or better, maybe the task force had a lead he would share.

Unable to reach Tanner, Harding left a message then texted him.

Waiting for a response, he began contacting the victims' families and friends, the people he'd interviewed earlier. Harding asked those he could reach if the police had given them any progress reports on the investigation.

No one was aware of anything. In fact, most had assumed Harding was calling to inform them of a break. Several had suggested that he was in a better position to learn of a development than they were.

After making his last call, he thought for a moment then scrutinized his maps and documents from the splayed files on his desk. He had more research on his computer. A few mouse clicks and he opened a growing folder on his hard drive. It held notes, scanned attachments and the photos that Jodi-Lee Ruiz had taken of the killer's letter.

Mining the material for clues, Harding lost track of time. He was oblivious to the office coming to life around him as other news staff arrived with the aroma of fresh coffee. He concentrated on the envelope until an earlier idea returned. It bore an Alhambra postmark—why not call Alhambra P.D.? See if they knew anything and if they'd share.

He was going through his electronic contact file for a number when he noticed the smell of strawberries as Allison Porter passed by his desk.

"Here's some snail mail for you, Mark. Nothing scary looking, this time."

"Thanks."

He glanced at the handful of letters and an old magazine subscription card from the U.K. How many times did he have to tell them he was no longer interested? He tossed that one and went on to a membership renewal from the press guild; an invitation to speak to journalism students at a college; something from a Beverly Hills charity seeking coverage; and a letter addressed to him in neat handwriting, with the return name:

Mea Gain
60606 Déjà Vu Avenue
Burbank, CA.

Mea Gain? Who's that? Mea Gain? Déjà Vu Avenue? That's a bit strange, is that a real address? Allison missed this. Two seconds later it hit him that the letter—*Oh, Christ—Me Again—Déjà vu.*

Using his cell phone he took pictures of the envelope. Then he hurried to the office kitchen and got a pair of rubber gloves from under the sink. He returned to his desk, fumbled for his scissors, noticing a stamp but no postmark, and his pulse kicked up as he sliced open the envelope. It was a standard letter size ten. It contained one page, a map to a location and the words "A gift for you and the Blue Meanies. Better hurry."

The Blue Meanies? Harding knew that was a term from *Yellow Submarine,* the old Beatles album. He also knew that San Francisco's Zodiac Killer had used the same term in his letters to the press.

His heart racing, Harding took several pictures of the map with his cell phone camera before carefully putting the page and envelope in a safe place at his desk.

He had to go now. He couldn't risk the chance that other reporters had been tipped, too. That someone else could beat him on this. He grabbed his car keys and nearly bumped into Magda, who was stepping off the elevator as he was stepping on.

"We need to talk about a follow-up story today," she said.

"I think we have one. The killer wrote to me again."

"What? Hold on, Mark!"

"I have to go, I'll call you." Harding jabbed the elevator button.

As the elevator descended, he reviewed the map and mentally planned his route. When he stepped off, he spotted Jodi-Lee Ruiz trotting toward him, juggling her camera bag with her take-out coffee and muffin.

"Hi, Mark— *Hold the elevator!*"

"You're coming with me on an urgent assignment."

"But I've already got two this morning."

"This is a priority. We'll take my car."

Harding's phone rang and he answered.

"What the hell's wrong with you?" Magda said. "Don't you ever do that to me again, you got that!"

Harding updated her quickly as he walked with Jodi, who struggled to keep up. After Harding calmed Magda and she understood what had happened she said, "Fine, I'll alert Sebastian in New York."

"Wait! Just tell him we're working on a tip that may be solid, don't oversell in case this falls through."

"All right, but take a photographer with you and be careful."

"I got Jodi with me. We're on our way. I'll call you when I know what we have. Then we'll sort out telling Tanner and the task force."

Once they got into Harding's car, he updated Jodi as he entered the map's information into his GPS. The drive time was an hour. They went east on Wilshire making their way to the 101. They were bound for Camarillo, a quiet bedroom community north of L.A., once known for its walnut, orange and lemon groves. It had evolved from a small farming town into a suburb of cookie-cutter homes, fast-food outlets, strip malls and big box stores.

Traffic was good.

As the morning sun climbed in a blue sky, Harding and Jodi said little until they neared the city.

"Don't you think we should call the police or something first, Mark?"

"Why?"

"What if this is a setup or a trap?"

"It appears we're headed for an open area. We'll size things up as soon as we get close. We'll be careful and apply common sense, all right? Look, we can't risk that he may have tipped other papers, too."

Eventually they left the freeway.

The map ultimately directed them to University Drive, a narrow two-lane road that twisted and turned along the rural fringes of Camarillo. As they moved along stretches of open land and fields bordered with small forests and brush, they saw fewer and fewer cars.

Jodi grew quiet.

They both knew the local history and geography. They were getting closer to the site of a former state mental hospital. Even though it had been redeveloped into a university in the late 1990s, some people claimed the area was haunted.

Harding's attention sharpened on his GPS and he slowed the car.

"Almost there," he said, passing her his phone. "Here, check the map again."

Jodi first raised her camera and took a few pictures of the surroundings. She consulted the map and notes on Harding's cell phone, then the GPS, and she surveyed the area before suddenly pointing.

"There! There's the spot! There it is, over there!"

She took more photos.

Just as the map directed, they'd come to a small path that paralleled the road near a deer-crossing sign. Harding stopped next to the sign and shut off the engine.

They got out and took stock of the area.

Jodi continued taking pictures.

No other cars. No other hint of life other than the chirp of a bird as the motor ticked down.

Harding turned to her.

"Nobody here but us," he said. "Let's do this."

She nodded.

The map indicated the "gift" was about forty paces from the sign into the grass and brush. Harding took one direction, Jodi took another. They counted off paces while examining the ground, uncertain what they were looking for, anxious about what they might find.

Sweeping the patches of grass aside, Harding scoured the ground as he hit the forty-pace point. He came upon a sun-faded beer can. He used a pen through the drinking hole to lift and inspect it. Nothing at all was unusual. Keeping his head down Harding resumed searching the area, working his way toward Jodi who was doing the same until she shouted.

"Found it!"

Harding's head snapped to Jodi. Her face was clenched

behind her camera as she adjusted her lens and took photos.

Harding rushed to her, then lowered himself.

Propped against two small rocks was a naked female doll about twelve inches tall with flowing dark hair. Her hands were bound with string behind her back. Her mouth was bound with tape. A small noose was fashioned around her neck and was tied to a tag bearing the words *"Her name is Amber. She's mine now. DWK."*

44

Downey and Camarillo, California

Tanner stared at Polaroid head shots of children displaying gap-toothed smiles as he sat in the dentist's waiting room ruminating on the murders' common denominator. *Was it social, professional, physical, geographical or movements? All of the women had traveled in the months before their deaths. But travel seemed like a weak connection. Still, there was no way these were random kills.*

Anxious at being away this morning Tanner checked his phone once more. Tips were being followed but he had no messages of significance from across the county or the supporting police agencies. No leads from the LAPD or the FBI.

As if impulsively reaching for help, he thumbed through his menu and played one of the short video messages from his wife. His heart warmed upon seeing Becky's face, and he lowered the volume to a whisper as she greeted him with advice.

"Eventually after I'm gone, you'll have to start building a new life. You'll have to find someone new." Becky brushed her eyes. "I want you to find someone, Joe. Sam will need a new mom for her life ahead, graduation, her wedding, her first baby. I don't want you to be alone. Okay?"

A door clicked open and Sam rushed to him with a report.

"No cavities, Dad!"

The dental hygienist made notes on a clipboard.

"She's lucky, Mr. Tanner. In Sam's age group we usually find a couple."

"She likes brushing and flossing," he said.

"Keep up the good work, Sam," the hygienist said. "I'll see you again in a few months."

In the parking lot, Tanner turned Sam to him, bent down and gave her a hug and kiss.

"You know I love you, pal."

"I know, Dad."

"Now, we have to get you to school and get me to work." At that moment Tanner's phone rang and he answered.

"Joe, it's Mark Harding. He wrote to me again and directed me to something you should see."

"What is it?"

"A doll with a woman's name."

"One of the five?"

"No, a new name—Amber. Isn't there a missing person named Amber?"

"Hang on. Are you at your office?"

"No, I'm in Camarillo at the spot where he left the doll."

"You're at the freaking scene?" Mindful of Sam, Tanner turned and dropped his voice. "What's going on? Who else knows?"

"No one else but the ANPA knows."

"Damn it! Don't move! Don't touch anything! Give me your location."

"We're not going anywhere. Stand by, I'm sending you my copy of the killer's directions to where we are."

Once Tanner got Harding's map, he forwarded it to task force members and alerted his lieutenant. Then he called Camarillo P.D. and the Ventura County Sheriff's Office and requested them to protect the scene and "keep things off the air." He didn't want a news carnival waiting for him. Then he alerted Brad Knox, advising him to get the FBI to dispatch its Evidence Response Team up to Camarillo to process the material. Then he called Harvey Zurn.

"Meet me at my house, Harv. It'll be faster for us to drop Sam off at school then go straight to the scene."

The whole time Tanner was on the phone, Sam amused herself by hopping along the sidewalk cracks. She was happy to be with her dad.

A knot of Ventura County sheriff's vehicles and ribbons of yellow plastic tape marked the site along University Drive. As Tanner and Zurn arrived, Tanner spotted Harding leaning against his car, talking to a deputy. Tanner's jaw muscles throbbed when he interrupted them to pull Harding aside.

"What the hell are you doing, Mark? You should've called me before rushing out to play detective."

"I called you. That's why you're here, instead of reading about it. Don't try to accuse me of being irresponsible or uncooperative. He didn't write to you, he wrote to me. I'm doing my job."

"Your job? Take a look around."

Puzzled, Harding scanned the area as more police vehicles arrived.

"This is a dirt road. You drove all over it. You and your friend with the camera tramped all over it and in the process you destroyed our chance for tire and shoe impressions. You contaminated the scene. Is that your job?"

"I could've not called you and you'd be reading about it in the *L.A. Times* or watching it on CNN."

"And I would've charged you with interfering with an investigation."

Harding looked off, saying nothing. He knew Tanner was under a lot of pressure, he heard it in his tone. Tanner looked to the scene and let a few moments pass.

"Are we going to slam heads all day out here?" Harding asked. "Or are we going to carry on professionally with our work? The latter, I hope."

Tanner saw the FBI's ERT people arriving, ran a hand over his face, then held up a finger to Harding.

"Don't you move, Mark, understood?"

Tanner left him to consult with Knox as the FBI set up. For the next couple of hours the scene specialists conducted a meticulous analysis of the site and surroundings. They made sketches, took measurements, photographs and searched for impressions. Tanner and Knox studied photos the techs took of the doll and note as deputies canvassed the rural area. A chopper thudded above them taking aerial photographs while Ventura County K-9 units attempted to pick up any trail.

In Los Angeles, the LAPD had sent its crime scene team to the AllNews Press Agency bureau on Wilshire. By that time Harding had made several calls to Magda, who'd alerted Sebastian Strother, who'd called the news agency's lawyers.

Again, the ANPA cooperated.

From Camarillo, Harding directed L.A. investigators by phone to where he'd placed the original letter and envelope so they could process it for any prints or DNA.

It was only a matter of time before the local press would be tipped to all the activity, descend on the scene and weaken his exclusive. Unable to wait any longer, he approached Tanner and Knox.

"I'd like a few comments before I file my story."

"I've got nothing to say right now," Tanner said.

"Off the record, then?"

Neither investigator said anything, so Tanner proceeded.

"Do you suspect this is tied to any specific case, any homicides or missing persons?"

"It's too early to speculate about that."

"Were you able to secure any fingerprints or DNA?" Harding asked.

"We're still processing everything, and that's not for attribution," Tanner said.

"Come on, Joe."

"Let me ask you a question, Mark. Did you notice the postmark on the envelope?"

"There was no postmark."

"That's right, which indicates he may have walked up to your building and delivered his letter by hand himself, or had someone else do it. We're getting warrants for your building's security cameras."

"I'm quoting you."

"No, you're not. I'm telling you this so you get that you've cost us time."

"Quit blaming me, Joe." Harding turned to his phone and retrieved his photo of the note the killer had tied to the bound doll. "Look, what do you think he means with this line after the name, 'She's mine now'?"

"She's either dead, or she's going to be."

A few tense seconds passed before Tanner's name was called. His partner, Zurn, was at their car, holding up his cell phone and waving it. "I gotta go," Tanner told Harding. "You and I will talk later. But you'd better call me before you write a freaking word. You got that?"

"I'll call. Count on it. Jodi?" Harding shouted. "Let's go back to L.A.!"

Tanner shot Harding a simmering glance, then turned and walked to Zurn. They huddled at their car.

"I think we've got something here, Joe." Zurn held his hand over the phone. "Detective Ed Belinski with Alhambra P.D. wants to talk to you now."

Tanner took Zurn's phone.

45

Above the United States

The charter jet climbed out of Detroit and Robert Bowen ran through his calculations again. After factoring in weather, he figured they'd touch down in Van Nuys by ten o'clock local time tonight.

This Gulfstream was a fine aircraft. He liked how the autothrottle performed and how the flight management system made takeoffs easier. As the plane leveled off, last night's phone call with Claire echoed in his mind.

"Something horrible has happened. One of my patients is missing. There was blood. Robert, please come home, I need you."

He looked into the endless afternoon sky, then glanced at Tim, his copilot, who had taken over controls for this leg of the return trip.

It gave him time to think.

Things were happening in L.A. and it felt as though he'd been away for an eternity. When the charter was in Toronto the other day, his passengers, seven executives from a high-tech startup in Santa Monica, had secured a new Canadian deal for remote areas. That meant extending the tour by adding a last-minute final destination: Iqaluit, the tiny capital of Nunavut, one of Canada's three territories.

At this time of year, Iqaluit's temperature was about 30 to 35 degrees Fahrenheit and there was snow on the ground. The group bought additional warm clothing in Toronto before making the four-hour flight northeast.

Iqaluit was in Canada's north, on Baffin Island, located in the eastern Arctic, near Greenland. A former military outpost, the town now had a population of some seven thousand people.

Bowen found that the air there was sweeter, clearer and, save for the sound of a plane at the airport, the tinny whine of snowmobiles or the lonely yip of a tethered dog, the silence was overwhelming. During his short stay, he'd kept to himself and embraced the isolation even as he enjoyed being in control of what was evolving a continent away.

There, in that cold, remote corner of the planct, he was warmed by a feeling of unstoppable power.

He'd walked to the town's original cemetery on the shore of Frobisher Bay. He'd been fascinated by the tale a local in the hotel had told him. Because of the permafrost, the gravcs were not that deep and at times when the earth heaved, you could see coffins in the gaps.

Beautiful, he'd thought.

He took pictures of the pretty white wooden crosses before returning to the hotel, which was on a hill overlooking the town and bay. That evening, he ate alone in his room. Afterward, he drew up his chair to his window and watched the aurora borealis. The dazzling display of colors swirling across the heavens underscored his sense of majesty, as if he were seated on a throne at the top of the world while all of nature entertained him.

After he'd gone to bed and drifted to sleep, his phone rang. It was Claire, still distraught at discovering her patient was missing. Her anguish tore at him, but at the same time his skin tingled.

And so it has begun, he thought.

He'd told Claire he'd be home within twenty-four hours.

After he'd comforted her, he'd been too excited to sleep.

Yes, work was proceeding but I never expected it would unfold like this, with Claire making the find.

His breathing picked up. Fully awake, he'd sat at the desk. As he digested this new twist his sense of power intensified, hot waves of adrenaline rolled over him and he'd become aroused.

He needed to savor the spoils again.

Bowen had turned on his laptop and navigated his way to a short video of Amber Pratt: alive, confined in a wooden box.

His shadow had fallen over her as he'd recorded.

Like the doll, her hands and ankles were bound. She was naked but for the duct tape sealing her mouth. He remembered how she'd pleaded, begged for mercy, how her cries had enthralled him. Now her beautiful eyes were bulging with terror.

She was magnificent.

Bowen inhaled then let it out slowly.

And I am just getting started. Look at that fire in the arctic sky. The glory is mine.

The celestial images of the aurora borealis in his mind dissolved into the distant sea of shimmering light as Los Angeles floated on the horizon.

"You want to take us home from here, Bob?" Tim said.

"Sure. Thanks."

Amid muted transmissions with the tower, Robert took control of the jet and prepared for landing. His blood rushed and he welcomed the familiar, intimate sensation of absolute supremacy over the world below. He gazed at the infinite immensity of L.A.'s twinkling lights rolling beneath him.

Let the mortals on earth tremble. He was the Dark Wind.

He decided who would live and who would die.

46

Calgary, Alberta, Canada

Private investigator Milt Thorsen was working in the basement office of his northwest Calgary home, occupied with the case on his computer monitor.

His wife, Jean, watched over him from the framed photo he'd hung on the wall after she passed away two years ago. The kids were grown and long gone. He lived alone with Tippy, Jean's cat, which he'd intended to give away, but had never had the heart.

As he scrolled through files, Tippy hopped into his lap.

"Scram, I'm busy."

Thorsen nudged her away and resumed examining the life of Robert John Bowen, a subcontract job for Julie Glidden, an investigator from Los Angeles. The case had begun as a straight-up search to confirm the location of Bowen's ex-wife, Cynthia, to establish whether she'd remained romantically involved with him after he'd remarried. Should've been easy, but it presented complications, including a Canadian aspect.

That's why Julie had turned to Thorsen.

He'd been a Calgary cop for twenty-eight years. He'd worked in Homicide, Major Crimes and Intelligence before retiring to start his one-man P.I. agency. Thorsen's reputation as a detective was well-known, Julie told him when they first met in Washington, D.C. at an international investigators' conference.

He turned to the red flags Julie had noted in her search.

A verification of education showed nothing. *Where the heck did Bowen go to school?* Some databases showed different dates of birth for Bowen. Thorsen, like all investigators, knew that data entry errors were always possible but discrepancies indicated areas of concern.

A troubling picture was taking shape.

Robert Bowen's records all appeared to dead-end in the U.S. around 2010, as if he didn't exist prior to that date. How did he maintain his pilot's license? Thorsen wondered. The TSA in the U.S. was supposed to be tough on screening and security of the certification of airline pilots.

Did he fall through the cracks?

When Bowen married his wife, Claire, in Mexico, he supplied his divorce decree. According to his current spouse, it was supposedly from Montana. A check with Mexican officials was futile. They could not supply a copy for verification and claimed they were unable to locate it. *Did he actually supply one? Was it genuine? Or did he bribe a Mexican official?* Because a check with all counties and court records in Montana revealed no marriage or divorce for a Robert John Bowen to a woman named Cynthia.

An update in the file from Julie indicated that new

information had recently arisen when Bowen revealed that he and his first wife had lived in Canada and were married there.

Thorsen removed his glasses, rubbed his eyes and dug into his work. He paged through the handwritten list in his notebook, an old detective habit he'd kept.

Since Julie had contacted him on Bowen, he'd already initiated much of the same probing in Canada as she had done in the U.S.

He'd checked through a range of databases, criminal, civil, court and social. He'd made calls through his network of sources.

Thorsen's detective radar was giving him a vibe about Bowen.

His life on paper appears to start in 2010. So what was he up to before then? Sure, it's common for divorces to be dripping with acrimony. People want to start fresh and scrape the past from their lives. Amputate all links to their ex. But for Bowen and his professional certification, there are huge security issues. Maybe he cleared everything with the TSA, with all the government and industry security gatekeepers?

Thorsen shrugged, replaced his glasses and reviewed his queries.

Like Julie, he'd also initiated a second name check and had contacted his sources in all provinces and territories for legal name changes. He'd submitted Robert John Bowen for them to check. In Canada, legal name changes are published unless there's an overriding concern about personal safety.

Ontario, the largest province, had nothing on Bowen for Thorsen. Neither did Quebec, British Columbia,

Nova Scotia and Saskatchewan. Then a friend in Edmonton, Alberta's capital, sent an email.

Stand by, Milt, I think I have something for you.

"Hear that, Tip? We could have something?"

The cat yawned, still nursing hurt feelings at being rejected.

"Get over it," Thorsen said as a new email from Edmonton arrived.

He opened it to a page from the provincial government's *Alberta Gazette*, going to the official record for the department of Vital Statistics: Notice of Change of Personal Name for November 2009.

Thorsen scrolled through the page.

"There it is."

Elliott, Leon Richard to Bowen, Robert John

"Bingo," Thorsen said. "Gotcha. Now we have some real work to do with Mr. Leon Richard Elliott."

He reached for his phone.

47

San Marino, California

Stiff from a fitful sleep, Claire stepped into the shower. As the water streamed over her skin she prayed for Amber.

Please keep her safe.

Claire was grateful that Julie had spent the night. She was already up and had busied herself in the kitchen making coffee, pouring a cup when she saw Claire.

"Milk, no sugar, right?"

"Yes, I see you're still the early riser."

"Just like the old college days."

"Thanks. For everything."

"Did you get any sleep?"

"Not much."

Julie set a steaming cup down for Claire then said, "The *L.A. Times* had Amber's case on its website, and it was on this morning's local radio news."

"Did they find her?"

"No. They just said that she's missing under suspicious circumstances and they're looking for her."

"I'm praying she's alive," Claire said.

"We can't give up hope."

"This is my fault, all my fault."

Claire's despondency surged and Julie went to her.

"Stop blaming yourself."

"I should've done more."

"What more could you have done? You had the creep arrested when he attacked her in your parking lot."

"It's that letter. It was a violation for him to contact her and I should've reported it but I thought I'd helped her see that the best thing for her was not to go back to him." Claire stared at nothing and shook her head. "I should've told the police that Eric had contacted her."

"Amber told you about the letter under patient confidentiality. You said it was an ethical call."

"But I could've encouraged her to report his violation. If I'd done that, he might've been arrested and jailed and none of this would've happened."

"He would've gotten out in a heartbeat. He would've been mad as hell and he would've looked for her."

Claire massaged her temple as a new realization dawned on her.

"My God, the burglary! Maybe that was Eric searching for Amber's address. What if it was disguised to look like a break-in, just like that detective suspected?"

"Claire, stop this."

"When we checked my computer, it appeared someone had tried to access it. Why didn't I report that letter?"

Julie took hold of Claire's shoulders.

"This doesn't help," Julie said. "Stop punishing yourself. You did everything right. Speculating is futile. Until we know the facts, we don't know anything. We have to let the police do their job, okay?"

Julie was right, but it didn't assuage Claire's guilt.

"Think positive." Julie smiled. "You reached Robert last night. He's on his way back to L.A. Maybe you should stay home today." Julie glanced out the window to the backyard. "Work off your worry in your garden. It's beautiful. I love those new planter boxes." Julie looked out the window to the backyard but Claire didn't.

She looked at Julie. Something was up.

"What is it, Julie?"

"What do you mean?"

"I get the feeling there's something you're not telling me. Did you ever find out anything more about Robert and Cynthia's life in Canada?"

Julie searched Claire's eyes for a long moment as if looking for the right words.

"Nothing yet," Julie said. "We're still working on it with the subcontractor in Canada. We're still checking things out."

"What sorts of things?"

"You're dealing with a lot right now, Claire, and we're still in the early stages of confirming Robert's history in Canada."

"What sorts of things, Julie. Tell me."

"Records, that kind of stuff."

"What about the records?"

"There might be some confusion on whether we are looking at the right Robert Bowen. It's going to take a while and we need to confirm things."

Claire studied her friend's face for any deception before Julie said, "Listen, this thing happens all the time in my line of work. This is not the time for you to worry about this. Let me confirm things, okay?"

Claire let out a long slow breath. "Okay. I'm going into the office."

"But you had Alice cancel all of your appointments for today."

"There's work to do. The insurance isn't settled and I want to re-read Amber's file. I'd feel better going in and waiting for news there."

"All right." Julie glanced at her watch. "I've got a few things to take care of. We'll get together later today, get a pizza or something, and I'll wait here with you until Robert gets home tonight."

"Okay."

After Julie collected her things, Claire walked her to the door.

"Be sure to call me if you hear anything," Julie said.

As Claire watched Julie drive away she was left with the feeling that Julie was holding something back from her.

Driving through San Marino, Claire couldn't escape her fear and guilt. At times she felt as if she were outside her body, watching herself trapped in a nightmare.

Before she'd left home for her office, she'd called her doctor to reschedule today's appointment. It was this afternoon, but she couldn't go through with it. Not today.

Dr. LaRoy surprised her when he got on the line.

"Is everything all right, Claire? We talked about how important it is that we adhere to your cycle with the treatment."

She steadied herself and explained. With a better understanding of her situation, Dr. LaRoy gave her scheduling options and some advice.

"It's crucial we not disrupt the regime, flexibility is limited. You're not pregnant, but your signs are promising. Given what you're experiencing, it's important that you control your stress. I'll see you at our next appointment. My thoughts are with you and your patient. Call me anytime."

Amber's safety consumed Claire until her unease about her marriage flashed in the back of her mind.

Did Julie learn something more about Robert? Is that why she'd hesitated when I raised the question?

The scream of a siren from a passing ambulance pulled Claire back to her anguish over Amber. A few minutes later she was in her office where Alice flew to her, giving her a tearful hug.

"It's been on the news. Is there any word on Amber?"

"Nothing."

They sat in the empty reception area, staring at the aquarium.

"How are you doing?" Alice asked.

"Hanging in there."

"After you called, all I could do was pray for Amber to be safe."

"Me, too."

"It must've been so awful for you to be the one to—I mean after you told me how you went to her house and then called police. I'm just so sorry and so scared."

"I know. Me, too." Claire exhaled slowly and stood. "I came in to take care of some things."

"Well, I've got the invoices, the insurance file and fresh coffee."

Alice brought files and coffee into Claire's office, then left her alone to work. In the quiet, Claire battled her aching need for police to tell her that they'd located Amber and that she was safe.

Please find her.

Over the next few hours, she took care of office matters. Then she revisited her notes on Amber. It was painful, but other than her failure to report Eric's letter, Claire found nothing she would've or could've done differently.

Setting the file aside, she retrieved business cards and started making calls to every investigator she knew with knowledge on the case. San Marino police officer Deena Freeman, who'd first arrested Eric, had no new information. Neither did Larry Cobb, the sad-faced detective who was investigating the burglary. He directed Claire to the Alhambra detectives she'd already talked to, Norm Seeton and Ed Belinski. They were leading on Amber's disappearance.

She reached Belinski, who was guarded, clearly a professional trait.

"Nothing much I can tell you since we talked yesterday, Dr. Bowen," Belinski said. "We're working on a few leads with other detectives. We're hopeful for a break soon." Before hanging up, he made a request that suggested what she'd suspected: Belinski knew more than he could reveal. "Please be sure we have all of your contact information, in case we, *or other law enforcement,* need to interview you further."

After that, there was little more Claire could do at her office.

As she prepared to leave, Robert texted her. He was set to depart from Detroit and estimated that with good weather he'd be home that night.

His last text was a question.

Did they find your patient?

No. I'm praying for her.

When Claire returned home she'd received a text from Julie telling her that she was running late.

Will be there as soon as I can.

Claire's neck and shoulder muscles had turned to granite. She took a hot shower, then made herself a tomato, lettuce and cheese sandwich. She ate half while skipping through TV channels, searching for any reports on Amber.

It was after sunset when Julie arrived.

"I have some news," she said. "A friend of mine at the D.A.'s office said there are rumors flying in justice circles that investigators are comparing Amber's case with others."

"What cases? What about Amber? Did they find her?"

"I have nothing on that," Julie said.

"Well, why don't the detectives tell me? Why isn't this on the news?"

Julie shook her head.

"My friend didn't have any details. Claire, at this point everything is speculation. It's routine for them to compare a new case with old ones. Until they tell us, we really don't know what's going on."

Claire took a moment to absorb the news on the rumor, accepting how it fit with Detective Belinski being so tight-lipped while indicating that police would want to talk to her further.

"And nothing at all about Amber?"

Julie shook her head.

"I'm sorry."

As Claire blinked back tears, she took a long, deep breath.

"Stay positive and pray, right?" Claire said, then offered Julie some wine. As she uncorked a bottle of California red, she looked out to her garden and planter boxes, beautifully illuminated in the evening by the solar-powered path and deck lights.

The cork squeaked loudly.

"Tell me what more you know about Robert, Julie."

"We're still working on it."

"You've been saying that for a while. I know you're being protective, but I deserve to know where you're at with this. Especially with him coming home."

She set a glass of red down in front of Julie.

"Claire, you've got so much else to deal with right now."

"Tell me, Julie."

Julie swallowed some wine, then nodded.

"We searched records of every Canadian province and territory and found that Robert may have lived in Alberta, Canada."

"Alberta? Is that where Cynthia's living now? Is that where they got divorced?"

Julie didn't answer. Claire looked at her.

"Well?"

"That's about all we have, we're working on it," Julie said.

At that moment, headlights raked through the kitchen from the breezeway to the driveway.

"Robert's home," Claire said.

He entered carrying his bag, which he dropped to embrace Claire.

"I wish I could've gotten home sooner, but they added another flight," he said, nodding to Julie. "Hello, Julie." Then he asked Claire, "Anything?"

"Nothing," Claire said.

"Not a word?"

"Just rumors. They won't tell me anything," Claire said, turning to Julie who was collecting her bag. "Are you leaving, already?"

"I should be going."

"Don't leave on my account," Robert said.

"I should be going."

"I'll see you out," Claire said.

She walked with Julie outside to the driveway.

"That seemed sudden," Claire said. "What's going on?"

"Nothing." Julie got behind the wheel of her car and started it. "I'm sorry, Claire, we've both got a lot going on."

"Is there something more you wanted to tell me?"

Julie shook her head.

"We'll say a prayer for Amber," Julie said. "I'll let you know if I hear any news and you promise me you'll do the same."

Julie took a long look at Claire's house. Lights went on in different rooms as Robert moved through it.

"Promise me, Claire."

"I promise." Claire lowered herself and hugged Julie, thanking her again.

As Julie Glidden drove off through Claire's San Marino neighborhood she called a number on her cell phone.

"Thorsen," the man answered.

"Milt, Julie in California. Do you have anything more on Bowen for me?"

"A little—his real name is Leon Richard Elliott."

Julie's stomach tightened.

48

Alhambra and Downey, California

Tanner and Zurn left Camarillo where the death doll had been placed and drove to Alhambra for an emergency briefing with detectives there.

It started in the afternoon and lasted into the early evening.

Ed Belinski had led the meeting. He and his partner, Norm Seeton, were running the investigation into Amber Pratt's disappearance. While Tanner was hopeful about the break, he was careful to protect the integrity of his case when Belinski asked him for an update summary.

"Key fact evidence found at our scene in Camarillo is linked directly to Amber Pratt and our five cold cases," Tanner said.

"And what's the evidence?" Belinski asked.

"That's holdback, Ed."

Belinski snapped his gum.

"We're all trying to catch the same guy, Joe."

"You know how it goes, Ed."

"I know you're friendly with the press."

"We had a strategy and it worked. We got a killer to go public."

Belinski stared at Tanner for one cool moment.

"If that's how you want to play it," Belinski said. "Let's get to work."

Belinski said Amber's psychologist, Claire Bowen, had reported her missing after she'd failed to make an appointment or respond to calls. Alhambra police had not yet detected any activity on Amber's cell phone, bank, credit cards or personal email account.

"She's made no contact with relatives, friends or her employer," he said, adding that her car had not been moved. The residential alarm system had been defeated and there was a lot of blood in her bedroom. They were still processing the property.

"Looks like foul play and Eric Larch is a good place to start," Belinski said.

After reviewing the history of the case to date, the group agreed all the signs pointed to Larch. Belinski then summarized the canvass and tip reports. Finally, before wrapping up, he agreed to Tanner's request for Alhambra to join the task force.

It was nearly midnight when Tanner got home.

He'd stopped off at his office first to collect files.

As soon as he got to the kitchen, his cell phone started ringing with a call from his lieutenant.

"We're getting squeezed by the politicians, Joe. People are scared. How did it go with Alhambra, is Larch our guy?"

"He looks good for it."

"Get some sleep. The captain's talking about a news conference tomorrow to blast Larch's face and that of his missing wife."

Tanner got a box of cold pizza from the fridge and a

beer. Piling his files on top of the pizza box, he settled at his sofa to eat and read. The files were thick with court records, transcripts, complaint histories, statements and reports about Larch. In a short time, Tanner became very familiar with Larch's life.

Eric Fenlon Larch, aged thirty-six, was born in Daly City, south of San Francisco. His father, Chet, was a trucker who'd abandoned Eric's mother, Lana, an alcoholic heroin addict, and their sons. Eric's mother frequently beat Eric and his older brother before giving them up to be raised by Eric's aunt and uncle across the bay in Oakland.

Eric had wanted to be a police officer. But he had a drug problem and anger issues which he seemed to overcome with the help of his aunt's church group. He studied electronics in community college and worked at installing industrial and residential security systems, finding work in the L.A. area.

But his drug problem returned and he started drinking heavily.

Women Larch had known complained that he had a violent temper and had abused them. Several made 9-1-1 calls, a few pressed charges, which were usually withdrawn because he was skilled at talking the women out of pursuing them. Larch cleaned up, got counseling. Eventually he married Amber and moved to Long Beach. After he'd abused her, she sought a divorce, underwent therapy and started a new life.

But Larch couldn't let her go.

So here we are, Tanner thought, before turning to statements from Amber's psychologist, Claire Bowen. Again, he'd read how she'd pepper-sprayed Larch in the parking lot of her office when he'd attacked both women.

Tanner liked how Bowen had gone to war with this guy.

Bowen knew Amber's state of mind before she'd disappeared and she'd had recent dealings with Larch's rage.

We need to talk to her tomorrow.

Tanner finished the last of his beer and dragged himself to bed. As he passed Sam's empty room, he felt a sudden longing to hold her. It seemed like a lifetime ago they were at the dentist's office.

He reached down for one of her stuffed toys, a lion, and touched it to his cheek.

49

San Marino, California

The next morning, Claire's eyes flicked open from a troubled sleep to see Robert standing over her at the foot of their bed.

She struggled to focus on him in the diffused light, motionless in his sweatpants and a T-shirt.

"Robert? Is there news on Amber?"

"No, nothing, I'm sorry."

"What're you doing standing there like that? Is everything okay?"

"It's the time change, I couldn't sleep. How about you?"

"I had to take a pill." Claire sat up, ran her fingers through her hair. "I don't know how much more of this I can take."

Robert sat on the bed near her.

"When I was watching you, I kept thinking how beautiful you are when you're sleeping."

She looked at him.

"Please don't," she said. "This isn't the time. I need to get to the office."

"I'm sorry, listen, I have an idea. Before you go to the

office, let me take you for breakfast at the old diner, like we used to. It'll help take your mind off this for a bit."

She cupped her hands over her face. She was tired.

"I know this is a bad time, Claire," he continued. "But when I was away I got to thinking about everything, about being a father, selling the cabin, us, our future, everything. God, I miss you."

She took several moments to consider his offer.

"All right. Let me get ready."

Before they left their house, Claire went online to check for emails from detectives and news reports on Amber. In the living room she switched on the TV and surfed channels for any local reports. She flipped through Robert's newspapers in the kitchen.

She found nothing new.

The stories reported the same facts. Police were searching for Amber Pratt, who'd recently been assaulted by her estranged husband, a "person of interest," they were attempting to locate.

Yet despite her fears connected with Amber, she could not brush away her concern for her marriage, especially after Julie had learned more about Robert's life with Cynthia in Canada.

They took Robert's SUV to the diner.

Claire sat in the passenger seat, holding her cell phone as if it were a lifeline while Robert, in an effort to melt some of the tension, told her about his brief visit to Iqaluit.

"Seeing the aurora borealis in that eastern Arctic sky was stunning."

Claire didn't respond.

As if he recognized that she was preoccupied with her

worries and only half listening to him, Robert let a few blocks pass in silence before raising an issue.

"Do you have any idea why Julie was so cool to me last night?"

"Excuse me?" Claire turned from the window to him.

"Why was Julie so cold to me last night?"

"She's worried about Amber and everything."

Robert rubbed his chin.

"Have you asked her to help, her being a P.I. and all?"

"Yes, she's checking a few things out for me."

Claire's phone rang.

"Speak of the devil," Claire said. "Sorry, I'll answer it and be quick." She smiled to Robert.

"Hey, Julie."

"Any news?" Julie asked. Her voice was raised, indicating she was talking through her speakerphone in her car.

Claire glanced at Robert. Thankfully a loud semi was passing and his attention was drawn to it.

"No, nothing." Claire tried to keep her voice soft. "Are you hearing anything?"

"No. Look, Claire, I'm sorry things got weird with me last night." Julie's voice was coming through loud and clear, and she was talking fast. "The fact is we discovered more on Robert's life in Alberta and we're digging a little deeper to make sure we're on the right track. But I know you got a lot on your mind right now, so let me worry about it."

Claire grew anxious. Maybe Robert could overhear her? She shot him a sideways glance, found some relief. The car slowly passing them was throbbing with loud music, annoying Robert, who seemed occupied with checking traffic in the mirrors. Claire's attention shifted back to the call when Julie said her name again.

"Claire? Are you with him now?"

"That's right, yes."

"Okay. I don't want to talk about this on the phone." Julie's voice remained clear. "It's best we talk face-to-face when I know more. I'll call you maybe tonight or tomorrow."

"Great. Thanks, Julie."

Claire hung up and brushed aside her hair.

"Everything all right?" Robert asked.

"Yes, she's just worried, like me."

Robert looked straight ahead into traffic and adjusted his grip on the wheel. The palms of his hands had moistened. The vein along his neck began pulsating and his breathing quickened.

Every word of the conversation had leaked from Claire's phone.

He'd heard it all with crystal clarity.

50

San Marino, California

Less than five minutes after Julie's call, Claire and Robert were coming to the diner when Claire's phone rang again.

This time it was Alice.

"Hi, Claire, are you on your way into the office now?"

"I'll be there in about an hour or so, what is it?"

"A Detective Tanner and Detective Zurn from the L.A. County Sheriff's Department are here to talk to you."

"Did they find Amber?"

"No."

"Did they say what it's about? I wasn't expecting them."

"No, but they say you should come in as soon as possible."

Claire told Robert about the call, they skipped breakfast and he turned the SUV around.

"Detectives from L.A. County?" He repeated as he accelerated. "Maybe they've got a lead on Amber's husband or something."

Fifteen minutes later, they arrived at Claire's office.

Two men were waiting in reception. They stood as Alice introduced them to Claire and Robert. Zurn, the hard-looking one, wore a sports jacket over a polo shirt and khakis. Tanner had long ago unbuttoned his collar and loosened his tie, suggesting his morning had already been stressful.

Shaking Tanner's hand and meeting his eyes, Claire found a measure of sadness mixed with strong gentleness that she liked. Something about him felt reassuring.

"Can we talk to you about Amber?" Tanner asked, turning to Robert. "Sorry, but privately. I'm sure you understand, Mr. Bowen."

"Certainly. I'll be right out here if you need me for anything, Claire."

"I'll make more coffee," Alice said. "And you're clear for appointments, Claire."

When the door to Claire's office closed, Alice busied herself with the coffee, but her face telegraphed worry.

"I'm so glad you're back, Robert, to be here with her. It's a comfort." She patted his shoulder. "You're such a good husband."

He gave her a smile and flipped through an old copy of *Reader's Digest,* oblivious to the articles.

Wheels turned as he made plans.

Inside Claire's office, Tanner and Zurn opened valises containing files on Amber's case. Tanner led the interview.

"We want you to know that police across the state, the FBI and several other agencies are working full tilt to find Amber," he said.

"Thank you."

"Now, we've spoken to Detective Belinski with Alhambra, Detective Cobb and Officer Freeman with San

Marino P.D. We've reviewed your statements and all the reports. We just need a little more help."

"I'll do whatever you need me to do."

"We're aware that patient confidentiality comes into play, but much of Amber's case is a matter of public record, arising from Eric's assaults."

"Yes."

"Tell us about Amber's demeanor, her state of mind, in the time leading up to her disappearance."

"She was in torment." Claire paused. "In previous sessions she'd told me that she'd sensed a presence in her house."

"A presence?"

"Like someone was watching her, hiding in her house in Alhambra."

"Was this reported at the time?"

"No, she had no evidence of anyone breaking into her house. I thought it was a psychological manifestation of the stress of ending her marriage to Eric. Still, I advised her to take precautions, to get her security system checked and make sure her emergency escape plan was ready."

"In hindsight do you think it could've been real?"

"In hindsight? Yes." Claire took a breath. "We were careful. After Eric's attack I got Amber to move temporarily into a women's shelter. Amber was battling to escape an abusive relationship with a man who was determined to keep her, to maintain control over her."

"How so?" Zurn made notes.

Claire looked into her palms.

"After the parking lot assault, Amber revealed to me that Eric had written to her begging her to reconcile, to go back to him. It followed the typical cycle pattern of an abuser. After an explosive incident he makes acts of contrition and urgent pleas for forgiveness. The man's a textbook case."

"Was this contact violation reported?" Tanner asked.

"No. I take responsibility for that. It was made known to me in confidence by a patient. She said Eric was going to file the letter with the court. Still, I should have reported the violation. I thought I was successful in counseling her to continue her work to rebuild her life without him. I told her that she was in danger from Eric."

"Did she agree?" Tanner asked.

"Yes, that's why she allowed the Alhambra police to do a security check on her home after the burglary here."

Tanner consulted his notes and went back to several points about Amber's sessions before changing the subject.

"Did Amber ever discuss places or locations Eric favored? This may help in locating him."

Claire shook her head.

"I read your statement on the assault several times," Tanner said. "Based on your firsthand experience with him, what more can you tell me about Eric's behavior that day?"

"I remember how his face burned with hate for Amber and for me."

"Do you believe he's capable of harming other women?"

Claire paused at the line of questioning.

"I do," she said. "Why?"

Tanner shot Zurn a glance and hesitated before continuing.

"Claire, we've reason to believe that Amber's case

is linked to several older ones and that Eric Larch may have been involved."

Her eyes widened slightly as she stared at the detectives. Claire swallowed hard as they allowed her time to comprehend what they'd told her. Tanner pulled a sheet of paper from a folder, containing the names, ages and addresses of the five cold case victims.

"Are you familiar with the names of any of these women?"

Alarm filled Claire's face as she read the death list.

"No." She touched her fingers to the corners of her eyes. "Why?"

"From the period 2003 to 2007 each of the women were murdered in the greater L.A. area. Their homicides have never been solved. Evidence recently discovered in one of the cases linked them to one killer."

"Wait. This is the case in the news, the killer who wrote to the press, the Dark Wind Killer case?"

"Yes."

"Oh, no."

"New evidence has surfaced linking Amber's disappearance to the person responsible for these others."

"Do you think Eric Larch is the killer?"

"We want to find him and talk to him about Amber."

"My God, you must think Amber's dead."

"We don't have anything to confirm that. You were in her home and know there's evidence pointing to foul play, but until we find her, we remain hopeful she's alive."

"What about the burglary here? Do you think that's how Eric obtained Claire's home address?"

Zurn shook his head.

"Detective Cobb's report and the forensic analysis

suggest the attempt to gain access to your electronic files failed. No files were taken," Zurn said. "Our theory is Larch could've used his sources in home security to find his wife's address. Even though she was house-sitting, the name of the person to contact in case of an alarm would be on file for insurance purposes. Maybe Eric paid for the information?"

Claire said nothing as a new concern surfaced.

"Dorothy."

"Excuse me?" Tanner said.

"One of my patients, Dorothy in East Pasadena, recently told me that she'd felt as if— Wait." Claire typed rapidly into her keyboard to find her file. "Here, she told me that late at night she sensed that 'there's someone in my house—a man hiding in my house.' But I reported her concern because it happened after the burglary."

"Yes, East Pasadena. We've been watching the residence out of Temple Station. Claire, it might be best as a precaution to provide us addresses for your patients. We'll advise them to temporarily relocate if possible, or we can put patrols on their homes. We know there are confidentiality and ethical issues, but this is an unusual situation. Tell them it is a temporary precaution until we locate Eric Larch."

"Of course, I'll call them and explain."

"Good. We'll work with the appropriate P.D. where they live to ensure their safety. We also think that since Eric Larch threatened you, that you should consider postponing your sessions and relocating yourself."

Claire said nothing. Tanner continued.

"We'll assign units to your residence, just until we locate Larch."

"I understand."

"Things are going to get intense, Claire. There will be a news conference and press coverage today about Amber's link to the five other murders. Do you have some place you could go? It might be best if you left L.A. during this time."

Claire's thoughts blurred.

"Yes, there are places I could go." As she nodded, she used her fingertips to stop the tears rolling down her face. Tanner leaned forward and passed her a tissue from the box on her desk, something she usually did to comfort her patients.

"You have to find Amber and arrest Eric," she said.

"We'll find them."

Tanner stood and gave Claire his card with his office, cell and home numbers, then asked Claire for all of her contact information.

"Whatever you decide to do, or wherever you decide to go, you keep in touch with me, okay?" he said.

Claire regained her composure and nodded.

"I'll talk it over with my husband. He's still out front."

"Okay, we're done here."

As Claire and the detectives emerged from her office, Robert and Alice, seeing her reddened eyes and the crumpled tissue held to her lips, moved to comfort her.

"They think Amber's disappearance is connected to that case in the news, the Dark Wind Killer," Claire said.

"Dear Lord, no," Alice murmured.

"There will be a press conference later today," Tanner said.

"Robert's been following the case in the news. He lived in L.A. during those years," Claire said.

Tanner and Zurn looked at Robert, appraising him for the first time.

"You look familiar," Zurn said to him. "You're that guy, the pilot who rescued the family from a burning car on the freeway? It was all over the news. You're a hero."

"Anybody would've done the same."

Tanner looked at him and for a moment felt a sudden tug of unease in a far corner of his memory. Then his phone rang. Before reaching for it, he said, "Mr. Bowen, your wife will tell you our concerns. We'll be in touch."

51

San Marino, California

Claire was still reeling from what the detectives had told her.

She kept twisting the cap of her pen while waiting for Martha Berman to return her call.

Through the window she saw a marked San Marino patrol car roll into her lot to keep a vigil on her office, underscoring the gravity of her situation.

Twenty minutes had passed since the detectives left and Claire sent Robert home. She was alone at her desk, battling her fears while staring at her patient list on her computer monitor. She had to take control of her situation but first she needed some advice.

For one selfish instant, Claire glimpsed at a calendar note for her new appointment with Dr. LaRoy and was reminded of what he'd said about disrupting her regime and avoiding stress.

I can't think about any of that now. I just can't.

As she waited for Martha's call, Claire reread the news clippings Tanner had given her and contended with the horror that was unfolding. Not only was Eric an abusive husband, police suspected he was the Dark Wind Killer.

Five women murdered.

And he is still out there.

Images of the blood in Amber's home and Eric's enraged face rose in the back of Claire's mind. Her knuckles whitened as she tightened her grip on her pen.

Please let police find him. Please let Amber be safe.

Claire's desk phone rang. It was Alice transferring a call.

"Dr. Berman, I'll put her through."

The line clicked.

"Hello, Claire, it's Martha."

"Oh, thank goodness. I need to talk to you."

Claire explained events, telling Martha everything and seeking her advice.

"I'm so sorry, Claire, it's a terrible situation," Martha said. "But you shouldn't feel guilty. None of it is your fault. You'll get through this, but you need to take several steps."

Claire took a breath and let it out slowly, grateful for her older friend's steady, calm voice as she guided her.

"First, call your insurer. I know malpractice is a sad part of our business, but tell them what police are directing you to do. Get it on record."

Claire made notes.

"Then when you call your patients, advise them of what's taken place, how you're working with police to be sure everyone is safe during this time and that there's going to be an interruption of therapy. Be certain you explain that this stems from the violent and unpredictable behavior of the abusive spouse of *one* patient and that the spouse is suspected of other serious crimes."

"But it's going to have such a negative impact on their states of mind. They're already vulnerable."

"I agree and I'll come back to that, but Claire, the alternative is worse. Should you not tell them and they learn about it later, they'll never trust you again. That would cause irreparable damage. When you talk to them, you must continually assure them that you're following police direction and you agree that it is for their safety and well-being."

"But some are going to have problems. It could reopen abandonment issues at a time they may perceive as threatening," Claire said.

"Absolutely, and it could go beyond that, so you have to be prepared. Your patients have a great deal of emotional dependency invested in you. There's every chance they'll feel frightened, frustrated, resentful and angry when you interrupt therapy, especially under these circumstances. Some may see it as so damaging and countertherapeutic that they may quit you. This could have a negative impact on your practice."

"I understand, but I'm more concerned for my patients."

"I know you are, and you should be. So start having those conversations with them now. Set up emergency calls, a clinic referral for them. For your exceptional cases, arrange to have short telephone sessions with them."

"I'm thinking now that I won't be leaving my house, or leave town," Claire admitted.

"Why? Police advised you to leave, if only temporarily."

"But how can I leave when they're still searching for Amber and there's hope they'll find her. Martha, if by some miracle they find her alive then she's going to need me."

"I understand, Claire, but a jet can take you to just about any point in this country in four or five hours. You could be with your patient in a short time."

Claire's silence confirmed Martha's point.

"Dear, you're one of the biggest factors in all of this. You have to be safe and you have to keep your mind clear. Otherwise you can't help Amber and you can't help your patients. Believe me, they need you now more than ever."

Martha was right.

"Come stay with me in Las Vegas, I've got plenty of room you can work from here. Or go to your cabin, or go to Berkeley and catch up with old school friends. I think Michelle Baker and Val Cummings are practicing in the Bay Area."

"I'll think it over."

"Whatever you decide, let me know. I'm praying they find Amber safe."

"Thank you so much, Martha."

Claire ended the call, cupped her hands over her face and let out a long, tense breath before getting to work with calls to her patients.

It took a few hours, but Claire got messages into most of her patients. She was determined to speak with each of them and had just finished talking to one when Alice knocked softly on her office door.

"It's on the news now. Turn on your TV."

Claire switched on the small flat-screen set on her credenza. She flipped through channels stopping at one of the big L.A. stations. It was running a *Live Breaking News* flag along the bottom. The screen was split.

One half showed aerial footage of police vehicles and investigators at a roadside area, identified as Camarillo. There was a small map showing its proximity to L.A. The other half showed a podium with a police official identified with a graphic as Captain Martin Bronson of the L.A. County Sheriff's Homicide Bureau.

He was taking questions from reporters.

"As we stated, we believe evidence found at Camarillo is linked to the case of Amber Pratt who has been reported missing from a residence in Alhambra."

"And you say the evidence is connected to the Dark Wind Killer, already suspected in five murders?" a voice asked the captain.

"That's correct."

"Can you tell us how you made the link?"

"No, we're not prepared to share that information at this time. All we're prepared to release is that a person concerned about her whereabouts visited her residence and called police."

Amber's picture appeared on the screen.

"Sir, can you elaborate on her husband, Eric Larch? Is he the Dark Wind Killer?"

Eric's photo appeared on the screen above his name.

"At this stage he is a person of interest, and we'd like to talk to him. We're asking anyone who has any information on Amber Pratt's whereabouts, or that of her estranged husband, Eric Larch, to call us."

The words "Person of Interest in Dark Wind Killer Case. Wife Missing. Foul Play Involved" crawled along the screen under Eric's face. Suddenly, another line of information zipped along the screen.

Eric Larch recently breached bail conditions after

assaulting estranged wife, AllNews Press Agency, reporting.

"Captain Bronson, did the Dark Wind Killer leave police a message in Camarillo, or an item linked to Amber Pratt?"

The camera made a quick cut to other police officials lining the wall near the podium. Claire recognized Joe Tanner.

"I'm sorry," the captain said. "That's about all the information we can disclose at present. Thank you, we'll wrap this up."

The news conference ended and the station resumed regular broadcasting. Claire saw a cooking demonstration on an afternoon talk show before switching the set off.

She covered her face with her hands.

Her heart was racing.

"God, please find Amber. Please find her alive."

52

San Marino, California

Robert Bowen paced in his home office.

Claire and Julie know. Damn it, they know. It can destroy everything.

The onset of panic rolled through him in waves as the words that had spilled from Claire's cell phone earlier, now echoed in his brain.

"…The fact is we discovered more on Robert's life in Alberta and we're digging a little deeper…"

Discovered what? What the hell did Julie discover?

Stop and back it up, he told himself, making a quick assessment.

It all fit now.

It explains why Julie was so cold to me when I got home last night.

Fingers of pain clawed the inside of his skull.

What did that prying bitch find out, Robert?

I don't know. I've got to remain calm, got to think clearly.

It was only through dumb luck with the phone that he'd learned Julie was nosing around his life for Claire. How could he have been so stupid about her? She was a private investigator and Claire's best friend, yet he'd never considered her a factor. Never thought she'd intrude into his affairs.

He'd let his guard down.

He stopped at his window and gave a small wave, acknowledging the San Marino police car that had been parked in his driveway for the past thirty minutes. That Detective Tanner had told Claire he would move fast to get patrol units to her patients and put cars at her office and her home.

Bowen smirked.

The Blue Meanies.

The fools were his puppets. Police weren't even close to the truth. A police car parked in his very driveway and they didn't have a clue of the power they were dealing with.

They're looking for Eric Larch.

A person of interest.

Everything on that front had played out beautifully in his favor.

Bowen had carefully planned the burglary of Claire's office building for some time. He'd bought old sneakers, bulky sweatpants and an oversize navy hoodie at a flea market in Chicago. He'd strapped cushions to his body to alter his build and appearance in any security camera footage. He wore gloves, broke in and tore up the place.

He'd intended for the burglary to deflect suspicion to an abusive ex-spouse of any of Claire's patients once he launched Project Amber.

And it worked.

Enter Eric Larch.

Bowen never knew or met him, but Larch played the part of moron so well. The attack Larch had unleashed on Amber and Claire in the parking lot was an unexpected gift. As long as Tanner and his people were looking for the idiot, Bowen had no big police worries.

Julie Glidden.

Now *she* was his concern.

What had she found out about Alberta so far? What had she told Claire? He could not—would not—permit Julie to get in his way. He went to his laptop, clicked to his hidden folder and his video collection and images of women. Looking at one stunning image after another, his breathing picked up as adrenaline pumped through his veins, stirring him to arousal. He'd taken such loving care with the process and was on the cusp of a masterpiece. He would not allow that meddling bitch to get in his way.

What are we going to do about her, Robert?

I'm going to take action.

On the earlier call with Claire, Julie had said she wanted to talk again with Claire face-to-face, tonight or tomorrow.

This was his chance, his only chance. He had to roll the dice.

Bowen had an arsenal of resources he could use.

He navigated farther into his drives and reached for his cell phone. About a year ago, at a restaurant during a layover in Gander, Newfoundland, he had befriended a Russian pilot, Dmitri Morozov.

Dmitri claimed he had been a pilot for Russia's Federal Security Service and that he was also an expert in counterintelligence and high-tech surveillance. Bowen had met him again in New York, where Dmitri sold him black market state-of-the-art software. Bowen figured he might be able to use it at some point.

It was known as spyware and it gave him the ability to use his computer to record all emails, instant messages, track all downloaded files and every keystroke of any targeted computer he secretly installed it in. The user never knew the spyware was there. With the software, Bowen could also intercept, delete or respond to any emails by posing as the targeted user.

Bowen had similar software for cell phones. It involved advanced technology and allowed him to clone a target phone. He could secretly monitor, or hijack all activity on the target phone using his phone or laptop. He could intercept texts, voice messages and calls without the user knowing. Months ago, Bowen had installed the software in the phone and computers Claire used, but he'd never employed it.

He'd never really had reason to.

Until now.

He activated the technology on his devices. Now he could secretly monitor and intercept Claire's communication without her ever knowing.

As for Julie Glidden....

Give her to me, Robert.

Bowen entertained the thought.

Shivers of pleasure ran up and down his spine.

53

Pincher Creek, Alberta, Canada

Driving south from Calgary along the rolling foothills at the eastern base of the Rockies, the mountains looked close enough to touch.

It was a breathtaking part of the world, Milt Thorsen thought, guiding his Ford pickup from Highway 2 to a western stretch of the Crowsnest Highway before leaving it for the road to Pincher Creek.

He was hopeful his drive to see a retired cop, a friend of a friend, would fill in a lot of blanks on this case for Julie Glidden.

Learning that Leon Richard Elliott had changed his name to Robert John Bowen was a big break. Thorsen had moved on it fast since it surfaced yesterday. But unlike TV, the movies or detective novels, real investigations seldom went smoothly.

Glancing to the passenger seat, at his worn leather briefcase with the broken strap that held his laptop and hard-copy folders on Elliott/Bowen, Thorsen assessed what he'd confirmed.

In 2008 Elliott had married Cynthia Marie Cote in Calgary in a small ceremony. So far, he was unable to locate Cynthia. A search of driver's records across Canada had yielded nothing. A search through Alberta Court of Queen's Bench archives revealed no divorce records.

A check of death records with Alberta Vital Statistics showed nothing.

He'd been unable to locate any relatives for Cynthia or Leon, but was reaching out for help from an expert genealogist he often worked with.

In 2008, the couple purchased a house in the southeast Calgary suburb of Lake Sundance, which was sold in 2010. Using property and tax records, Thorsen did some door-knocking but he could not find anyone who recalled Leon and Cynthia. The house had been resold twice and the current owners knew nothing of the couple.

Other aspects of Leon Elliott's life remained a mystery.

Thorsen had not yet located a birth record. Nothing surfaced in Canadian military records, nothing in business and corporate affiliations, no lawsuits, judgments, liens or bankruptcies. A credit check showed no outstanding debt. And there was nothing in the way of criminal records.

As for employment, Thorsen was able to confirm that at the time Elliott was living in Calgary, he was a pilot with First Canadian Western, a national airline. Cynthia was a flight attendant with the same airline. But the company ceased operations in 2011. Getting further records or information on Elliott from a defunct airline was going to take more time.

Again, as with Bowen, a disturbing picture was forming.

There's not a lot of data. It's as if this guy was covering his tracks.

Fortunately, not long after Thorsen had put out a call for help to his network of confidential sources, he got a response. Ted Sedaynko, a former Mountie with Major Crimes South out of Calgary, called.

"Go see Keith Brophy, down in Pincher. He's a retired member, lives like a hermit. A bit of a character. Keith will only talk face-to-face, but he's got something for you on your guy. I'll call him and set it up for you."

Now this is intriguing, Milt thought. *Why would the Royal Canadian Mounted Police be familiar with Leon Richard Elliott?*

Thorsen set out on the two-and-a-half-hour drive over two hours ago.

He searched the foothills flowing by his window and consulted his GPS as he rolled up to a dead and twisted tree, the landmark for Brophy's property just northwest of Pincher Creek.

Brophy had a log home on three acres tucked in a rugged foothills valley that had a small waterfall. A forest nearby ascended the mountains. A man, who must be Brophy, was out front chopping wood when he greeted Thorsen.

He had thick white hair and a barrel chest that stretched his T-shirt. He patted his whiskered face and moist brow with a towel, then invited Thorsen inside.

"Don't like to waste time, seeing how you drove all this way," Brophy said. "Ted Sedaynko told me to give you a hand on this business with Leon Elliott. I got everything set up there. Coffee?"

He pointed to the kitchen table where he had some files and a shoe box filled with worn notebooks, which made Thorsen smile. *Old cops,* he thought, *we're all the same.* Brophy had been with the RCMP posted in British Columbia. He was a major crimes investigator.

"Sure. Thanks, Keith. Black is fine."

After pouring two cups, Brophy joined Thorsen at the table.

"So Leon Elliott changed his name and is now living in California?" Brophy said.

"Yes and his wife's friend, the P.I. in Los Angeles, has asked for some background on him."

"I see. Well, I'm happy to help."

Brophy slid on his bifocals, wet his forefinger and began slowly flipping through the pages of a notebook.

"I interviewed Leon Elliott a few times in 2010. I'll say this—the guy's bad news. But I had nothing to prove it. Nothing. I'm going to tell you what the official report says happened. Then I'm going to tell you, confidentially, cop to cop, what I believe really happened with Leon Elliott and his wife, Cynthia."

Brophy lifted his ice-blue eyes over his bifocals to meet Thorsen's.

"It was my case, Milt, and it haunts me."

54

San Marino, California

"Help me! God, please help me!" Amber's screaming...then...Claire's father is yelling, "I'm gonna kill all of you fuckers for dragging me down!" "No, Daddy!" Claire's baby brother, Luke, is crying. Claire's mother is shouting for her to "Get out of the house! Go next door! Call the police!"

Claire woke, her chest heaving.

Robert sat up with her.

"Are you all right?"

She covered her face with shaking hands.

"A nightmare, I'll be okay."

It was 7:30 a.m.

Claire had taken a pill to help her sleep and had slept in.

She got up and went to the kitchen and started brewing coffee. She was still rattled and consumed with worry for Amber. Yesterday's news conference, and suspicions that Eric was the monster who'd already murdered five women, was overwhelming. Claire was thankful police didn't reveal that Amber was a patient, allowing her to privately prepare the others for this whirlwind of horror.

Please find Amber. Please.

Claire checked her landline home phone for any updates from Tanner or Belinski.

There were none.

She checked her cell phone, but it took longer than usual. *What's wrong with this thing? It started acting up last night.* Finally, it cooperated. She had messages from Alice related to office matters, but Claire had received nothing new from Tanner or Belinski.

Claire logged on to her laptop for emails and was frustrated again. It froze several times before finally allowing her access to her account.

Again, nothing.

Very quickly she searched online news sites, nearly all were reports on Amber and Eric, stemming from the press conference. No new developments had surfaced. She switched on her TV for local news reports then checked the newspapers.

Nothing.

When the coffee was ready, she prepared a mug, taking it outside to the patrol car in her driveway. She offered the fresh coffee to the officer who'd drawn the early shift. Williams, his name tag said.

"Thank you, ma'am."

His police radio crackled with muted dispatches.

"Is there any news on Amber or Eric since yesterday?"

"No, ma'am, I'm afraid there's nothing to report from overnight. You've got to figure the task force will advise you if anything breaks."

Claire nodded her thanks, squinting in the morning sun.

"I'll be taking Detective Tanner's advice and leaving

L.A. soon. I appreciate having you here but police won't need to watch over me much longer."

"Let us know when you plan to depart. Don't forget to give the task force your new contact info. Thanks again for the coffee."

When Claire returned to the house, Robert had showered and was standing at the window, staring at the patrol car.

"Did the cop say if they found Amber or Eric?"

"No, there's nothing new."

Claire had work to do.

After a breakfast of fruit and whole-wheat toast, she showered, got dressed, went to her home office and got busy. There were more calls to make. She hadn't reached all of her patients yesterday, and was determined to talk with each one before she left.

Claire had already taken most of the steps Martha had urged her to take. She'd advised her malpractice insurance provider of the situation and she'd arranged referrals. She'd taken all the right precautions.

Claire decided she would leave L.A. and stay with Martha in Las Vegas for a few days. She would put in short telephone sessions with her most troubled patients from there. If things went right, they would all get through this. She wanted to drive to Nevada, to be in control. She would risk a few extra hours on the road for not having to face airport delays and cancelations.

Besides, if they find Amber, I could still fly back to L.A. God, please let them find her, safe and alive.

In between calls to patients, she double-checked her calendar for her next appointment for treatment with Dr. LaRoy.

It was in five days.

She could be back by then, but did she want to continue? Did it matter at this point? The other day amid the maelstrom of Amber's disappearance, Robert had indicated that he'd reevaluated things about their future, about being a father, even selling the cabin.

But his change of heart did not suddenly erase her unease about him.

It left her torn.

At the same time Julie said she'd found information about Robert's life with Cynthia in Alberta. Maybe it would lead to answers to help Claire make the right decision.

Julie had promised to tell her more, but so far Claire hadn't heard a word.

What's up with Julie?

Claire texted her and waited for a response.

When none came, she attempted to start packing as a distraction. She wanted Robert, the technical genius, to check her slow laptop and phone. Walking through the house, she was unable to find him until she heard the buzz of his saw and went to the garage.

To her surprise he was building another planter box.

"How many of those are you going to make?" she asked. "Didn't you already take some up to the cabin?"

He lifted his safety goggles and shrugged.

"I don't know. I like making them, gives me peace of mind at a time like this. I can always give them to the neighbors."

"Have you got a minute? I need you to help me with something."

"Sure."

"I need you to look at my phone and laptop. They keep freezing up."

"Now?"

He set down his power saw.

"As soon as you have time. I'm going to do what the detective suggested. After I finish postponing all therapy sessions at my office, I'm going to visit Martha Berman in Las Vegas for a few days, or until they arrest Eric and find Amber."

Robert thought for a moment.

"Are you flying? I'll go with you. Maybe we could see a show and take your mind off things a bit."

"No, I don't want to take my mind off things. I'm going to drive. I want the time alone to think. I'll stay with Martha at her house."

Robert let a few seconds pass.

"Forgive me, Claire, but I was hoping we could find a minute or two to talk about us, you know, about everything."

"I'd like that, but this is a bad time. How about when I get back and we know how things are going to go?"

"Sure, if that's what you want."

"I think that's the best way for now."

"When are you leaving?"

"Might not be for a little while yet, I still haven't reached everybody."

He unplugged his power saw and dragged a forearm across his brow.

"Okay, let me take care of your computer and phonc for you."

55

Los Angeles, California

Later that day, LAPD Officer Will Tollson walked out of a little taco place on South Alvarado carrying two large take-out coffees to the parking lot.

His partner, Arnie Veck, had found a patch of shade big enough to swallow their new Chevy Caprice black-and-white.

Tollson passed him his coffee.

"Thanks." Veck ceased scrutinizing the patrol car terminal to take the cup. Then he readjusted his seat behind the wheel. "You know, I prefer the Crown Vics."

"Old dogs like you don't like change," Veck said, swiveling the terminal.

Veck studied the street as dispatches crackled over the radio.

"I'm thinking of dropping in on Bill Cruger's retirement party tonight. Want to come meet some embittered old bulls?"

"Sure, all part of staff development." Tollson tapped the monitor. "Look at this. We got to watch out for a gang funeral. Cruger's retirement, gang funeral—the circle of life turns the right way for once."

"Let's head that way, fly our colors out of respect."

Veck slid the transmission into Drive and they started patrolling. They'd turned down a local four-lane boulevard and were eastbound about a mile from the Staples Center. They were rolling by low-rise office buildings and fast-food outlets when they approached the Palms of Paradise Motor Inn, a two-story hellhole. Veck hit the turn signal.

"Let's sweep the lot for BOLOs first," he said.

"Roger that." Tollson took a hit of coffee, then cued up the monitor for his notes from the rotator, looking for information on wanted suspects.

Veck slowed the car to a crawl through the lot, which by Tollson's estimate, had some two dozen vehicles.

They had alerts for a 2009, possibly a 2010, blue Dodge Challenger with left rear taillight damage sought in the shooting of two gang members on Eighteenth Street's Westside. They were also looking for a lime-green lowrider Civic with the last character a 9 in the tag. The Civic was wanted by L.A. County for an armed robbery.

"Hello." Veck swept by a white 2012 Jeep Patriot, without stopping, reciting the seven-character California plate to Tollson for submission. "I think there's a BOLO for a white Jeep Patriot." Veck rolled out of the lot so that anyone watching them would assume they were done.

The terminal gave a soft ping.

"Bingo," Tollson said. "That tag comes up with a big-time want by Alhambra P.D. The registered owner is Eric Larch, of Long Beach, wanted for breaching a protective order, now sought in the disappearance of his estranged wife, Amber Pratt. Christ, this is real bad. It just goes on. Hell, it looks like he's a 187 suspect. He's already had one assault on her. According to his bail terms, he's not to set foot in the Southland."

Both officers looked at Eric Larch's recent arrest photo.

"Okay, call it in," Veck, said. "We'll swing back and block him. Odds are he dumped his SUV. When backup arrives, we'll shake the building."

Veck and Tollson T-boned Larch's Patriot. A quick visual of the interior indicated no one was inside. Within minutes, two additional units arrived. The officers got out and used earpieces to mute their radios as two took the back and one each took the side of the motel.

Tollson and Veck entered the small office.

It was cramped with plants and wired carousel trees filled with tourist brochures about L.A., Hollywood and the sights. The clerk, a soft-spoken slim man in his forties, cooperated fully, checking his registration records and tapping his finger in his record for Room 134.

"That is the one with the white Jeep," the clerk said. "It's on the ground floor, near the pool breezeway. Here it is on the map."

"No back entrance? No adjoining room entrance?" Veck asked.

"None, sir, only one door."

"Are there people, guests, in the adjoining rooms or above?"

The clerk studied his records.

"None. They are vacant."

Veck turned and whispered into his radio before he and Tollson headed to Room 134. Two more officers joined them. The pool was empty. The courtyard showed no signs of life and the upper level balcony appeared quiet. Paint blistered on the door, which rattled when

Tollson banged on it. The other officers kept to the side, each had a hand on the grip of their holstered sidearm.

Nothing.

Tollson banged again, harder.

Movement on the inside.

"Los Angeles Police, step outside with your hands on your head!"

Locks clicked, the chain jangled, the handle turned and Eric Larch opened the door. He stood there bewildered, wearing only boxer shorts.

Tollson, Veck and the others charged in, put Eric down on his stomach and began placing his wrists in handcuffs behind his back.

"Hey! What the hell is this?"

"You're under arrest." Tollson snapped the first cuff.

"What for— Fuck, hey that hurts!"

"Violation of the protection order."

"What? No way, I'm keeping my distance. I'm in L.A., not Alhambra."

The other cuff snapped.

"You're not supposed to be here at all, asshole," Veck said. "Let's go."

The other supporting officers checked the bathroom. It was clear. Veck told them to sit on the room.

"The techs are going to want to process this and his SUV."

As they escorted Eric to their patrol car, Veck read Larch his rights.

"Want to tell us where Amber is?"

Larch remained silent.

As Veck and Tollson approached their car in the rear parking lot, the two officers posted there had taken serious interest in the back of Larch's Patriot.

"Hey, Arnie, come over here and take a look," one of them said.

He pointed to an area on the rear gate and some rusty-red smears.

"Does that look like blood to you?"

56

Commerce and Alhambra, California

Joe Tanner studied the files on his desk.

Since yesterday a puzzling ping of recognition had been sounding in his brain but he didn't know why. He couldn't put his finger on it. He'd been searching reports, exhibits, handwritten notes, photos, records and statements from the five cold cases and the new one for Amber Pratt.

For much of the morning the task force had been following tips from the news conference. But Tanner was dogged by a persistent niggling in the back of his mind since meeting Robert Bowen.

The reason eluded him.

"Why is Bowen familiar to me? The answer's got to be in here."

"I told you," Zurn said, setting down a clipping from the *Los Angeles Times*. "Look at the headlines. Robert Bowen is the hero pilot who rescued a mother and her baby from their burning car."

"I don't think that's it."

"That's it, Joe. You're overthinking this. Now get

moving on some of these new tips. We may find a lead there."

Tanner couldn't shift his focus. He continued scanning the documents, until he heard his name shouted by a detective across the office.

"Hey, Joe, call coming for you!"

Tanner grabbed his line.

"Joe, this is Belinski in Alhambra. The LAPD just picked up Eric Larch. We're setting up to let you talk to him."

"You find anything about the girl?"

"Nothing. How soon can you get here?"

"On our way." Tanner hung up and pulled on his jacket. "Let's go Harvey, Alhambra's got our suspect."

Some twenty-five minutes later Tanner and Zurn were in Alhambra police headquarters standing on the dark side of the one-way glass looking into the Alhambra Police Department's interview room. It had dull white walls, an acoustic-tiled ceiling, fluorescent lighting, a plain table with two empty hard-back chairs on one side.

Eric Larch was alone in a chair at the table, facing the one-way glass with his arms folded over his chest—the embodiment of anger.

Is this the Dark Wind Killer?

Since his arrest by the LAPD, he'd been transferred to Alhambra where he'd been jailed in a holding cell while awaiting a court appearance for violation of his bail and the protection order.

"What do you think, Joe?" Ed Belinski stood next to him and Zurn.

Without taking his attention from Larch, Tanner tapped his file folders against his leg. He had studied Larch's history and was concerned with several aspects.

Throughout his life Larch was obsessed with true-crime shows and had aspirations of being more than what he was, "being famous for something," "being a somebody with power," according to psych reports filed with the court after he'd assaulted Amber.

He was an expert at bypassing security and surveillance systems.

He'd lived in cities tied to two of the five murdered women at the time they were killed.

All of these points raised red flags for Tanner.

"So what do you think?" Belinski repeated, eager to help the task force. "He looks pretty good for Amber Pratt and your cold cases."

"That's what we're here to find out."

Tanner and Zurn entered the interview room. Larch's head snapped up.

"Eric, I'm Detective Joe Tanner, this is my partner, Harvey Zurn. We're with L.A. County and we'd like to talk with you."

Chairs scraped as they seated themselves.

Tanner pulled a photocopied document from the file and slid it to Larch.

"Before we can help you, we need to confirm that you've been read your rights and that this is your signature confirming that you waived your right to a lawyer."

Larch glanced at it.

"Yeah, my lawyer's useless. I got nothing to do with all this bullshit on the news about Amber missing. Christ! She told me on the phone that she wanted to talk about getting back together, so I came down here to see her, to work things out. I told Belinski I wish to hell I knew where she was!"

"Don't lie to us, Eric. You know what this is about.

You violated the order and your bail conditions. Your brother stands to lose the money he put up for you."

"He knows I'll pay him back."

"Where's Amber?"

Larch tightened his arms over his chest. His right leg started bouncing.

"Eric." Tanner exhaled. "You've been down here for two days. What were you doing? You couldn't miss the news reports of Amber's disappearance. Where is she?"

"I don't know." Eric shook his head. "That's what I want you to tell me."

"What were your activities here for the last two days?" Tanner asked.

"When she called me and said she wanted to talk, I came down here."

"We got that, asshole," Zurn said. "What were you doing in L.A. for two days?"

"She wasn't home when I rang the bell. I couldn't find her. Then I saw on the news that she was missing and I freaked out. I was already messed up, you know, trying to fix things with her. I didn't know what to think."

"So what did you do?" Tanner said.

"All of a sudden I got real scared. I thought maybe this was some sort of elaborate trap to nail me, put me back in jail, you know, something cooked up with her shrink and that bitch cop that arrested me. So I pretty much kept a low profile."

"Were you not concerned for your wife, seeing how she vanished?" Tanner said.

"Yes, absolutely. But I was screwed up, I couldn't think straight. We were going through what we're going through, then she goes missing. I was freaking right out, and between driving around looking for Amber by her house, her job, her shrink's office and our old place in Long Beach, I stayed in my motel room and got drunk."

Zurn's jaw muscles began pulsating as he eyeballed Larch.

"You're a three-coil piece of shit. You know that, don't you?" Zurn said.

"The court ordered you to stay away from Amber," Tanner said. "Why did you violate the order?"

"I'm still her husband. She's confused by lawyers, by judges, by her shrink. All this crap. I'm doing my part. I'm taking counseling."

"It's not working out so well. Is it, all-star?" Zurn's gaze burned into Larch. "Seeing how you attacked Amber and her shrink on the street. You disgust me."

Larch glared at Zurn. "This good cop, bad cop?"

"Why did you violate the order, Eric?" Tanner asked.

"Amber told me she wants to reconcile. She called me and I drove down here to talk to her. Where is she?"

Tanner opened a folder and showed Larch a colored photograph of a reddish smear on the tailgate of Larch's Jeep. "You know what that is?"

Larch studied the photo.

"That's blood, my blood."

Larch held up his right fist, displaying scraped knuckles.

"I banged up my hand fixing a loose battery cable. What's going on?"

"Not long ago there was a burglary at your wife's therapist's office in San Marino. Someone defeated the security system and attempted to look through confidential files. You're an expert at security systems, aren't you? And you're familiar with that office. You were arrested there."

"What the hell is this?"

"Tell us where Amber is, Eric. Cooperate so we can help you."

Larch said nothing.

"Eric, we know you wrote to her, we know you called her and left a threatening message on her machine the night she was last seen. We know you drove to Alhambra. Your credit card was used to buy gas there. We found blood in her residence and blood on your Jeep."

Larch said nothing.

For the next thirty minutes Tanner hammered Larch with the same questions before he changed the subject and placed a photo of a pretty smiling woman before him.

"Ever meet Esther Fatima Lopez, Eric?"

He looked at her face and shook his head.

"Her body was found in Topanga in 2004, the same year you lived there."

Tanner let the minutes pass by before he set another picture of another woman before Larch.

"You also lived in Temple City, in 2007—" Tanner tapped the photo "—that's the same year Bonnie Bradford lived there. Her home had a security system that was expertly disarmed."

"What's this got to do with me?" Larch asked.

"Both of these women were murdered by the same killer."

"Why are you telling me this? You think I killed somebody? You're fucking crazy."

"You have a serious interest in true-crime cases—legendary murder cases like Jack the Ripper, Son of Sam, the Zodiac Killer, Green River, Ted Bundy, that sort of thing?"

"So do millions of other people, so what?"

"According to a psychiatric assessment filed with the court after you smashed your fist into Amber's face a few times, didn't you say you fantasized about being famous, about having power over people, especially 'bitches who didn't know their place'? Isn't that right, Eric?" Tanner tapped the files.

Larch blinked like a man who didn't trust the ground under his feet as Tanner placed photocopies of newspaper articles about the Dark Wind Killer in front of him.

"What's this? What do you guys want?"

"We want you to tell us where Amber is, Eric," Tanner said.

"I told you, I don't know."

"Maybe you argued with her?" Zurn said. "Slapped the bitch around, to help her understand that she belonged to you?"

"You're very possessive of her," Tanner said. "In one of her complaints she said you told her that you 'owned her.' Are you familiar with the phrase, 'she's mine now'?"

Larch shook his head.

"You were trying to pound sense into her, weren't you?" Zurn said.

"But she refused to listen to reason," Tanner said. "Maybe things got out of hand? Maybe you went a little too far because you loved her a little too much. You didn't mean to hurt her. You didn't mean for this to happen. Things got out of control. Maybe she came at you?"

"Did she come at you?" Zurn asked.

Larch shook his head.

Tanner stood and leaned into Larch's space.

"Just like with the others, right, Eric? You tried to make them understand but things went too far. It's something inside you that you can't control, a pressure, a force or sickness that just takes over and makes you do these things. You're a slave to it, a victim, too, but part of you likes it, likes the power. Then you feel bad, you didn't mean for all this to happen."

"I don't know what you're talking about."

"Yes, you do," Tanner said. "Eric, you don't have to live the lie any longer, you don't have to carry it around alone. Tell us about it. Unburden yourself. Let us get you the help you need."

Larch swallowed.

"We know you had your truck serviced in Sacramento a few days ago. We checked the odometer and did the calculations. You've done a lot of driving since you returned to L.A. Have you been up to Camarillo, Eric?"

"No, I never went there."

Tanner didn't answer. He sat down, letting silence mix with the tension, waiting before proceeding.

"You know, at this moment," Tanner said, "we're executing warrants on your Jeep, on your motel room, on your apartment in Long Beach, your brother's home in Sacramento and his office."

Larch looked at him.

"That's right. Sooner or later we'll get to the truth."

"I got nothing to hide."

"We're going to find out, but it would be better if you cooperated now."

"There's nothing I can do."

Tanner slid a pad and pen to Larch then went to a file for a page with printed text.

"Would you copy these sentences, print them in block letters for us?"

Larch's face whitened as he stared at the passage of text.

> THANK YOU FOR THE RECENT INTEREST IN MY WORK. IT HAS BEEN A LONG TIME AND I WAS BEGINNING TO THINK THAT THE BRILLIANT MINDS OF L.A. LAW ENFORCEMENT WOULD NEVER APPRECIATE THE MEANING OF THE BEAUTFUL GIFT I'D LEFT THEM.

"What's this? I don't know if I should do this," Larch said.

"Thought you said you got nothing to hide. Was that a lie?" Zurn asked.

"No."

"Then do it."

Larch picked up the pen, turned it over several times, then carefully started printing the sentences in block letters.

57

Commerce, California

"Pay attention to this guy." Detective Terry Metcalf, with the task force, pointed to a figure in surveillance camera footage on the big flat screen in the boardroom.

The heavyset subject was wearing a large navy hoodie, bulky gray sweatpants and sneakers. The subject approached 5900 Wilshire and deposited an envelope in the mail slot. An enlargement showed details on the envelope matching the one that the reporter had received.

"This person delivered the death-doll letter to the L.A. bureau of the AllNews Press Agency wire service. Note the clothing, the body shape and gait. Now watch."

Tanner and Zurn, along with other task force members, studied the footage. The investigation was moving fast. They'd found upon their return to the homicide bureau in Commerce from interviewing Eric Larch, that some of the results from leads, search warrants and analysis of evidence had been completed.

Metcalf clicked his remote control and new footage appeared, showing a heavyset person in a large navy hoodie, gray sweatpants and sneakers.

"This footage was taken from cameras at a gas station near Claire Bowen's medical building at Huntington Drive and Garfield Avenue in San Marino. Our subject is walking in one direction down the street in front of the gas station and less than thirty minutes later he's walking by in the opposite direction. This was recorded within the time frame of the burglary. Note the clothing is identical to the Wilshire images, leading us to conclude that it's the same person," Metcalf said. "But after executing warrants on all locations tied to Eric Larch, we found none of the clothing items."

"He coulda tossed them," a detective said. "Also our guy here also coulda bulked up for the cameras."

"That's right, so while it's the same person in the footage, we are inconclusive on whether it's Larch."

Tanner flipped through his notes.

"The time on the gas station footage could rule out Larch. I have him in Sacramento for that date and that time frame, but we need to confirm that. Our information's been wrong before."

"That doesn't rule him out for Amber," Metcalf said.

"It doesn't rule him out for anything. It means that we need to triple-check everything. We have a lot of other areas we're looking at. Thanks, Terry."

Returning to his desk, Tanner stopped to drink from a water fountain. The political heat to advance the investigation was intensifying from politicians downtown and in the Capitol. There was pressure from the department brass to issue a press release on Eric Larch's arrest before the LAPD did it for them.

Tanner resumed working at his desk for less than five minutes when his cell phone rang.

"Tanner?"

"Mark Harding. Got a minute?"

"Not really. What's up?"

"I'm hearing from some police sources that you've made an arrest."

"Is that so?"

"I'm hearing you arrested the Dark Wind Killer."

"I can't discuss anything."

"You're not denying it."

"I'm not saying anything."

"We have an agreement and I've kept up my end."

"Listen, we've got a lot on the go right now. Keep in touch."

After the call, Tanner exhaled, knowing they were running out of time. Larch was charged with his bail violation, but unless they had a good case to show he was behind Amber's disappearance they wouldn't be able to hold him long, and they wouldn't be able to keep his arrest under wraps much longer.

We've got a ton of suspicion, but no hard evidence, Tanner thought as he resumed work, going back to a key piece of holdback evidence. A report had come in from the lab that morning confirming that Amber Pratt's bloodied fingerprint was on the tag affixed to the death doll the killer had placed in Camarillo.

Every initial indication pointed to Eric Larch as the suspect in Amber's disappearance and the murders of five other women. There were so many factors that pointed to him. He'd lived in L.A. at the time of the murders. He was obsessed with infamous killers. He had a history of violence toward women. He fantasized about fame, power and control.

So much about him fit.

But it didn't fit well, Tanner told himself.

"Joe, the blood analysis from Eric Larch's vehicle just came in."

Detective Metcalf passed him the report. It showed the blood on the rear and in the interior of Larch's Jeep was A positive. Larch was A positive. Amber Pratt, from the medical report filed with the court in the assault, was O positive.

It was not Amber's blood in Larch's vehicle, but it was her blood with the death doll the killer left in Camarillo.

"All right, thanks." Zurn had finished a call. "That was the FBI. They said that a preliminary analysis of Larch's handwriting sample, or printing in this case, strongly indicates that he's not the author of the Dark Wind Killer notes sent to our reporter friend."

Waves of doubt about Larch swept over him.

So, back to square one.

This Dark Wind Killer is playing us, but my gut tells me the answer is in our hands. It's in here somewhere, he thought.

Tanner took a deep breath, let it out slowly and surveyed the files on his desk. Time was hammering against them. His focus flicked to the *L.A. Times* clipping Zurn had set at the edge of his desk earlier.

Nearly buried by other files, a corner of it reached out as if pleading for his attention.

Tanner reached for it.

He studied the headline Miracle Rescue in Fiery Freeway Crash. The news picture of a car in flames and a small picture of Robert at the hospital with the caption Hero Pilot Robert Bowen Saved Mother and Baby.

Pilot, Tanner thought.

Why was that familiar?

Pilot.

Tanner blinked at all of the cold case files as understanding began dawning on him. His heart began beating a little faster. At first he was mistrustful of what was emerging.

Is it a reflexive reaction to Larch being ruled out?

Am I that desperate?

Tanner studied the clipping, rubbing his chin.

The facts: in the last six months of their lives all of the women had traveled, but he had not pursued that angle, until now. He began flipping through the cold case notes he'd made on each victim.

Leeza Meadows had flown to Boston to visit a friend in college.

Esther Fatima Lopez had gone to Las Vegas and Atlantic City to work.

Fay Lynne Millwood—she'd gone to Denver for a conference.

Bonnie Bradford had gone to New York to talk to a literary agent.

Monique Wilson had visited Chicago, Houston and Philadelphia.

But here it is, the remark Wilson's sister had made back in 2005.

Monique had flown so often she got to know some of the airline crews.

That meant she'd used the same airline.

What airline? Did they all use that airline?

Tanner checked the older reports on the files.

StarBest Airline.

What about Bonnie Bradford?

StarBest Airline.

Fay Lynne?

StarBest Airline.

Esther?

StarBest Airline.

Leeza?

StarBest Airline.

Was this it? Was this the common factor?

Tanner's keyboard clicked as he typed rapidly, consulting the files and compiling a list of flight numbers and dates for each of the women. As soon as he was finished, he'd send it to FBI Special Agent Brad Knox with an urgent request to work with TSA and the airline to obtain flight crew manifests for those dates.

As he typed, Robert Bowen's photo stared back at him.

58

Los Angeles, California

Julie Glidden got back to Los Angeles sooner than she'd expected.

She'd been in San Diego working on a fraudulent compensation claim, but the case was now miles behind her.

For much of her trip, she'd focused on Claire.

Driving north along the 5, Julie had listened to radio news reports of Amber Pratt's disappearance and its link to the Dark Wind Killer. But police still hadn't found Amber and there were no updates on whether they'd arrested her husband. And now, on top of Amber's tragic situation, Julie's digging into Robert's past was becoming more disturbing.

As a private investigator she knew that it was not uncommon for people to change their names. The story was always in the reason.

Why did Leon change his?

Where was his wife, Cynthia, and was he still in love with her?

While Milt Thorsen kept investigating in Canada, Julie had only managed a superficial search of Leon's background in the U.S. But the fact that "Robert" had never told Claire about his past troubled Julie.

If he'd deceived her on his name, what else was he hiding from her?

It was early evening, but traffic flowed smoothly as Julie made her way downtown. Her agency was in L.A.'s Bunker Hill district in a thirty-five-floor postmodern skyscraper. She parked in the building's near-empty underground lot and took the elevator to the twenty-fifth floor where her small office was slivered between a global accounting corporation and a law firm.

As the elevator rose, Julie texted Claire.

Again.

I'm back—will be working @ office for a few hrs. I could come over after or meet you? Anything to help.
love & prayers,
J.

She waited for a response. Claire's reply was usually instantaneous but nothing came, as was the case earlier when Julie had texted her before she'd left San Diego.

Claire had a lot to deal with. Julie's heart went out to her. In pursuing the truth about Robert and his first wife, Julie was fearful of what more Milt Thorsen might uncover.

How much more bad news could Claire endure?

Stepping from the elevator, Julie went to her office, unlocked the door and entered. Everyone had gone for the day. She glanced at the time, growing a little uneasy that she hadn't heard anything from Claire.

Julie was also expecting an update from Milt in Canada. The last time he'd contacted her, he said he had a lead on more information on the history of Leon Elliott and his wife.

Julie got a bottle of juice from the fridge in the kitchen, along with some cheese and crackers. She went to her desk and began fine-tuning her report from San Diego, then moved on to catching up on work she'd missed while away. It took close to an hour to get through her emails. She'd finished responding to the last, an invitation to address a security conference, when a new email from Milt Thorsen arrived, along with several attachments.

Julie opened it.

Milt had more on Robert's life in Canada.

Julie held her breath as she burned through Milt's covering email.

Leon and Cynthia Elliott had embarked alone on a full day hike along the Iceline in Yoho National Park in British Columbia. Parts of the trail were steep with the hazard of fallen trees where trail ridges ascended over a river gorge. Leon Elliott stated to investigators that he was off the trail, making a small day camp for their lunch, when Cynthia walked off out of his sight to take in the view over the trail edge. At that point Elliott heard a scream. Cynthia had lost her footing and fallen into the gorge.

Milt's information went on to say that her body was recovered by park wardens later. An autopsy showed her injuries were consistent with a fall and being battered amid the rocks on the fast-flowing mountain river.

Officially, the Royal Canadian Mounted Police and Medical Examiner attributed her death to a wilderness accident. But as Julie continued reading, her jaw dropped, tears filled her eyes and she covered her face with her hands. She skipped along passages listing the impressive scope and findings of Milt Thorsen's work. Records attached…led to law enforcement familiar with…a former Royal Canadian Mounted Police officer… Arising from his own investigation of the subject, provided further insight about Leon Richard Elliott and his wife, Cynthia…

Julie began printing off pages, reading as fast as she could, the words blurring by.

…No record of divorce, no separation…former Mountie indicates that according to a friend, to whom Cynthia had confided, there was stress in the marriage which led to Cynthia contemplating divorce…the Mountie pressed Leon Elliott on the matter and he made a bizarre revelation…

Elliott claimed that months before his wife's death, he'd been approached by an international drug cartel to make an illegal delivery flight. Elliott refused and suspected the drug dealers had followed him and his wife into the mountains, and that they killed Cynthia to send him a message. Elliott stated that he was too frightened to report it to authorities. When pressed, Elliott could not provide the Mountie with any information, a name, number, contact, or phone record, to support his cartel claim…

The Mountie discounted Elliott's drug-flight-wife-death story and had discussions with the prosecutor on possible charges against Elliott for his wife's death. The prosecutor said there was no solid evidence to support the charges. The case was closed.

In his covering letter, Milt wrote that upon obtaining this new information, he made a number of urgent calls to his trusted sources, including those with U.S. national security, as well as those with Canadian and U.S. aviation security, to confidentially enquire about the link between Leon Richard Elliott and Robert Bowen.

Milt learned that Elliott had managed to persuade federal officials, some of whom were friends, of the real possibility that drug dealers may have been behind his wife's death. As a result, Elliott was successful in having his federal friends arrange for his professional flight records as a pilot—in fact his whole life, Social Security Number, everything—changed smoothly to his new name without raising any red flags. They helped erase, or nearly erase, his previous identity.

Oh my God, Julie thought, she was right to check on Robert. *I'm so sorry, Claire, I should have done a background check when you were first seeing him. I always got a weird vibe from him. How did I let this get by? At least you're not pregnant. God,* please *don't be pregnant.*

Julie sent Milt an email thanking him, then collected the documents.

Robert's first wife died under suspicious circumstances, yet he wants Claire to believe he was divorced. The man's a liar. Or worse.

Julie took a deep breath.

She had to get to Claire now, give her the facts and let her make a decision on what to do about what they now knew about "Robert."

Julie reached for her phone and started texting.

Claire, please answer. I know it's a bad time but just received new disturbing data on Robert. Important I see you to discuss.
J

After sending the text, Julie touched her phone to her chin and said a prayer while still processing the new information. She'd tell Claire to stay with her tonight. That would be best.

Before she could form another thought her phone pinged.

Claire had responded.

Are you still at your office, Julie?

Yes.

Can you come to my house now?

Yes, on my way.

59

Los Angeles, California

Julie gathered her documents and her bag.

As she prepared to leave for Claire's house, she hesitated before shutting off her computer. She sat back down and searched online news sites for updates on Amber's case.

She was still missing and police hadn't found her husband.

Damn, what's happening with that task force investigation?

Julie picked up her office phone and called her friend in the D.A.'s office. After three rings the line was answered.

"Bartley Green."

"Bart, it's Julie, I need a minute."

"What can I do for you?"

"Friend to friend, what're you hearing on the Dark Wind Killer?"

"Well..." Green exhaled. "They still haven't found Amber, but—" he dropped his voice "—this will be made public soon. The LAPD in Rampart grabbed the husband, took him to Alhambra where the task force questioned him."

"Good."

"Not good. They've ruled him out."

"They don't have him for the five unsolveds and his wife?"

"Nope, they've got no hard evidence. He's not the guy, which means the killer is still out there."

Julie considered the situation.

"Are they looking at anyone else specifically?"

"If they are, we're not hearing anything. We know they're chasing a number of tips."

She shot an uneasy glance at her pages of new information she had on Robert Bowen, a.k.a. Leon Richard Elliott. Her mind was racing. She was angry at him. She'd never really liked him. And she was angry at herself for not watching out for Claire when she'd first met Mr. Community Hero.

Am I wrong for thinking what I'm thinking?

Before Julie knew it, she'd wedged her phone between her shoulder and ear and started typing on her keyboard.

"You've got friends on that task force, right?" she asked.

"A couple."

"And you protect your sources, a lawyer-client privilege thing, right?"

"What are you getting at, Julie?"

Her conscience cautioned her about ethics, about revealing confidential information relating to a client's case, *unless it concerned a crime or public safety.*

This damn well does, she told herself.

"I'm going to send you some information right now, several attachments. It's on its way to you. It all deals with some questionable history of the husband of Amber Pratt's psychologist."

"Are you suggesting they take a look at him? On what basis?"

"You'll know when you see the material. This is likely nothing. It'll likely dead-end. Still, under the circumstances, I think you should pass it to the task force and let them assess it quietly. That's all I'm suggesting, Bart."

"All right."

"And remember you didn't get it from me. I trust you on this."

"You know I'm bound, Julie."

"Okay, gotta go."

Once again, she got ready to depart. After sending the information to her friend in the D.A.'s office, Julie held off sending it to Claire. She thought it best to first talk to her face-to-face about Robert. She picked up her cell phone and texted Claire, hoping she would keep responding.

Is Robert with you now?

No, we'll be able to talk. What did you find out?

I'll show you some documents when I get there.

OK.

Any word on Amber?

Nothing. I'm going out of my mind.

Be there soon.

After sending the text Julie bit her bottom lip; she considered her gun locked in the office safe.

Should she take it?

No, she thought, she was visiting Claire at home to talk and convince her to stay with her for a couple of nights. In gathering her things and hurrying to the elevator, Julie was stung by second thoughts over what she'd done, and what she may have set in motion.

As Julie's elevator descended, Leonard Fitzhugh, the guard at the main concourse security desk, set his comic aside and unwrapped his Tex-Mex submarine sandwich. He'd been looking forward to this moment for the past few hours, since he'd picked up his dinner on his way to his late shift.

As Fitzhugh lined it up for that first joyous bite, there was a flash on the console bank of twenty-four security camera monitors. Three cameras for Level Four in the underground parking garage went out.

They were showing a static snowstorm.

"Crap," Fitzhugh whispered.

He set his sandwich down, flipped through the laminated binder for a number and then called the dispatcher for the surveillance company that maintained the cameras. This was the fourth time this year they'd had a problem. He wrote up the issue in his log. It would be about an hour before a tech showed up.

Fitzhugh returned to more important matters, opening a bag of potato chips and soda, before picking up that glorious sandwich.

He'd eat first, then go down to Level Four and take a look.

Julie's elevator went directly to the underground garage.

As she walked to her car, which was parked on Level Four among the sprinkling of vehicles that remained at the far end of the lot, she continued grappling with the action she'd taken.

Given the situation, she hadn't overcompensated by alerting the task force. She doubted much would come of that, but she needed to help Claire get some distance from Robert, Leon, whoever the hell he was.

On top of all else that was happening, this was going to crush Claire. She'd need some time and space to think and Julie would be there for her.

Her steps echoed as she neared her car, parked near a column and whitewashed wall under a fluorescent light. She reached into her bag for her remote key lock. It beeped twice when she unlocked her doors. Reaching for the door handle, she gave the area a quick scan.

As she opened her door Julie caught her breath.

The security camera on the pillar above her car had been smashed from its mounting and was dangling by its wires. A sudden rush of movement caused her to turn at the moment she felt metal prongs pressed into the flesh of her neck. Her body was paralyzed with a million-volt jolt of tingling burning electricity and she dropped.

Just like the cows at the slaughterhouse.

60

Greater Los Angeles, California

The tear tracks had dried on Claire's face miles ago.

She'd set the radio on her Toyota Corolla to scan AM stations so she could monitor news reports on Amber's case.

There was nothing.

It seemed like an eternity since she'd left her home in San Marino for Las Vegas. Traffic had backed up in stretches along the 210 as it wove through the eastern sprawl, taking her through a gamut of emotions.

All she knew was that they still hadn't found Amber, or Eric.

She'd heard nothing from the detectives or Julie, and the horror that Eric Larch was suspected in the murders of five other women continued exacerbating Claire's guilt over the tragedy.

She couldn't escape it.

She'd tried to find solace in Martha Berman's comforting words, that it wasn't her fault. And in the aftermath, she'd done all she could for her patients. Some were so supportive and concerned for her but now, as miles rolled by, Claire felt as if she were running away.

Like I've been running all my life.

As the road flowed under her, Claire saw herself at eight, running from her home carrying her baby brother, Luke, before he died in her arms. Her heart was breaking. Then she saw herself pinned by Cliff as he raised his fist to hit her before Robert saved her. Then she saw her dream of a family with Robert coming true before it began crumbling when she'd sensed he didn't want one with her because he was still in love with his first wife.

Should I continue my treatments with Dr. LaRoy?

She didn't know.

Julie had said she'd found more information on Robert's past but Claire hadn't heard any more from her. Suddenly Claire had to brake to let a van in ahead of her.

Catching her breath, she went back to her thoughts.

What should I do about Robert?

She was confused. He'd seemed to have a change of heart about selling the cabin.

Claire thought of their honeymoon, the happy time they had together at the cabin and how she'd wished she'd had more chances to get out to it.

As she approached the exit for 15 North and Las Vegas, she came upon an idea: *I could go to the cabin now. I could work there instead and be back in L.A. in two hours if I needed to be. Martha will understand.*

She checked her rearview mirror and adjusted her grip on the wheel. She didn't take the exit for Las Vegas. Instead she continued east.

Claire always loved how this leg of the drive transported her from the metropolis as it climbed into the San Bernardino Mountains.

Rolling through the small mountain towns and the ribbon of highway that connected them was good therapy. She dropped the windows to inhale the cool, sweet pine-scented air.

She took in the stunning lake views as she traveled along the north shore before stopping a few miles from the cabin at the tiny Lone Post Store and Gas Bar.

"Could you fill it up, please?" Claire asked the lanky teenaged attendant before she went to the store.

A Lab napping on the store porch greeted her by lifting an eyebrow. Transom bells rang when she entered. Claire smiled at the woman at the counter before browsing the well-stocked aisles. The wooden floor creaked and the air smelled of suntan lotion and baked bread.

Unsure of what Robert had in the cabin fridge, she picked up a shopping basket and got some milk, lettuce, tomatoes, fruit, yogurt, bread, salad dressing and a box of granola cereal. When she put it all on the counter to pay, Claire followed the woman's attention through the window to the pumps.

"Looks like you got some trouble."

"Excuse me?"

The front end of Claire's car had sagged. The boy was crouched, running his hand over the tire.

"Oh, no," Claire said.

"Bobby will change it for you if you let him get to your spare."

"Thank you, yes." Claire went to the car.

After they'd emptied her trunk and Bobby got to the mini-spare he shook his head.

"It's gone, too. The stem's shot."

"Oh, no, I was heading to my cabin, but I'm on call and may need to get back to L.A. in a hurry. Is there anything you can do? Can you sell me a tire or something? What about this can of tire sealant?"

"We don't carry tires and sealant's not going to work. The flat's too damaged." Bobby made note of the tire's specs on a grease-stained pad. "We can make some calls about getting a tire for you."

"Thanks."

Bobby and the woman, who it turned out was his mom, Flo, called garages in the lake area using the phone at the counter.

Claire used the time to call people in L.A. on her cell phone but her attempts were futile because it kept freezing, even though it was fully charged. Frustrated, she resorted to using her credit card and the store's public pay phone near the door.

While the dog ambled inside to yawn at her, Claire called Robert but got voice mail, then Julie and left a message. Then she tried reaching Tanner, leaving a message on his cell phone. Then she tried his office line, but he was out and the person who took the call wouldn't discuss a word of the investigation. Finally, Claire called Martha and left her a message.

"Good news and bad news on the tire," Bobby said. "Pixely's in Victorville has one but Donny won't be able to get it here until the morning."

"Where's your place?" Flo asked.

"Vista Lane."

"That's not far," Flo said. "We'll load up your stuff in our truck. Bobby can drive you to your place. After we fix your car in the morning, I'll send Bobby out to bring you back here. How's that sound?"

"Overly generous," Claire said. "Thank you."

61

Commerce, California

Joe Tanner stood at the windows of the Cold Case Unit of the Los Angeles County Sheriff's Department, his cell phone pressed to his ear.

With his free hand, he kneaded the tension in his neck while clarifying the wording of the press release before it went out the door.

"No, Mindy," he said. "We're only saying that Eric Larch has been arrested for bail and protection-order violations and he's cooperating in the investigation into the disappearance of his wife, Amber Pratt."

He waited as the wording was read back to him.

"Estranged wife, fine," he agreed. "That's it. That's all we'll say. We know the people downtown want it out now, so let it go."

The press release wording was crucial to buy time and ensure the real killer believed Eric Larch was their suspect.

Finished with the call, Tanner returned to his desk, hopeful that his instincts were right. All he needed were those manifests. He had hoped to have them by now. His line rang. It was Shirley, out front.

"Joe, you got a message from Bartley Green with the D.A.'s office. He says it's important you call him back ASAP."

Tanner took down the numbers. Green's name was not familiar and he figured it was a status check. It happened with high-profile cases. He'd get back to him as soon as he could.

"That it?"

"And you got a call from Claire Bowen. She wanted an update and to inform you she'd left town. She's in Big Bear Lake and left contact info."

"Good, thanks."

It was getting late in the day.

Tanner downed the last of his cold coffee. Before returning calls he checked his email just as the first of several attachments arrived in his box from Knox at the FBI bearing the *StarBest* flight crew and passenger manifests covering the flights for the period in question.

Tanner printed them off and looked over to Zurn, thinking he'd ask his partner to help study the manifests, but he'd just taken a call.

"Bartley Green?" Zurn leaned forward at his desk. "With the D.A.'s office? Put him through."

Tanner held his tongue. Whoever Bartley Green was, he was persistent. Let Harvey deal with him, Tanner thought, collecting his pages.

He started with Leeza Meadows, who'd only flown once in the time period before her death. It was to Boston. The captain listed for her flight was Leon Elliott. Tanner then went to the list for Fay Millwood. She'd flown once to Denver in the period. The captain for her flight was listed as Leon Elliott. Tanner thought, fine,

Elliott was a pilot for *StarBest*. But the name Robert Bowen hadn't surfaced at all so far.

So much for instincts and hunches.

Shuffling through the pages, he went to the flight for Bonnie Bradford to New York. The captain was Leon Elliott.

This Leon Elliott was everywhere.

Esther Lopez had gone to Las Vegas and Atlantic City to work. Leon Elliott was captain for one of her flights. Tanner flipped to the pages for the most frequent flyer of all five women, Monique Wilson. She'd flown to Chicago, Houston and Philadelphia. According to a note in the file, Wilson's sister had said that Monique flew often enough to get to know some of the airline crews. On two of her flights, Houston and Philadelphia, Leon Elliott was her captain.

What the hell?

"Hey, Joe." Zurn had finished his call. "You're not going to believe this."

Still contending with the flight lists, Tanner turned to Zurn.

"We got a tip from a source with the D.A.'s office to check out Robert Bowen," Zurn said. "You know, the husband of Amber Pratt's psychologist, the guy we met in her office? The freeway hero pilot. Turns out he changed his name in Canada after his wife died in a wilderness accident a few years back. She fell while they were hiking in the mountains. The Mounties up there had nothing to charge him with, but got a bad read on the guy."

"Robert Bowen changed his name?" Tanner asked.

"Yeah."

"From what?"

Zurn looked at his notes.

"Used to be Leon Richard Elliott. We're going to get some paper on him and a Mountie contact in British Columbia— What is it, Joe?"

"It's him."

"What?"

"It's Robert Bowen."

"How do we know that?" Zurn asked.

Tanner stapled the flight manifests together and tossed them to Zurn.

"Go through those flight lists where I highlighted. I don't know how it happened—if he fell through the cracks or what, because I thought the TSA vetted pilots and that the airlines helped screen them with security checks and deep background. Look, Elliott is the common denominator. He was captain of the flight for each victim. He must've selected and stalked them."

As Zurn raced through the pages, he started shaking his head.

"And now," Zurn said, "he's back, stalking his wife's patients."

Tanner grabbed his jacket.

"We need to get warrants now."

62

Big Bear Lake, California

Stones pelted the floorboards of Bobby's old Dodge pickup as he and Claire bumped along the gravel road that was Vista Lane.

"Thanks again for all your help," Claire said.

"No problem."

"I meant to ask, how's the wireless reception out here? I've been having trouble with my cell phone and need to work on my computer."

"It's mostly good since they put up the new towers, but people down your way without landlines say it's still really sketchy."

"Great," Claire said, sighing.

"Just keep your phone charged and keep trying. Calls seem to get through, eventually."

"I will, thanks.

At the big granite rock they turned onto the pathway. Branches swept against the doors as the truck bumped along through the short stretch of dense forest before coming to the cabin.

The sight of it stirred memories.

Claire loved the soothing way the sunlight pierced

the arching treetops and dappled the property. For a moment she blinked fondly, as if seeing an old friend. But the sentiment was eclipsed as she walked to the door.

It took several tries before she unlocked it.

After Bobby unloaded her bags and groceries from the truck, Claire offered him two twenties but he refused.

"Thank you again."

"No problem. See you tomorrow sometime," he said, then drove off.

Claire stood alone in the quiet of the cabin, wishing the tranquility were a sedative. She remained tense, from the trip, the day, everything. She checked her cell phone, the signal was good, but there were no new messages. *Is anybody going to tell me what's going on?* She set up her laptop on the kitchen table, logged on and checked her email. No responses to her calls. She reviewed online news sites. Nothing new on Amber's case.

All right, you've got things to do.

She put her groceries away and went to the master bedroom, remembering that Robert had kept an ancient portable TV around somewhere to catch Lakers and Dodgers games. She found it in the closet, took it out, turned it on and adjusted the antenna until she picked up an L.A. news channel.

She left it on to monitor reports on Amber while she unpacked a few things. Claire then undressed and went into the bathroom. It'd been a long, hard day and she wanted to wash off the grime and stress of the drive.

She'd eat something and then start work.

Reaching into the shower to turn on the faucet she stopped.

What's that on the stall floor?

Claire lowered herself.

A dried stain webbed around the drain, lacy pinkish and with some muddied residue. Claire hesitated, guessing it was from Robert after he'd done some work outside—*maybe he'd cut himself?* She poured some shampoo over the stain, turned on the hot water. As she washed it away, she thought it had been ages since the cabin had a good cleaning. She considered hiring a cleaning service to scour the place.

While Claire showered, she planned the rest of her day. She'd go over her patient files to ensure she hadn't overlooked anything in her more difficult cases.

Overlooked anything? Who am I kidding?

Her ever-present guilt over Amber resumed gnawing at her. Claire resurrected Martha Berman's advice and tried to concentrate on the things she could control. She stepped from the shower and toweled off. As she started dressing, her attention went to the TV and live news coverage of a motel under the graphic *Arrest Made in Missing Woman Case.*

She turned up the volume.

"...Again, KTKX has breaking news. The AllNews Press Agency is reporting that the LAPD has arrested Eric Larch at the motel behind me, the Palms of Paradise Motor Inn on West Olympic Boulevard in Los Angeles...We now have on the line Mark Harding the ANPA reporter who broke the story."

A still photo of Mark Harding appeared in a lower corner of the screen.

"Mark, what can you tell us?"

"Eric Larch was identified as a person of interest in the case of his estranged wife, Amber Pratt of Alhambra, who has been reported missing. Police say they have not yet located the woman…the L.A. County Sheriff Department's Cold Case Task Force has said that the Pratt case is linked to five unsolved murders of women across the L.A. area but so far they're not confirming if Larch, who I am told is facing questioning, is suspected of being the so-called Dark Wind Killer who has written to the ANPA. Police refuse to discuss any aspect of their investigation into this very gruesome case."

"Thank you, Mark… Again, an arrest has been made in the case of… KTKX will monitor this breaking development…"

Claire's heart raced.

Oh, God, please find Amber.

Maybe Eric took her somewhere to talk? Maybe she got away and hid in a women's shelter until they arrested him? Maybe she'll try to call me?

A thousand more thoughts blazed through her mind.

If they find Amber tonight, how would she get back to L.A.? She'd call the store and pay Bobby or his mother to drive her. But how would Tanner or Robert reach her? Her phone seemed unreliable. She'd keep checking it and her email for messages. She'd call Tanner. She'd call Robert, Belinski, Julie, everybody. That's what she'd do.

She'd call until she got answers.

Claire took a deep breath. Okay, calm down.

Eric's arrest was a good thing. It might be the beginning of the end of this nightmare, she thought, and finished dressing. She stood in front of the dresser mirror and began brushing the tangles from her damp hair.

She stopped in midstroke.

Reflected in the mirror were the spindles of the bed's headboard behind her.

Claire turned around.

Two sets of white braceletlike loops hung from the headboard—one at the lower end of each spindle at the separate side of the bed. Puzzled, Claire took one in her hand before realizing what the loops were.

Plastic handcuffs.

Small brownish clouds lined the edges, *like dried blood.*

Claire drew back the bedsheets and inspected the pillow, finding a few strands of long hair. She held them to the window, up to the fading afternoon light. The hair was not hers and it was not Robert's.

Claire took a step back from the bed.

Suddenly she was engulfed in a storm of betrayal.

Robert had brought a woman to the cabin, to their bed. Was it Cynthia? Is this why he hesitated about selling it? He's using it to bring her here for what? Some kind of bondage sex?

Claire bit back on her tears.

I've been such a fool.

She gathered her clothes and her bag and hurled them into the next room. Anger and pain pummeled her as she tried to think.

She couldn't think.

She couldn't breathe in this place.

She had to get outside.

63

Big Bear Lake, California

The screen door whacked against the cabin as Claire shot through it.

Nothing made sense.

Grappling with her rage, she followed the path that twisted and turned to the secluded edge of their property. It led to the lookout and gazebo where she and Robert would go to enjoy the lake view and the mountains.

By the time she reached the scenic spot, she was in tears.

How could you do this? How could you? We spent part of our honeymoon here. We planned our life here. We dreamed here.

Bile rose in the back of her throat and she felt sick to her stomach.

God, she hoped she was not pregnant. Her world had been turned upside down. Not long ago she'd ached to have a baby—had planned to have a baby with Robert and now—*now this.*

How did it come to this?

Everything was crashing down around her.

Claire gripped the railing to steady herself.

I am the dumbest person on earth. How could I have been so stupid and so blind to all the signs?

There was Robert's brooding at the time Dr. LaRoy said they'd be able to have a family. And Robert's solo trips to the cabin; and the way he'd let her know that he'd lived in Canada with Cynthia; and the way he'd run his hands over those young women at the banquet; and the fact Julie was uncovering more about his past.

Why haven't I heard from her? Why hasn't she called or texted me?

As Claire cast around for answers she saw a planter box near the gazebo, one of the new ones Robert had built, mocking her like a monument to his betrayal.

Still, Claire was drawn to it.

I thought he'd made them for me. Maybe he made them for her.

The box was about six feet long, two feet wide, stood about two feet tall. Looking upon it, tears rolling down her cheeks, Claire saw how he'd filled it to capacity with her favorites, wild roses, fireweed and lilies. Bits of petals had fallen to the ground, like confetti.

Confetti, how fitting.

Claire glanced at it, then started to turn away when one small petal caught her eye, a shiny one. At first she thought it was like others on the ground surrounding the planter.

But it was different.

It was the size of a small postage stamp, bright red with tiny bright pink stripes.

With gloss.

She picked it up.

It was a fingernail. Amber's fingernail!

Claire's stomach spasmed.

She searched around the planter and froze.

On the opposite side of the box, halfway down, poking through the latticework, Claire saw fingers in a desperate futile escape posture.

"Amber!"

Claire touched them.

They're warm! She's alive. Oh, God please let her be alive!

With her bare hands, Claire began ripping out the flowers, stopping when she'd discovered a rubber hose that surfaced from somewhere deeper in the box. *A breathing tube?* Claire continued attacking the soil, clawing at it, then her fingers hit something solid—wood a sheet of plywood.

The hose continued down through a circular hole in the plywood.

"Amber, it's Claire! Can you hear me? I'm going to get you out! Tap if you can hear me."

In the stillness, Claire heard a soft knock on the wood.

"Oh, thank you! Good, good!"

Claire ran her hands along the wood that served as a coffin lid, looking for a way to remove it, but it was no use. Screws held it down tight. She'd need a tool, something to pry it off.

I walked by a shovel and wheelbarrow leaning against a tree near the back of the cabin.

Claire ran back and grabbed the shovel.

Her heart racing, pulse thudding in her ears, she rushed back to the gazebo, never hearing or seeing the SUV stop in the front of the cabin.

She returned to the box.

"Amber, I'm going to get you out now!"

Gripping the shovel, Claire began smashing at the

latticework on one side. Then she attempted to work the shovel's tip between the one-inch plywood lid and the lower body of the box. She made several attempts to force the blade tip into position, either missing or finding that the seam was just too tight.

Grunting and cursing, Claire refused to give up.

Finally, she found a spot that yielded enough play for her to thrust the blade tip in with enough purchase to leverage the area.

The seam cracked, surrendering a few more critical inches.

Claire pulled out the shovel and as she steadied herself to make a second punch, she stopped.

What was that? A footfall or a twig snap?

As Claire turned to face the cabin, the last thing she saw was a silhouetted figure before the sky exploded with a million constellations, propelling her into darkness.

64

Big Bear Lake, California

Claire's eyes opened to a watery haze.

What...where...

The swollen side of her head throbbed, making her woozy. Her blood pumped hard as she tried to see, tried to...

What happened?

Swimming through disorientation, she smelled the cabin and recalled the fragrance of flowers as she focused in the dim light. She was facing the fireplace. Yes, she was in the cabin.

Crickets.

Evening.

Inside, the cabin was lit only by candles flickering from various shelves and tables. The air was silent but for the crickets.

And the roar of remembering.

Amber.

Claire's head was pounding and she tried to think. Okay, she was sitting in a hard-back chair but it felt so strange, so weird.

In the dull stillness, large shapeless shadows danced along the walls.

Okay, I have to get Amber out of the box, get her to a hospital but— No. It was a dream. No. Robert was cheating here with Cynthia? No, it was a dream. I must've fallen, got a concussion or... I have to get up and call an ambulance. Get up now!

Claire's effort to stand was halted.

Her legs were bound at the ankles to a wooden kitchen chair. Her wrists were bound to the armrests. With plastic handcuffs.

"Help! Somebody help me!"

Breathing hard in the quiet, she struggled in vain until she cried out in frustration. Squirming in her chair, she strained her neck to turn to the kitchen. On the floor she saw…Robert!

First she saw his travel bag. Then she saw him in the kitchen, his back to her, standing at the table, in jeans and a T-shirt, casually flipping through newspapers by candlelight.

"Robert! Help me!"

Nothing.

"Robert, please help me!"

He didn't react.

It was as if she didn't exist.

This isn't real. I'm having a nightmare. So wake up, wake up!

She strained against the handcuffs and felt pain.

They're real.

Claire went numb, time raced with her fear rising as she struggled to comprehend what had befallen her. It was incomprehensible. She had to think. She must get through to him; convince him to release her.

What are the levers, the triggers?

She swallowed hard and tried to keep the fear out of her tone—tried to talk to him as his wife.

"Robert, I love you with all my heart. We've both been through so much lately. We can help each other. Whatever you're going through, we can help each other. I love you. I want to help you, let me help you."

He didn't respond.

"Robert, I understand it can be painful to talk about these things."

He continued ignoring her. She tried a direct approach.

"Robert, what have you done with Amber? Show me where she is. We need to help her."

Like a tradesman whose break was over, Robert took his bag and left the kitchen for the hall to the bedrooms. Then she heard the shower running. Alone in the living room, she struggled against the plastic handcuffs until her wrists bled.

It was futile.

She began writhing in her chair. If she could tilt it so she could stand maybe she could crab-walk to the kitchen and a knife. It was not easy. Her position afforded her little strength, but after several attempts she succeeded.

She was on her feet in a spine-breaking posture. The chair was heavy. Its weight threatened to pull her back down.

She had moved about a foot when the shower stopped.

Startled, Claire lost her balance and slid back into a sitting position, a prisoner again. Then she heard humming.

What was he doing?

She listened.

Forgetting how long it had been since the shower stopped, she prepared to try again when there was movement in the hall.

"Robert, please, I'm begging you!"

He emerged from the darkness like a ghost.

"Robert is gone, Claire."

She gasped.

He stood before her, naked.

In the near dark of the candlelight his face glowed white but Robert's features had vanished in the brilliant makeup, the streak of bright red smeared across his upturned mouth, his cheeks, a fury of cuts, his eyes burned from huge black smudge pools with fierce streaks for eyebrows, amplifying his rage.

"You know who I am."

Claire's heart hammered against her rib cage as she nodded weakly.

"Say it."

Claire was speechless.

"Say it!"

"What have you done with Amber?"

"Tell me who I am and I will show you wonders."

"Please, let me help you, Robert."

"Robert is gone." Suddenly he thrust his face within inches of hers. *"Tell me who I am. Say it."*

"You're the killer in the news." She choked back her sobs. "The Dark Wind Killer."

He stood up and thrust out his chest.

"I am a deity, spawned in hell. I control life and death."

"Please."

In a heartbeat he moved behind her chair, with his superior strength he tilted her back as if she weighed nothing and dragged her into the bedroom, which was lit by candles.

He turned her to the bed.

"A masterwork in progress, don't you think?"

Claire's breathing stopped, her skin prickled with gooseflesh.

Amber was naked, spread-eagled on the bed, each wrist and ankle restrained by plastic handcuffs. Her thinned, weakened body was muddied and bloodied. Her face laced in blood and bruises. Barely conscious, she sensed Claire's presence and groaned.

Claire's chair tilted as he dragged her into the second candlelit bedroom where a naked woman was bound on the bed in the same way as Amber. Her face was bloodied, but when Claire recognized her, she cried out, "Julie! Oh, God, Julie!"

"She meddled and now she's a very special project."

He dragged Clairc back out to the living room.

"You lied, Claire. You were supposed to go to Las Vegas. No matter. I can adapt. Your time was coming. You're just like Cindy. You and Julie interfered but you failed. Just like Cindy did."

Claire sobbed.

"When I'm done tonight, I'll move on. The world's a big canvas and my fan base is growing. Now, if you'll excuse me, I need to resume my work. It's going to be a long, glorious night."

He drew his hideous, horrifying face to hers, opened his mouth wide and extended his tongue, and when she averted her face in disgust, he gave her a long, reptilian lick from her neck to the top of her head.

Then as if in a cobra strike, he seized her throat.

"I'm saving you for last."

Left alone in the living room, restrained to her chair, the only sounds Claire heard were crickets and the hammering of her heart, then the screams from the bedrooms. The pain and outrage hit Claire again and again.

He's going to kill us all.

Every vein in her body stood out as again, Claire battled to stand. Breathing hard and straining like a power lifter, she got to her feet. Slowly, steadily and by sheer will, she progressed to the kitchen for a knife. But Claire's chair leg clipped the kitchen table, toppling the candle onto the newspaper, igniting a fire.

The newspaper burned in seconds, the flames spread to the wooden table, smoke rising. Thinking fast, Claire turned her chair to the flames and moved her plastic-cuffed wrist into them. The heat was excruciating, and she fought through her tears as her skin cooked, pulling against the restraint until it gave way.

As her burned flesh throbbed, she hobbled to the drawer, got a serrated knife and cut herself free as fire spread.

The flames now reached from the kitchen to the living room.

Claire seized the fire poker and ran into the bedroom where Robert was on top of Amber. Raising the steel poker like a club, her two-handed swing knifed through the air as she brought it down, striking him repeatedly. As he turned to defend himself, she continued beating him until he fell to the floor—then she stabbed him, forcing the poker's point into his stomach.

Claire cut Amber free and began pulling her to safety out the rear door. By the time she'd returned for Julie, the fire had spread to the hallway. The smoke was choking, the heat was intense.

Claire had to get down on her hands and knees.

She cut Julie free. They started for the rear door, hindered by the flames, heat and smoke. Using all of her strength, she got Julie through the door, but Claire couldn't get out.

Something had locked on to her lower leg.

She turned. In the churning inferno of smoke and flames, Robert had crawled on his stomach, bleeding and dying, to seize Claire in a death grip. His grotesque face contorted as he growled.

"I'm taking you to hell with me!"

65

Big Bear Lake, California

It was just after dark when the call came out of the Los Angeles County Sheriff's Department.

"Captain says this is a priority, Lee."

"All right, raise Marv. He's at Thirty-eight and Pine Oak. Get Duke to send the Marine Unit, so we're covered from the water and we need air support to stand by. We're on the way."

Lee Hespler, a deputy with the San Bernardino County Sheriff's Department, was posted to the Big Bear Sheriff's Station.

Any thought of a sleepy night shift had just gone out the window.

The urgent request from LACSD came from Joe Tanner. They wanted Big Bear sheriffs to secure a property on Vista Lane, belonging to Robert Bowen of San Marino.

If they were to encounter Bowen, they were to exercise extreme caution, meaning get backup, arrest him and alert the task force.

Warrants were signed.

From what Hespler gathered from the call, guys

across L.A. and up in Van Nuys were executing warrants, as well.

As he rolled out of Big Bear and over Stanfield Cutoff, he grabbed his microphone again for his dispatcher.

"Allison, tell Marv and Duke no lights or sirens. We'll keep this low-key."

Hespler could get to the address in twenty minutes, but he'd wait until the others were in position, he thought as he sailed along North Shore Drive. It was not long after that, about eleven minutes beyond Stanfield Cutoff, Hespler would later write in his report, that he first saw the flicker of the fire at the Bowen property.

He called for fire and paramedics, then hit his lights and siren.

Don't this change everything? Hespler thought.

Emergency crews found the cabin fully involved with flames soaring into the night sky.

After rapid work they kept the blaze from igniting the surrounding forest, but the structure was lost.

Paramedics rushed the survivors to Bear Valley Community Hospital.

The Coroner's Office was alerted to stand by.

One victim with third-degree burns to eighty-percent of their body was airlifted to the Burn Center at USC in Los Angeles.

66

Big Bear Lake, California

Claire Bowen stared up at the hospital's blurry ceiling lights flowing by as they wheeled her into the E.R. where emergency staff worked on her.

That was all she remembered.

When she woke the next morning, the horror overwhelmed her like a tidal wave and she cried out.

The nurse in the chair set down her magazine and went to her.

Claire was in a private room with a large window. When she lifted her hand to accept the tissue from the nurse, she felt the hospital wristband over her bandages, the IV tube in her arm.

She was groggy from sedatives.

"Can I get you anything, Claire?"

"Water, please."

The nurse helped her sip from the cup at her bedside.

"How are you feeling?"

Claire swallowed and nodded her thanks, then finished drinking.

"Amber?"

"She's stable, heavily sedated, but the doctors say she'll recover."

"Julie?"

The nurse blinked several times and Claire knew.

"She'd suffered trauma to her head. It led to bleeding in her brain. She did not survive her injuries. I'm so sorry. Her family in Minnesota's been contacted. They're making arrangements."

Claire covered her face with her hands and sobbed.

Then the nurse said, "Robert died at USC in Los Angeles."

Claire felt nothing for him.

A short time later the nurse allowed Claire a private moment with Amber. She entered her room quietly, rolling her IV pole. She sat in the chair next to her bed. Amber was unconscious. Claire took her hand.

"Please, please forgive me. I'm so sorry."

She held on to Amber for a very long time.

Back in her room, Claire mourned Julie as she sat by her window, thinking of her friend until more tears came. As she wept she tried to remember Julie's smile, her laugh. She was lost as she struggled to come to terms with it all until they allowed Martha Berman to visit her.

"I'll never understand what happened," Claire said.

"It's okay. It's all right. Right now you need rest," she said. "I'm going to stay with you in San Marino. I've been making calls. There are people who want to help you—Kallski at Irvine, and Constance West-Hatcher at USC. And they're already arranging help here in California for Amber, too. She's going to need it."

"I want to help her."

"You already did, Claire. You saved her life. You're

not in any shape to help her further. Let other experts take it from here."

Understanding, but not understanding, Claire nodded.

"I've been in touch with Alice to take care of things," Martha said. "We'll extend your absence while we decide how to deal with your practice. We'll take care of everything. I'll be back to see you."

"Thank you, Martha."

After Martha left, a doctor checked on Claire while the nurse waited.

"You've got some first-degree burns, smoke inhalation and lacerations. We'd like to keep you here for another day or two," he said. "Taking everything into consideration, you're doing well."

About ten minutes later, Detectives Tanner and Zurn visited her.

They spoke with her on the case for nearly an hour. They told her that they'd gone to USC the moment Robert arrived to question him, but he died one hour after his arrival.

Claire had no words for his death and looked away.

Through her tears, she cooperated but was still unable to overcome her guilt.

"It's because of me that Julie's dead."

"No." Tanner snapped his notebook shut. "It's because of Leon Elliott, or whoever the hell he was."

"It's my fault. I should've known. How could I not know?"

"Listen," Tanner said. "Leon Elliott was a deceiver, that's how he existed. He fooled air-industry security people, he fooled cops, he fooled a lot of people for a long time, but not you. You stopped him. It was only through your suspicions about him that Julie and Milt

Thorsen dug into his past. Julie's actions saved lives. Your actions saved Amber, remember that."

Claire appreciated the kindness in what Tanner had said.

Zurn told her how the news of the events concerning the Dark Wind Killer was all over the internet—that press requests for interviews with her were coming to the task force and the hospital.

"Satellite news trucks from L.A. are in the parking lot," Zurn said, "but you don't have to talk to them."

Claire shook her head.

"I don't want to. I don't want to answer questions about how I could be married to a monster and not know it, or how it feels to be the idiot psychologist. No one will ever understand."

"I understand," Tanner said. "Believe me."

Claire found warmth in his eyes and the beginnings of her healing.

After the detectives left, Claire called the nurse.

"I need to know something confidential, something important."

"Anything I can do to help you."

"Does my chart show that I'm pregnant?"

The nurse cleared her throat.

"You're not pregnant."

Claire shut her eyes.

67

San Marino, California

The Forever in Peace Cemetery was situated on twelve acres of immaculate grounds south of Huntington Drive, west of Del Mar Avenue.

In the time after the funeral, Claire visited nearly every day, placing flowers at the headstone for Julie Dawn Glidden. Each time, she thanked Julie for saving her life, asked forgiveness and whispered a prayer.

It was her way of coming to terms with it all.

Healing a day at a time.

Like the burns on my wrist.

And whenever she could, Claire went to see Amber, who was staying with a friend in Torrance. For weeks after, Amber's face still bore the traces of cuts and bruises.

"I have good days and bad days," Amber told her over tea.

Her divorce from Eric was final. He no longer contacted her. It was over and she was rebuilding her life with the help of the "excellent" psychologists Martha Berman had arranged.

"Claire," Amber said. "You don't have to keep checking on me. I never ever blamed you. Eric's loser relatives thought I should sue you. I told them we were both victims of the same monster. If it wasn't for you, I'd be dead. I told them that he wanted to kill you, too. I got the whole story from Detective Tanner."

This time, Amber took her hand.

"We have to move on, Claire."

That's what Amber was doing. During Claire's last visit she'd noticed a bouquet of fresh roses for Amber. They were from Les Campbell, the Alhambra police officer. "He's been very nice. I like him," Amber said.

Now, as Claire sat on the bench near Julie's headstone, a warm soothing breeze caressed her, as if nudging her to take the next steps.

After police had released the crime scene at Big Bear Lake, Claire hired a contractor to remove the charred ruins and erase any trace of all structures on the property. Then she listed it for sale. A film executive, known for notorious acquisitions, was interested.

Claire also listed the house in San Marino.

Martha was helping her transfer her practice, ensuring Alice would remain employed while Claire considered her future.

Listening to the birdsong, she thought of the business card in her purse from Mark Harding, a reporter with the AllNews Press Agency. He had come to her door several times.

He'd been respectful in his persistence that she break her silence and give him an exclusive interview. Tanner had vouched for him, indicating that Harding's cooperation early in the investigation was critical. "But you don't owe him anything. It's entirely up to you if you want to talk to him," Tanner had written in an email.

Yesterday, over the phone, Harding told Claire that he

wanted to write "A dignified tribute to you, Julie Glidden and Amber. I'd like to tell the human story of what you did to stop this monster. You're the heroes. You can set the record straight on any aspects."

There were many. Word had emerged that Ruben Montero's group, the Great Light and Hope Association, revoked its honor for Robert Bowen. Shaken by what some called, "shock, disbelief and betrayal," the board also ordered that Bowen's framed photo be removed from the community hall and destroyed.

As expected, there'd been a lot of online chatter accusing Claire of being "too stupid to live," for being married to the devil and not knowing it. "Was she blind to his tail and cloven hooves?"

While Claire's anonymous defenders said, "Ask the woman he saved in the freeway miracle if she knew a monster was rescuing her baby. This guy outsmarted everyone."

Claire considered agreeing to an interview with Harding, but not today.

She stood and touched Julie's headstone, then left.

As she neared her car, she saw another one parked next to it. Tanner was leaning against his front fender, arms folded, watching her.

"Martha Berman said you might be here."

"Hi, Joe."

"I don't mean to intrude."

"It's okay."

"I've been getting calls from the L.A. County Coroner. They said they've been calling you. His ashes have not yet been claimed."

"I don't want them. I don't care what they do with them."

"Leave the matter with me. I'll see what I can do to

make it official." Tanner took stock of her, her bruises had nearly faded. "How are you doing, really?"

Her chin crumpled but she maintained her composure. Her voice was strong.

"I'm hanging on. Some days I need to be alone, some days I need to be with people, you know?"

"Yes, I do."

"I realize that I've been very selfish in many ways."

"What do you mean?"

"When I was a child, I lost my family, and ever since, I wanted to replace that ideal, to have my own family, something to hold on to. I'm sorry if that doesn't make sense."

"I understand about losing something and what it does to you."

"I guess for me, I've been searching in all the wrong places for what I wanted. I guess that's evident."

Tanner thought for a long moment.

"Well, Claire, sometimes it doesn't matter what you want. Sometimes it's a matter of what you need."

"Excuse me?"

"And right now, we need ice cream. There's a place a couple of blocks from here. We'd love it if you would join us."

"Us?"

Tanner nodded to his car where Samantha was waiting inside.

"My daughter, Sam."

"Hello. You're pretty," Sam said, smiling.

Claire blushed.

"Hello there, sweetheart."

"So," Tanner said, "want to ride with us?"

"Yes." She smiled back. "I think I need ice cream, too."

* * * * *

Acknowledgments & Note

The inspiration for *Into the Dark* was loosely drawn from several real cases. While some readers might venture to guess which ones, I ask that you forgive any inaccuracies in the story. In crafting *Into the Dark,* I employed creative license, taking liberties with the geography of greater Los Angeles, police jurisdiction, investigative procedure and the field of psychology.

The completion of any book is never ever a solitary effort.

My thanks to Amy Moore-Benson, to Miranda Indrigo, and to the incredible editorial, marketing, sales and PR teams at Harlequin and MIRA Books in Toronto, New York and around the world.

Thanks to Wendy Dudley, who made this story better.

To Teresa Mofina for her editorial help at the eleventh hour.

Very special thanks to Barbara, Laura and Michael.

It's important you know that in getting this book to you, I benefited from the hard work and generosity of many people, too many to thank individually.

This brings me to what I hold to be the most critical part of the enterprise: you, the reader. This aspect has become something of a creed for me, one that bears repeating with each book.

Thank you very much for your time, for without you, a book remains an untold tale. Thank you for setting your life on pause and taking the journey. I deeply appreciate my growing audience around the world and those who've been with me since the beginning and who keep in touch. Thank you all for your very kind words. I hope you enjoyed the ride and will check out my earlier books while watching for my next onc. I welcome your feedback. Drop by www.rickmofina.com to subscribe to my newsletter and send me a note.

Rick Mofina

www.facebook.com/rickmofina
www.twitter.com/rickmofina

New York Times Bestselling Author

ANDREA KANE

Each day is a struggle for Amanda Gleason's newborn son as he battles a rare immune deficiency. Justin's best chance for a cure lies with his father—who was brutally murdered before Amanda even realized she carried his child.

Or was he?

One email changes everything—a recent photo of a man who looks exactly like Paul. But tracking down a ghost when every second counts is not for amateurs.

Forensic Instincts is the one team up for the challenge.

Forensic Instincts has built their reputation on achieving the impossible, and when they take the case, nothing will stop them from uncovering the shocking truth that transcends the line between here and gone.

Available wherever books are sold.

Be sure to connect with us at:

Harlequin.com/Newsletters

Facebook.com/HarlequinBooks

Twitter.com/HarlequinBooks

MAK1445